"I am not so naïve that I don't know what happens between a man and a woman when they are lovers."

In the sanctuary of Rian Connor's magnificent ancestral estate, Catherine Davenport struggles to remember who she was before he found her wandering practically naked on the docks of London. She has little memory of the vicious attack that brought her there, but she can't deny the feelings Rian awakens in her. In danger of losing her heart to a man tormented by the dark secrets of his own past, Catherine questions what an innocent like her has to offer such an experienced man of the world.

"You have no idea what you are doing to me—how much I want you, how much I need you!"

On the night of his brother's wedding ball, Rian proves exactly how much he wants his beautiful young protégé, only to be lured by his former mistress into committing the ultimate betrayal. For Isabel Howard will stop at nothing to do away with Catherine and destroy her future with the man they both desire above all others . . .

Visit us at www.kensingtonbooks.com

Resolve

Corsets and Carriages

Part Two

Carla Susan Smith

LYRICAL PRESS
Kensington Publishing Corp.
www.kensingtonbooks.com

First Electronic Edition: January 2018
eISBN-13: 978-1-5161-0591-5
eISBN-10: 1-5161-0591-5

First Print Edition: January 2018
ISBN-13: ISBN 978-1-5161-0594-6
ISBN-10: ISBN 1-5161-0594-X

Printed in the United States of America

Books by Carla Susan Smith

A Vampire's Promise
A Vampire's Soul
A Vampire's Honor
A Vampire's Hunger

Published by Kensington Publishing Corporation

Chapter 1

The hardest part of leaving for Oakhaven was not so much having to say goodbye to everything that was familiar to her, but being confined in a claustrophobic carriage with Rian Connor for the duration of the journey. Under normal circumstances being in the company of a well-bred gentleman for any length of time would not have made Catherine anxious, but these were hardly normal circumstances. And it did not help that her thoughts and feelings about this particular gentleman were like a treacherous quicksand. One wrong step and she was in danger of being pulled under.

Catherine would be forever grateful to him saving her life, but she nevertheless had no words to describe the swell of feeling that rose within her whenever he was near. She only knew that it was something far more complicated than gratitude.

Catherine's complete loss of memory was devastating. Other than her first name, she had no idea who she was. When Rian had stopped her from throwing herself in the Thames one dawn just a few short weeks ago, he'd had no idea why she'd been down at the wharves all alone, wearing nothing but a cloak. Her reasons for wanting to end her life had soon become evident. The vicious whip marks scarring her flesh were proof of the violence she had suffered at another's pleasure.

Now, part of her was grateful that she was unable to recall the details of that assault. She was not certain her sanity could bear to know. Had she meant to give herself up to the river? It certainly seemed to have been her intention, until fate intervened, offering her another path. One ushered in by strong hands, brown eyes, and a trust that promised to be unbreakable.

Along with the mystery regarding her identity was the confusion over where she had come from. London was not her home. Descriptions of landmarks and well-known places elicited nothing from her but blank stares and sighs of frustration. The lack of recognition could easily be put down to her current amnesia were it not for her voice. Her accent, while not particularly strong, was enough to make her sound different from those around her. If she didn't live in London, could she have been visiting a relative? Anything was possible, but neither she nor her rescuer knew the truth.

And being saved by Rian Connor had been the source of yet another type of confusion for Catherine. A confusion that was more than a little disconcerting. Like it or not, she felt an intimate connection to Rian, one she was determined to ignore.

It would be completely different if Rian gave any indication he had feelings for Catherine, but he remained aloof, keeping his thoughts to himself. It was a quality she wanted to emulate, if only as a way of calming her racing heart and churning stomach. This journey would be a test. One she was determined not to fail, and so she sat opposite Rian in the carriage, ignoring his dark good looks as best as she could. And it seemed that he was more than willing to help her in this regard. Other than inquiring after her comfort before setting out, his attention was absorbed by the book he was reading. So much so that neither of them noticed the nondescript figure across the street who witnessed their departure.

* * * *

Rian closed the book with a sigh. He had read the same paragraph three times now and it still made no sense. Surreptitiously he glanced at Catherine. She kept her face turned to the window, giving every appearance of enjoying the view, but he had felt her eyes stray toward him when she thought he wasn't looking. He couldn't begin to imagine what it must be like to lose your memory. If not for his own remembrances he might not have survived some very dark moments when the pride and temper of youth had made him leave home, and pledge himself to the captain of a seafaring vessel. Memories of himself and his brother Liam as children had been the lifeline to which he had held fast. And the knowledge that his brother would always welcome him back had made his return to the land of his birth an easy one.

What he had not been prepared for was the notoriety he'd gained by his relationship with Lady Isabel Howard. Seeking nothing more than a pleasant distraction, Rian had not been surprised when the notorious young widow invited him to her bed. A night of witty repartee and flirtation had led up to the proposal, but Rian was not without scruples. He would not bed the exotic beauty until she understood exactly what he could offer her, as well as what he could not. He'd been delighted when she gave every indication she grasped, and accepted, the parameters of their attachment. Apparently he'd been wrong.

Isabel, like many of her peers, thrived on gossip, especially if she was the subject of wagging tongues, but for Rian it was something he accepted only grudgingly and with a certain measure of distaste. Still, he couldn't deny he'd enjoyed Isabel's company, as well as her bed, and he was mature enough to ignore whatever was being said about him until the gossips included the subject of matrimony. Rian, himself, had considered the idea, but for him marriage had to be founded on more than physical attraction. That alone would not sustain a lasting relationship. As husband and wife he and Isabel would be incompatible, and his suspicion that she might be the source of these new rumors only emphasized the need to end their association. It was a decision that fate seemed to confirm by guiding his feet to the wharf and the lonely figure in need of rescue.

He couldn't say what drew him to her. What quality she possessed that made him want to make her part of his life. Whatever it was, it went much deeper than the male protective instinct that rose on seeing the bruises on her face and body. And it was a feeling that Isabel had never aroused. But Catherine's memory loss made him hesitate. It would be wrong to expect more from her, and yet her very presence was enough to unlock doors Rian had thought never to open. And make him want again.

Never had he envisioned the two women meeting, but just the evening before, Isabel had presented herself at the Connor townhouse, suggesting an interview with Catherine. He still was not completely sure why his former mistress had requested to meet the young woman he'd taken into his home. The idea that Isabel might recognize Catherine or know her family had not been without merit, but Rian hadn't been able to shake the feeling that Isabel's reasons were far less noble. He ought to have trusted his intuition. Though he didn't know what had been said, the fact that the two women had exchanged angry words was enough to make him act. Taking Catherine to Oakhaven was the most sensible solution for all involved.

Rian stared at Catherine as she continued to gaze out the carriage window. The slight tug on her mouth and the crinkle at the corner of her eyes when she noted something pleasing released an unexpected warmth in him. Along with a great many other feelings that were slowly awakening. He blew out a resigned breath. Whatever had happened between Catherine and Isabel, it would be better to get it out in the open, and not let it fester.

"I apologize if Lady Howard said anything to distress you," he said quietly as the carriage rumbled on. "That was not my intent in introducing you."

"I know." Catherine kept her gaze fixed on the trees and rolling hills in the distance. She found this bucolic view far more appealing than London.

"Did she upset you a great deal?" Rian probed.

Now it was Catherine's turn to sigh. Accepting his roundabout apology was not going to be enough; he wanted to know what had happened. Taking her gaze from the changing landscape, she fixed him with a stare as the memory of Isabel's grossly unjust accusations flushed her cheeks. "Yes, she did."

There was no anger or trace of histrionics in her reply, but that did not stop the muscle in his jaw from tightening. He was angry with Isabel for upsetting her. "I will speak with Lady Howard on my return," he said.

"You'll do no such thing," Catherine retorted.

"But I can see that you are still troubled by whatever passed between you." It was impossible to ignore the flush on her cheeks or the spark in her eyes.

"You're confusing anguish with anger."

Rian raised a brow in surprise. "You're angry?" She nodded. "You're angry with Isabel?" Curiosity was getting the better of him, especially as Catherine nodded again, keeping her lips compressed in a tight line. "But why?" he asked. "What do you have to be angry about?"

"I allowed her to provoke me into losing my temper," she snapped.

"And?" Rian leaned forward slightly, knowing there was a lot more that wasn't being said.

Catherine found herself staring into his eyes. Deep brown with flecks of gold that made her feel light headed. He wore his hair loose and it framed his face in such a way she was unable to organize her thoughts into any sort of coherent pattern. With an effort she redirected her gaze and looked down at her lap. "And I said some things that I should not have said, things that you most certainly will not persuade me to repeat!"

His gaze weighed heavy on her. Surely he was not going to make her reveal that Isabel saw her as a rival for his affections. That the only reason she had wanted to speak with Catherine alone was to make wild allegations and insist she not pursue Rian. As if Catherine even knew how to do such a thing!

"Well, it isn't often that someone gets the better of Isabel," Rian said with a chuckle, "but judging from the haste of her departure, I would say you managed quite well." He watched as Catherine smoothed an imaginary crease on her dress before returning her gaze to the view beyond the carriage. "And you are quite certain I cannot persuade you to tell me the, uh, substance of your conversation?" he teased.

"Absolutely not!"

Though he did not doubt her resolve, Rian thought he saw the corners of her mouth lift slightly in the window's reflection. He wished he could have been a fly on the wall during that conversation. Whatever had been said had upset both women. And he knew it was so because the Connors' motherly housekeeper had wasted no time in coming to him.

"What happened?" he asked in response to Mrs. Hatch's description of Catherine's agitated state.

"I don't know," she replied with a look of concern.

"She has not confided in you?"

Mrs. Hatch shook her head, which told Rian that whatever had taken place was serious indeed. Catherine trusted Mrs. Hatch implicitly. "She refuses to discuss the matter, Master Rian, but I can tell it upset her a great deal."

They both agreed another encounter with Isabel was to be avoided at all costs, and, at his suggestion, Mrs. Hatch made certain Catherine was ready to leave first thing in the morning. Rian had not been fooled by Isabel's hasty departure or her flimsy excuse of a headache delivered by note barely an hour later. She had been furious about something, but he could not imagine what Catherine might have said to provoke such a reaction. He sighed in frustration, wishing Catherine would confide in him. And then, unexpectedly, a chuckle escaped him, bubbling up from inside. He was going to have to watch himself if Catherine had a temper that could best Lady Howard.

* * * *

Isabel crumpled John Fletcher's report, and threw it on the floor. A few moments later she picked it back up, smoothing the page so she could read the informant's words again. The Connors' young footman had not been in service long, and felt no disloyalty in spilling secrets. Lured by the weight of the purse promised, and with a growing family to feed, he had shared with John all he knew of the mysterious guest in the upstairs bedroom. While the information was not as detailed as John would have liked, it was as much as anyone else in the house knew. Except for the housekeeper and the one maid, and neither of them were about to confide in him.

The footman proved his worth by managing to send a note regarding the sudden change in plan for the departure to Oakhaven. The house was in an uproar, but over what the young man could not say. John had smiled, knowing full well that Isabel was the reason for the sudden state of chaos. Unfortunately getting his benefactress to see the positive aspect of the situation would be challenging. But John was a master at manipulating people, at learning secrets and disclosing them for the right price. With his long experience of Isabel Howard, he had no doubt he would prevail. Eventually.

With a wild shriek Isabel tore the carefully worded report into little pieces and scattered it about the floor like confetti. All she saw was a confirmation of Rian's feelings for the girl. What other reason could there be for him to decide to personally escort her to the family estate? If he felt no attachment, then he could have easily sent her with a servant, or better yet that meddlesome housekeeper. Hands on her hips she tapped her foot impatiently. No, there could only be one reason that would make him leave London, especially this close to his brother's wedding day.

Grudgingly, Isabel admitted to being outfoxed. The girl was a clever little minx. Smart enough to have held her tongue, but still quick enough to make Rian dance to her tune. Well, two could play at that game, and Isabel had experience on her side. It made her by far the more proficient participant.

She paced about the floor, trying to decide what her next move should be. John's report had stated that no one in the household appeared to know any particulars, but it was generally believed that a disagreement had occurred between the guest and her visitor. Isabel snorted. It was only a matter of time before she would be able to completely expose the little fraud for who she truly was. And if, by chance, she was able to save Rian from being humiliated in the process, so much the better. His gratitude would surely know no bounds.

Unfortunately it was too late to circumvent his trip to Oakhaven. She had no choice now but to wait for his return, and yet this did not worry Isabel. Indeed, the smile that curved her mouth was positively triumphant. At least when he came back, he would be alone, having left the trollop behind with the other country bumpkins. Keeping this in mind she occupied herself for the next half hour writing instructions for John Fletcher.

Chapter 2

The long drive that led up to the main house was lined on either side with trees. From the distinctive twist of the limbs, the lower ones almost scraping the ground, Catherine recognized them as apple trees. She imagined they must be a glorious sight to see in the spring with pink and white blossoms, and then later as the branches groaned under the weight of rosy fruit. Would she be here long enough, she wondered, to witness the season's growth?

No matter, the barren trees welcomed her as they stood silently beneath a snow laden grey sky. Seated next to Catherine, her maid Tilly shivered and snuggled deeper inside the heavy blanket she had wrapped herself in. They had all noticed the drop in temperature, forecasting a possible storm.

"Does it seem much changed to you?" Catherine asked Rian shyly, knowing from her conversation with Mrs. Hatch, it had been many years since he had last seen his home.

"No," he said with a rueful smile, "although I must admit the house does seem a little smaller."

"Perhaps that is only because you are a little bigger." Looking back out the carriage window, she asked, "Why apple trees?"

He shrugged. "A whimsy. They were planted as a wedding gift by one of my forebears as a way to welcome his new bride. Supposedly she had expressed a fondness for apples. Something to do with fertility, I believe, but I doubt she was expecting more than one or two trees."

"What do you do with so much fruit?"

"The bounty has always been shared with our tenants, and Mrs. Hatch makes a positively sinful cider," he added with a roguish grin.

As the carriage neared the house Catherine was astounded by the number of people who spilled out from behind the massive carved doors. Despite the cold, they were all smiling and laughing, and seemed genuinely happy to welcome them. Rian insisted on carrying Catherine into the house, and was still holding her in his arms when a voice made him turn around.

"Well, you certainly made good time. I only received your note yesterday."

"Hello, Liam, good to see you again." Rian greeted his brother with a smile. "I wanted to get Catherine settled as soon as possible, and there seemed no reason to delay."

The slight hesitation in his voice produced a thoughtful look on the younger Conner's face, but he did not comment on it.

Catherine stared at the other man, bewildered by the lack of physical resemblance he bore to Rian. Was it possible he had had a different mother? Or one of them a different father even?

"Hello, Catherine. It's a pleasure to welcome you to Oakhaven," Liam said, and the smile he gave her said he was genuinely pleased to see her.

"Thank you for allowing me to be here."

Though she was pale, and no doubt fatigued from the journey, Liam was pleased to see that Catherine was much improved from the last time he had seen her. And he was not fooled by his brother's hasty arrival. Bringing Catherine to Oakhaven might have been his suggestion originally, but the suddenness of Rian's departure, along with a lack of explanation in his communication, told him something unexpected had pushed his brother to act. He was not unduly worried. Rian would tell him once they were alone.

"So you are Liam," Catherine said. "Mrs. Hatch told me about you," she added, sounding apologetic.

"Only the good parts I hope," he countered. A smile twitched the corner of his mouth as Catherine continued to stare at him. Ordinarily her behavior would be considered quite rude, especially when she turned her head and gazed at Rian, a frown furrowing her brow. She was as surprised as many others on seeing them together for the first time, especially since the blood connection was known. "As you can see," Liam explained with a boyish grin, "I inherited all the good looks in the family."

Deciding it was best not to comment, Catherine shifted slightly in Rian's arms. "You can put me down now," she told him. "I assure you I can stand perfectly well, and I promise not to run off."

"At least not until after you've got to know us better!"

The feminine voice made all three heads turn in the same direction as a petite brunette emerged from an arch and crossed the room to join them. Liam obligingly kissed the cheek he was offered before the young woman turned her attention to Rian. Her smile was warm and welcoming, though she appeared to be secretly amused by something.

"Hello, Rian, it's good to see you managed to grow up relatively unscathed."

It took a few moments before Rian was able to find his voice, but when he did Catherine understood the reason for the woman's private mirth. His voice sounded incredulous as he stammered, "F-f-felicity?"

Apparently being at a loss for words was a rare occurrence for the elder Connor, but it had his brother grinning from ear to ear as he introduced his fiancée to Catherine. No comment was made, or surprise shown, at the introduction being made using her first name only. Felicity stepped forward, and, taking Catherine's free hand, she greeted her as if they had known each other all their lives.

"Come, you must be exhausted," Felicity said. "There will be time enough to talk later." She turned and gave her husband-to-be a quizzical look.

He hesitated only a moment. "If you have no objection," Liam said, addressing Rian, "we thought Catherine might be more comfortable in Mama's room."

"Of course. It would have been my choice," Rian assured him, his long easy stride headed for the staircase.

Catherine pursed her lips in frustration. She could only hope the room was not situated at the other end of the house as it appeared Rian had no intention of putting her down. Thankfully it was closer than expected, and, as Rian waited for Felicity to open the door, Catherine felt the slight quiver in his arms. Her first thought was that perhaps he had been holding her for too long, and his arms were growing weary, but then she realized the tremor had nothing to do with her. A muscle jumped as Rian clenched his jaw and his thick, dark lashes made a shadow on his cheek as he closed his eyes. With no other thought than to offer some small token of comfort, Catherine placed her hand against his chest. Her palm over his heart. She did not need to feel the tension in his body to empathize with him, and she wondered if perhaps giving her his mother's room was a mistake. The request for a different accommodation was on her lips when she felt the press of Rian's fingers as he pulled her a little more tightly against him. He looked down, his expression thankful for her understanding and telling her he wanted her here. She did not move her hand as Felicity opened the door and Rian carried her over the threshold.

* * * *

He steeled himself for a rush of emotion once he was inside the room. Rian had loved his mother dearly, and the helpless feeling that consumed him as he watched illness steal her vitality had never quite left him. Taking a deep breath, he moved farther into the room.

Oakhaven had been built to withstand the passage of time. A stout edifice, it adapted itself well to the seasons. Warm summers would send its inhabitants seeking relief in those rooms that were cooler, while a bitter winter had them gathering together around a large fire and hot bricks warming every bed. Rian was pleased to see a fire blazing in the hearth. He reasoned Liam must have ordered one lit every day since making the decision to have Catherine occupy this room. It took time to chase away the pockets of chilled air that always seemed to stubbornly linger.

Carefully, he carried Catherine toward the hearth, and set her down on the chaise. After satisfying himself she was comfortable, Rian turned his attention to the room. His mother's presence was a lingering bittersweet memory here, but there were other subtle changes he noticed. Whoever had taken pains to prepare the chamber had harmonized her own personality with that of the previous occupant. The chaise he had placed Catherine on, along with the delicately painted table next to it, were both new additions, but the bed, washstand, and dresser were all familiar. He was surprised to find he remembered the delicate floral pattern that decorated the washstand ewer and basin. The curtains and counterpane on the bed, though vaguely reminiscent, were too bright, too fresh, to have been the same ones used by his mother.

"Felicity found the exact material and had replacements made," Liam said, seeing the slightly puzzled look on his brother's face.

Two heads turned to stare briefly at the next mistress of Oakhaven, who sat talking to Catherine in a low voice.

"What a kind gesture," Rian said. Going to the dresser, he noted that the hand mirror and hairbrushes were new as were the array of small, colorful sachets he was certain never belonged to his mother. "What are these?" he asked.

"Dried herbs and flowers. Dr. MacGregor mentioned something about the underestimated power of the sense of smell, and how certain perfumes can stir a memory. I told Felicity about it," Liam continued, "and she made these up for Catherine. Each one contains something different."

He looked slightly abashed, making Rian wonder if his sibling's dismay was because he'd been discussing Catherine, or that his fiancée had decided to act on her own initiative. "I remember the same conversation, but doing something like this would never have occurred to me," he said, picking up a small silk packet and detecting the unmistakable scent of lavender.

"Me either," Liam admitted.

As if knowing she was being talked about, Felicity rose from her seat next to Catherine just as Tilly entered with a tea tray, followed by a burly footman carrying a trunk. "I think we should all give Catherine some time to herself," Felicity suggested, joining the Conner men and ushering both of them toward the door.

Feeling Catherine's eyes on him, Rian paused at the threshold and looked back over his shoulder. He was pleased to see a smile momentarily lift the fatigue from her face, but obviously she still had misgivings. He couldn't say if they were for herself or for him. He raised his hand and placed it on his chest where hers had been. Her gesture meant more than he could express. Clearly she had understood his hesitation as he entered the room, and he suspected her intuition told her unresolved issues lingered, affecting his return to the family home.

Rian watched as Catherine's expression suddenly changed, displaying a warmth and supportive reassurance in her bright blue eyes. His mouth felt dry and he was forced to swallow a couple of times. An all too familiar need was beginning to stir, but he knew if he allowed the feeling to continue unchecked, he would be forced to confront things he wasn't sure he was ready to acknowledge.

Things that had nothing to do with his feelings for Catherine.

Things that had everything to do with his feelings for Catherine.

Chapter 3

"Why Rian, Catherine is simply adorable!" Felicity exclaimed as the three of them sat having tea of their own.

"Has my brother told you everything?" He was strangely relieved by her candid affirmation. "He thinks bringing her here to Oakhaven will help speed her recovery."

Felicity arched an amused brow as she set her cup back on its saucer. "And how could it not? The very air is a balm after being in the city."

For the next hour or so the three of them sat and spoke of inconsequential matters, and in many ways Rian felt it was almost as if he'd never left. The easy companionship that warmed him was comforting, but soon the lengthening shadows said it was time for Felicity to leave.

"Thank you, again," Rian said as he took her hands and kissed her cheek.

The catch in his voice seemed to take her by surprise, making her ask, "Whatever for?"

"For agreeing to marry this no account brother of mine"—Rian grinned as he linked her arm through his—"and becoming the sister I always wanted."

"Be careful what you wish for, big brother! The girl you pushed in the duck pond has long since grown up."

"And I wouldn't have it any other way, although"—Rian paused and looked over Felicity's head at Liam—"which of you will admit to thinking getting married in December was a good thing?"

"It's considered lucky to be married at Christmastime," Felicity told him.

"Besides," Liam added with a sheepish grin, "my bride thought a winter wedding sounded very romantic, and I could find no argument compelling enough to dissuade her."

"I doubt you searched very hard," Rian observed.

"True, very true," Liam agreed affably. "I barely considered it."

A light, feminine laugh supported his statement as Felicity relinquished her hold on Rian. "I really must leave," she told him. "And I am certain both of you have a lot of catching up to do." When she stepped through the huge front door a groom was already waiting with Felicity's horse, a beautiful chestnut colored mare. After being boosted into the saddle with Liam's help, she took the reins in her hands, giving her prospective brother-in-law some sage advice. "Don't worry so. Catherine could not be in a better place to get well again. With rest and time, I am certain she will soon find her way back, and I promise not to keep you from her for very long." She checked her horse, which was impatient to be moving. "You have been missed, Rian, and I am happy to see you home once more."

The sincerity of her words made him regret the duck pond incident.

* * * *

If no ghosts sought Rian's company in his mother's room, then they were waiting for him in his. Although the chamber had been scrubbed clean, and his bed had new linens, no fresh hand had sought to provide new furnishings or redecorate. Liam would never consider doing such a thing, and Felicity would think it too intrusive. She was not mistress of Oakhaven yet, but Rian doubted she would invade his privacy even when she had the right to do so. The bedroom looked much the same as when he had left so many years before. Childish animal carvings greeted him. The shelf was littered with a good many horses and dogs, along with some cows and a few pigs. He smiled as he took down the crude figures, and held them in his hand. Losing himself in the memory, he recalled as many nicked thumbs as completed pieces. He smiled until his father's voice interrupted his walk in the past.

Once more Rian heard the sting of words that made a disappointed parent disown a headstrong child. No pain was quite as deep as that of a father and son arguing. Each stubbornly clinging to the belief that he was right, refusing to accept another point of view. In his mind Rian could once again see Liam standing woodenly in the open doorway, knowing that something momentous was happening, but not grasping just how far-reaching the impact of their father's inflexibility would be. Rian shook his head. The hot-headed youth who had bucked against the parental yoke had vanished during his first month at sea.

"Father was a fool." Turning, Rian once more saw his brother standing in the doorway. Only this time Liam was no longer a young boy trying to hide his fear. Now he leaned against the doorframe, arms folded across his chest. "I loved him very much, Rian, but it does not change the fact that he was a fool. A stubborn fool."

"'Tis ancient history now, and best forgotten. All families quarrel." Rian gave him a tight smile. "Nothing we do can change what has happened, and we cannot summon the dead from their graves in order to make amends. No matter how much we might wish it."

His words resonated with Liam. "Would you like to go today?" he asked gently. "The light is fading, but we could take a lantern."

Rian shook his head. "Now is not the time. Perhaps after I've seen you wed, then I can come back and pay my respects. To Mama at least." He sighed and carefully set the carved animals back on the shelf. Each in its place. Life was too short to be filled with bitterness. Sophie had taught him that, but now, feeling old resentments resurface, he wasn't sure he could so easily put the past behind him. If he couldn't make peace with his father, then he needed to make peace with himself. "Come," he said, putting an arm about Liam's shoulders. "I am famished. Let's see what cook has made for dinner."

Later, when their hunger had been assuaged, Liam commented on the noticeable improvements in Catherine's physical condition. Rian checked to make sure a tray had been taken to her, but was concerned by how little she had eaten. He made Tilly promise to let him know if Catherine's appetite did not improve.

"Does she remember anything?" Liam asked.

"Nothing of any significance," Rian replied.

"I thought not."

"What makes you say that?"

"I saw something in her face. It's as if she's searching for anything that might be familiar."

"Well I think you are right about her preferring the country," Rian told him. "Once we left the city she seemed more comfortable, as if the sight of rolling hills and open pastures were familiar to her. Unfortunately she couldn't say if she recognized anything. It's all so damn frustrating!"

"Try putting yourself in her place," his brother said sympathetically. Rian sighed and for a while neither man spoke, until Liam asked, "So what prompted this sudden departure of yours?"

"I let Isabel meet Catherine."

In the process of taking a mouthful of wine, Liam spluttered, and, once he had stopped coughing, stared at his brother, aghast.

"I really didn't have a choice," Rian told him, explaining Isabel's surprise visit and the way she'd practically barged into Catherine's room.

"I'm almost afraid to ask what happened."

"I think it's safe to say it did not go well." It was hard suppressing his grin, but Rian did his best. "They met, exchanged pleasantries, and then Isabel asked to speak with Catherine alone—something about wanting to ask questions of a personal nature that she wouldn't want me to hear."

"I'm surprised Isabel would care."

"Not Isabel, you idiot. Catherine."

"Then I'm surprised you agreed," Liam said, ignoring the rebuke.

"It seemed a perfectly reasonable request at the time, and Catherine didn't refuse."

"And?"

Rian shrugged. "I don't know. Isabel left the house a short while later without speaking to me. She sent a note apologizing for the haste of her departure. Apparently she had a headache."

"Did you believe her?"

"I'm not that stupid," Rian said in exasperation. "Of course I didn't believe her."

"Well, what did Catherine have to say about it?"

"Nothing. She won't tell me what was said by Isabel, or what she said in return, but she did admit that Isabel provoked her enough she lost her temper, and said some things she shouldn't have."

"That doesn't bode well." Liam sounded ominous, and now he wore a frown across his brow.

Rian nodded in agreement. "In any case, I think it's safe to conclude one thing."

"And what is that?"

"Isabel has no more idea who Catherine is than we do."

Dividing the last of the wine between their glasses, the brothers sat in silence, each mulling over his own thoughts, until Liam asked, "And what is the state of your affair with Isabel?"

His brother gave him a sour look before recounting his failure to dissolve the relationship. Completely open with Liam, Rian spoke in a gloomy voice, leaving nothing out, and taking the blame for succumbing to Isabel's seduction.

"She's a hard woman to let go of," Liam offered supportively.

"We coupled Liam. It meant nothing more."

"I very much doubt Isabel will view it that way," the younger Connor pointed out succinctly. "But that was then. How do things stand between you now?"

"I am escorting her to your wedding as I agreed to do, and then I will return here to Oakhaven."

"Alone?" The question was forthright.

"Yes. Alone."

"And Isabel has accepted this?"

Rian sighed and emptied his glass. "We didn't really discuss it, but I'm inclined to say I don't think Isabel accepts very much that is not her decision to begin with." He paused, a troubled frown on his brow. "Now that she knows not to expect a proposal of marriage, I suspect she may look for a way to vilify me. I will understand if she needs to lay fault at my feet, and as long as she doesn't malign me too badly, I'll not contradict her."

"That's very honorable of you."

"I'm not thinking of only myself," Rian pointed out.

Swirling the wine in his glass, Liam watched as the candlelight made pockets of color in the deep red liquid. Rian's words filled him with the very real worry that his brother might be getting more attached to Catherine than he would admit. It was not a baseless concern. The last time Rian had loved, it had ended tragically with his wife Sophie's death.

"Liam?" Recognizing the look on his brother's face, Rian knew something still troubled his sibling. "What is it?"

His brother sighed. "What has happened between you and Catherine?"

"What makes you think anything has happened?"

"Two people who are strangers do not look at each other the way that you and Catherine do. Not unless they have shared something of significance."

"You think Catherine looks at me?" Rian sounded pleased by the notion.

"Oh yes, she looks at you, and you, brother mine, you look at her. So what happened?"

The need to speak was undeniably compelling. If he didn't share how he felt with someone he would explode, and who better than the one person he trusted more than anyone else? Keeping his voice low and his tone solemn, Rian described how in the delirium of her fever, Catherine had fought against him as her own personal demons manifested themselves.

"But then something unexpected happened. It was as if I suddenly woke up and knew I'd been waiting my entire life for her, Liam. As if every other woman I had ever known was nothing more than a distraction."

"Even Sophie?" Liam's mild disapproval was apparent.

"No." Rian shook his head in denial. "Never Sophie. She was not a distraction, and my love for her was very real, but it felt different somehow." Worried the mood between them was in danger of taking a decidedly mawkish turn, Rian gave a self-deprecating laugh. "I don't expect you to understand, brother. You have always been very clear minded about what you wanted." He gave Liam a wry grin. "Does Felicity know you've been in love with her since that one summer we were all together?"

"Was I truly that obvious?"

"Only to me, little brother, only to me."

But Liam was not to be dissuaded. "What if, when Catherine is fully recovered, she decides her future does not lie with you?"

The gold flecks in Rian's eyes seemed to shine a little brighter. He had considered this, but only in a very academic way. To hear another pose the same question gave his fear a substantial weight. "If Catherine tells me so, rest assured I will let her go," he replied stiffly.

"Well it's obvious she feels *something* for you, but I suspect it is too soon to measure the depth of that feeling."

"You think perhaps it is gratitude, and nothing more?"

Liam shrugged, unwilling to commit. "Be careful, Rian. She is young, and, I would imagine, impressionable. Taking into consideration what she has already suffered, you would not wish to cause her more harm, unintentional though I know it would be."

It was a cautious warning, but one that needed to be heeded. Though Liam's confirmation filled him with a cautious hopefulness, Rian decided he had no other choice but to bide his time and wait for Catherine to give him a sign.

Chapter 4

Liam sipped his glass of wine and watched his wife as she moved effortlessly about the room. She stopped to speak with a group of people, distant relatives from the Pelham side of the family, although he was at a complete loss to recall their names even though he knew they had been introduced. Then again, both he and Felicity had met so many new faces in the past twenty-four hours it was difficult to keep track of who was related to whom, at least on his wife's side of the family.

As for the Connors, it was a relatively simple matter keeping track of only himself and Rian. Their father had been the only child in his family to reach adulthood, and their mother's people had strongly disapproved of her choice of a husband. Defying her family's wishes and being married in secret had made her an outcast to them. Thankfully the large and colorful Pelham clan had more than enough females eager to welcome both Connor men into the family fold.

Felicity had left Pelham Manor the day before Rian and Liam's departure from Oakhaven. Naturally she had resided at her parents' town home until the wedding, and would spend her wedding night with Liam in his house before they returned to the country.

It had been the longest five days of Liam's life, but it had all been worth it when he had watched Felicity walk up the nave of the church toward him. Her wedding dress was pale blue with silver embroidery work decorating the bodice, outer skirt and pleated panels that fell from her shoulders down her back. White bows decorated the front of her bodice and each elbow where the tight-fitting sleeves ended in a cascade of ruffles. Bows continued down the front of her gown. With the addition of pearls, they ran either side of the gown's front split, accentuating the white petticoat that was also embroidered with silver thread. Liam found himself mesmerized as she came ever closer, and he might have forgotten entirely why he was there if not for a well-timed poke in the ribs from Rian. The look on Felicity's face, shining with joy as she repeated her vows to him, was one Liam knew he would remember for the rest of his life.

Sipping some more wine, Liam realized he was starting to feel a little lightheaded, and so he put his glass down on a nearby table. He had no intention of being anything but sober when he consummated his marriage. A movement at his side made him turn his head, and he found himself face to face with Isabel.

There had been no need to remind Rian of his promise to be her escort on this day. He was a man of his word. Besides, he had little to worry about with Catherine safely tucked away at Oakhaven, and Isabel had wasted no time reminding him what a charming companion she could be. No mention was made of their last meeting, or the apparent quarrel between her and Catherine. Instead it was almost as if they were meeting for the first time, and Rian could not help but be delighted by her conversation and general gaiety. A charming Isabel was as difficult to resist as the accomplished seductress.

Liam bent to kiss Isabel's proffered hand. "Thank you for coming, Isabel," he said, hoping his tone would not make a liar of him.

"Your bride is very beautiful, and I wish you both many years of happiness."

The smile she gave him seemed genuine enough, but it did not persuade him to drop his guard. Women like Isabel unnerved him. The boldness of her character was enough to guarantee he would never, by his own choice, seek her out. He glanced across the room at the woman he had chosen, who, at that very moment, lifted her eyes and met his. A frown of concern momentarily creased Felicity's brow as she noted who stood next to her husband.

Your reputation has managed to precede you even to our little backwater, Liam thought to himself, as he gave Felicity a reassuring smile.

"I will be certain to pass on your kind words to my wife," Liam told Isabel. A small shiver of delight ran through him at being able to refer to Felicity in such a way.

Isabel tapped him on the arm with her closed fan. "Now you must promise not to be a bore and keep Felicity locked away in the country. I expect both of you to come to town often, and I insist you both visit me when you do." Her smile turned positively feral. "After all, I want Felicity and me to become the best of friends. Just as I'm sure Catherine and I will soon be."

"Catherine?" Liam feigned innocence, though he was shocked at hearing Catherine's name being spoken out loud by his brother's former lover. Common sense told him that Isabel would assume her meeting with Catherine would not be unknown to him. Rian would have told him, but she could not have known it was Rian's idea to avoid mentioning Catherine's name. As far as Liam knew, neither Rian nor Mrs. Hatch nor even Catherine herself had actually used her first name in Isabel's presence. So how was it she was able to now speak of her with such familiarity?

"Oh come now, Liam," Isabel said, narrowing her eyes, "don't pretend that you have no idea to whom I am referring." Her voice was as smooth as silk. "You would be amazed at the secrets I know. I hope Catherine is enjoying her stay in the country. The air at this time of year can be so...invigorating."

Liam's protest was silenced before it even had time to form in his head. The tap from Isabel's fan was a little sharper this time.

"Ah, here comes your brother. I do hope you take advantage of his expertise should you be in need of instruction on your wedding night." She arched a brow. "Would you like me to have a quiet word with your bride? Offer some advice of my own perhaps?"

Her question took him by surprise. He could conceive of no situation that would benefit by Isabel giving his wife advice on any subject. It was an idea so repellant Liam was unable to successfully disguise his dismay.

"Don't fret so," Isabel chided with a laugh. "I have no experience with virgins, at least not those of my own sex!"

Liam muttered something unintelligible as his brother joined them.

"Rian, how wonderful!" Isabel declared, taking the glass of wine from his hand.

"What have you two been talking about?" Rian asked, noting the slightly horrified look on his brother's face.

"Oh, nothing in particular," Isabel said, tapping Liam once more with her fan. "I was just asking your brother if his bride might like to avail herself of my expertise."

"In what area?" The muscle in Liam's jaw began to jump alarmingly.

"A wife's expectations on her wedding night," Isabel laughed.

"And how would you know what Felicity should expect?"

Isabel laughed again, and put a finger to her lips. "Don't worry," she said, addressing Liam, "I promise it will be our secret!" Giving both men a conspiratorial smile, she left with a swish of her skirts.

Liam looked at Rian, the color beginning to creep above the collar of his shirt. "I swear to you, Rian, Isabel and I have never—"

"I know, I know," Rian soothed, his hand on his brother's shoulder. He knew only too well that this type of teasing, the kind filled with sly innuendos, made his brother uncomfortable. And it was positively unnerving when it came from a woman. He sighed quietly. He was not going to have Liam upset on his wedding day and certainly not by Isabel. "Unfortunately that's just Isabel's way of being humorous. She means no harm by it."

"Really?" Liam gave his brother a scathing look. "Forgive me if I beg to differ with you on that particular observation."

Rian drained his glass. Liam was being overly sensitive but, given the strain of the day, he was willing to overlook it. Like his bride, his brother preferred not to be the center of attention. "I'll speak with Isabel," he promised quietly. "In the meantime I think your beautiful wife needs rescuing." He pointed across the room, where Felicity seemed to be surrounded by a group of middle aged matrons. Giving the groom a push, he was pleased to see any concerns about Isabel vanish as Liam crossed the room to join his wife.

It didn't take long for Rian to find her. Surrounded by a group of young bucks, Isabel looked delighted as each man hung onto every word she uttered. She reminded Rian of a queen holding court, and there was a collective sigh of disappointment when he apologized, and led her to a secluded alcove. "Do not make me regret bringing you here today," he told her in a low voice, keeping his smile fixed.

"Regret?" Isabel sounded genuinely puzzled. "Whatever are you talking about?"

"I know my brother better than anyone else in this room, yes, better even on this day than his wife." Rian bent his head, and to the casual observer it would appear as if he were murmuring in her ear. "I will not have you playing games with either Liam or Felicity. Not today, and not ever. Do I make myself clear?" Pulling his head back, he looked down at her.

For a moment Isabel's eyes turned a hard, glassy green as rage made them glitter with an unnatural light, but then she relaxed and let out a peal of laughter loud enough to be noted by those nearby.

"Darling, nothing could be further from the truth." She placed her hand on Rian's chest. "I apologize if your brother misunderstood me, but if it makes you feel better, then I gladly give you my word that I shall behave myself as far as the newlyweds are concerned. Come now, you're being tiresome, and I thought we were getting along so well." Looking over his shoulder, she gave a small wave. The alcove, it seemed, was not so private after all. "Now if you will excuse me, there's someone who's been trying to get my attention, and I've been ignoring him for far too long."

He caught hold of her arm as she slipped past him. "I will be keeping a close eye on you, Isabel."

"I wouldn't want it any other way, lover," she said, tilting her head up and pressing her mouth to his, making certain the inappropriately intimate kiss was witnessed by at least two or three other couples.

Rian watched her walk away from him and wondered what she was really up to. There was always a purpose behind everything Isabel did, even when she was teasing, but before he could speculate further he was surprised to see Liam advancing on him once more. "Did I not send you to rescue your wife?" he asked.

"It seems my mother-in-law beat me to it," Liam answered in a tone that indicated wounded pride.

"Not to worry. Let them enjoy what little time they have left together. Felicity is your wife now. You can afford to be generous, brother." Lowering his voice, he added, "Isabel will apologize if you so wish it."

The new husband shook his head. "No, that won't be necessary, but there is something else I think you should know."

"Don't let her get you riled up with her foolishness Liam, not today of all days," Rian admonished gently.

Liam shook his head again. "I won't, but that's not what this is about." He frowned. "She talked about Catherine, and mentioned her by name."

Rian looked thoughtful. "What did she say?"

Momentarily forgetting the promise he'd made to himself, Liam seized two full glasses of wine from a servant carrying a full tray. He passed one to Rian, drained the other in one go, and then repeated his conversation with Isabel, word for word.

"Bah! Isabel has no intention of becoming friends with any woman, let alone one who could draw a man's attention from her," Rian said with a derisive snort. "She dislikes competition in any form."

"The real question is how did she know Catherine's name and the fact that she is already living at Oakhaven?" Liam asked

Rian shrugged it off. "Most likely one of the servants talked. It is of little consequence, and perhaps this is Isabel's way of saying she intends to find out who Catherine is. I am sure there are doors she can open that we cannot." He clapped his brother on the shoulder. "Lady Howard is a clever woman, but she knows no more about Catherine, or her circumstances, than we do. She holds no advantage." He took the glass from Liam's hand. "For God's sake, man, wipe that look of doom and gloom off your face. It's your wedding day." Liam gave a weak smile. "Better. Now let's go and find that wife of yours so I can indulge myself in a time-honored male Connor prerogative."

"Time-honored?" Liam was suddenly wary at the glint in his brother's eye. He'd never heard of such a thing. "And what might that be?"

"Dancing with the bride, of course!"

* * * *

At last, the happy couple managed to slip away from their guests, and, after a long, circuitous carriage ride guaranteed to discourage any would-be pranksters, they finally arrived at the Connor townhouse. Mrs. Hatch was the only member of the household to witness Liam carry his bride across the threshold. She had given strict orders that she alone would tend to the needs of the new couple. Most of the staff had been given the night off and those who remained knew better than to leave their rooms unless specifically called upon. The only exception was the night footman whose duty it was to make sure the front door was bolted securely after everyone was abed.

With a smile on her face, Mrs. Hatch led the way to the master suite, and, after closing the door behind Liam, she sat quietly on a chair at the end of the hall. Experience told her to wait, and a few moments later she heard the door open, and the new groom came out of the room.

"Mrs. Hatch?" His tone was as anxious as his expression.

"Master Liam?"

His nervousness made him appear far younger than his years. "Um...I was wondering if you could assist Felicity. Too many ties and things..." He stared at his hands as if he'd never seen them before.

She patted him gently on the arm. "Why don't you go downstairs to the library and get yourself something to drink, but only one, mind. I'll come fetch you when your bride is ready."

With a grateful look over his shoulder, Liam did as he was told. Mrs. Hatch knocked lightly on the bedroom door before entering. Her new mistress stood in the middle of the room, anxiously twisting the wedding ring on her finger.

"He tried to help me but his hands shook so much he was fearful he would tear the material," Felicity explained.

"Well now, we can't have that, can we, Miss Felicity."

Felicity caught hold of the older woman's hands, letting her feel the trembling in her own. "He's not the only one. I can't seem to stop my hands from shaking either."

Carla Susan Smith

"What you're feeling is perfectly normal," the housekeeper assured her. "I was nervous on my own wedding night, as is every new bride I imagine." She poured a small glass of blackberry brandy and handed it to Felicity. "Just a sip or two to help calm your nerves," she instructed with a twinkle in her eye. Turning the new bride around, Mrs. Hatch began unlacing the wedding gown. "Do you love him?" she asked softly.

"Oh yes, I do. Truly."

"Then put your trust in him, my dear. I have known Master Liam all his life, and believe me when I say he will never hurt you." With the back now loosened, she helped the new Mistress of Oakhaven step out of her beautiful, but cumbersome gown, and then proceeded to remove the layers of petticoats she wore. "Now let's get you into something that is sure to please your husband."

Liam poured himself a brandy but did not drink it. Instead he set the glass on the fireplace mantel as he stared into the flames. Although he was not as experienced as Rian when it came to the fairer sex, he knew what it was to lie with a woman. He remembered all too clearly his first time. Filled with a mix of excitement and dread, he'd been awestruck by her breasts, while remaining confused and bewildered by everything below her waist. Thankfully, she was the experienced one, and he would be forever grateful not just for her role in helping him through the physical act, but her kindness to him afterwards. Though he knew losing one's virginity was markedly different for a woman, he promised to be as kind to Felicity. A knock on the door brought in Mrs. Hatch, whose gentle nod told him he could return to his bride.

Together they walked up the staircase and then along the hallway, stopping outside the bedroom door. Liam turned to look at the woman who had been a surrogate mother to him for so many years. His head was suddenly filled with a hundred things he wanted to say to her, but he couldn't think of how to phrase a single one.

"She's a wonderful young woman, Liam, and I have no doubt she will make you a wonderful wife. Your mother would have been very proud of you. As am I."

"Thank you."

In a rare display of emotion, Liam gathered the housekeeper to him, holding her in his arms as though she truly was his mother. Leaning down, he kissed her cheek and received a kiss in return before he freed her from his embrace. She smiled up at him and then retraced her steps, leaving him alone to stare at the closed bedroom door behind which lay the rest of his life.

Chapter 5

The only light in the master suite came from the blazing fire in the hearth, creating shadows that danced on the walls. Liam remained standing by the door, waiting for his eyes to adjust to the dim light. He looked toward the bed and saw Felicity propped up against the pillows. She held the bed coverings up to her neck. He didn't recall his bed being so big. Now it seemed to dwarf the rest of the furniture in the room. He swallowed as a sudden attack of nerves made his stomach roll. Being nervous was not going to help his bride.

An anxious smile played about her mouth, and Liam could tell she was doing her best to try to relax, and failing miserably. Carefully he sat down next to her on the edge of the bed and gently managed to pry open her fingers, releasing the fierce grip she had on the sheet. He held her hand, turning it over so he could gently stroke her palm with his fingers. A woman like Felicity could not be rushed in such a sensitive matter. Like a high-strung thoroughbred, she needed to be coaxed into following his lead. And with his concentration focused solely on his bride, his own nervousness evaporated.

Liam was pleased to see that a light supper, along with an excellent bottle of wine, had thoughtfully been provided. He poured a glass for Felicity before joining her with his own glass and a plate of food. He saw the hesitation and curiosity in his wife's eyes as he began to remove his elegantly embroidered wedding coat and shoes, able to hide his smile as the look turned to disappointment when she realized that was all he was removing. Still clad in his fine linen shirt, waistcoat, breeches and silk stockings, he lay down on top of the bed next to his wife. The invitation to get beneath the covers must come from her.

He chose to seduce his wife with conversation.

Liam reflected on the day's events, talking about all that had happened, and watched as Felicity began to relax. She sipped her wine and nibbled on the light delicacies he fed her, laughing out loud at some of Liam's anecdotes regarding their wedding guests. None were directed at her closest relatives, and Liam was clever enough to weave outrageous fabrications with enough truth to make the stories sound believable. He wondered how many men spent their wedding night thus, concocting fantastic tales in order to calm an anxious bride. He didn't mind. The stories were having the desired effect.

At one point Felicity laughed so hard she reached for his hand, clinging to it as she fought to recover from a fit of the giggles. Liam simply stared back at her, a smile playing at the corners of his mouth. Candlelight, coupled with the glow from the fire, bathed her skin with a soft warmth, and sparks of light filled her eyes. Light that he was confident would soon be replaced by the blaze of passion. He reached forward and stroked his fingers lightly down the column of her neck, sliding inside the open neckline of her nightgown to trace a path across her collar bone. Felicity's breath quickened at his touch, but it was with anticipation not fear. Leaning forward, Liam kissed her softly on the mouth, feeling her momentarily tense as his tongue pushed against her closed lips, seeking entrance to the warmth beyond. She opened for him as she had before, moving her hand to his arm, and clutching tightly as she savored the feel and taste of him.

Liam released his lips and smiled at the look of astonished wonderment filling Felicity's face. Although he had kissed her like this once before, it felt different now. Apparently his wife thought the same. Wanting to repeat the experience, she greedily searched for his lips with her own, and in response to his coaxing, found herself kissing him ardently, not wanting the moment to end.

With a laugh Liam pulled away. "Patience, little mouse," he whispered as he tapped her gently on the nose with his forefinger. She gestured impatiently, reaching for him, and making a small, frustrated mewling sound. It was the invitation he'd been waiting for. He rolled off the bed, got to his feet and undressed quickly. Felicity shyly turned her head away. She had never seen a man naked before, and her face was on fire.

"Felicity." Liam's voice was gentle, coaxing, and the absence of rustling material said he had removed all his wedding finery. His wife however, kept her gaze averted. "Felicity, look at me." Now the tone was firmer, and years of obedience made her automatically yield to the underlying authority she heard. "Open your eyes, love."

He watched her throat move once, twice, and then a third time before she was able to do as he asked, and when she did, the look on her face told him he was neither ugly nor repellant in her eyes. Indeed, Felicity gazed at the lean lines of his body with its well-muscled frame with a hunger that was positively covetous. Liam could practically feel the heat rushing through her, making her skin flush, and causing a faint tremble in her limbs.

"I promise I shall try not to hurt you, darling."

His wife nodded, her trust in him absolute as she watched him pull back the covers and slide in beside her. Somehow the bed didn't seem quite so big.

Liam ran his hand down Felicity's arm, feeling the soft material bunching beneath his fingertips. The nightgown was lace, and as befitted her status, virginal white. But though it covered her completely from neck to ankles, it revealed more of her shapely figure than it hid as the delicate fabric clung seductively to every curve of her body. Now it was Liam's turn to stare. Unbeknownst to him a temptress had been hiding within Felicity's corset and layers of petticoats. A familiar stirring in his loins now increased in intensity as he ran his eyes over her, pulling her to him and kissing her slightly swollen lips once more.

With a mounting passion he carefully pulled up the lacy garment until he could slip his hand beneath the material and feel the smooth skin beneath. Felicity gasped at his electrifying touch, and as he moved his lips over her cheek, her closed eyelids, and the corners of her mouth, his restless hand continued to stroke the inside of her thigh. His lips moved down her neck, his tongue pausing at the dip in the base of her throat, tasting the drop of sweat pooling there. He moved his head, wanting to stroke his tongue across her collar bone, but the delicate lace became a barrier denying him access. Without saying a word, Felicity removed his hand from her thigh and pressed her own against his chest, motioning him to wait. She slid out of the bed, making him miss her already. Quickly she slipped the small pearl buttons free until her nightgown fell from her shoulders to the floor.

Liam's breath caught in his throat. "You're so beautiful," he murmured, extending his hand and helping her back into bed.

Felicity's body was compact, and sensuously curved. Small, perfectly round breasts sat high on her ribcage with pink nipples that begged for his touch. He leaned toward one, his tongue flicking across the taut bud before he took it between his lips and suckled, gently pulling her flesh inside his mouth as she gasped at the sensation. Then he gave the same attention to the other, and Felicity trembled as waves of pleasure ran through her.

Liam continued to nibble and suck hungrily on his wife's flesh. Exploring all her secret places with his fingers and his tongue while she held onto him tightly. With her fingers caught in his thick hair, she unconsciously guided him, riding the crest of one rippling sensation after another. Each one more exquisitely glorious than its predecessor. She stopped thinking, responding only to the physical wants and needs of her body.

Gently stroking the soft skin of her inner thigh, Liam could feel his own hunger rising as the heat from Felicity's body began to envelop him. His hand moved closer to her core, parting the delicate folds of skin as he eased a finger inside her body. Though her desire pulsed in waves like molten lava, he knew she was far from ready to receive him. She was still too dry, and penetration would be painful, so he began to suckle her breasts again, teasing the hard, swollen buds with his tongue.

Felicity moaned, and answering a need deep within her, she surged against him. Again and again she rolled her pelvic bone against the heel of his hand until the hot wetness flowing from her told him she was ready. Liam's own body was more than willing, his erection hard and jutting and growing increasingly impatient to find release.

Kissing her once more, full and hard on the mouth, he nudged her thighs open with his legs and then positioned himself between them. His voice was thick with emotion, and husky from his own wanting. "Darling, this may hurt, but it will be just for a moment, I promise you."

She opened her eyes and looked at him, and for a moment all Liam saw was fear, but then the all-consuming hunger raging through her smothered that emotion. Closing her eyes once more, Felicity nodded. "Do it," she whispered.

With one thrust Liam was inside her, stopping when he felt himself tear through the membrane that was her gift to him. His body trembled as he braced his weight on his forearms, but he gave his wife the time she needed to adjust to the feel of him, and recognize the aching throb inside her. He watched as a single tear slipped from beneath her closed eyelids and he thought his heart would break, understanding fully the reason a woman's virginity was so highly valued.

For what seemed an eternity Liam held himself suspended above his bride, not daring to move, his cock twitching inside her, desperate to complete the act that had been initiated. They were close, and yet still worlds apart. Slowly he eased himself down until, without realizing it, Felicity bore the weight of his body on her own slender frame. He felt the tremor in her arms and legs as she opened her eyes.

"Darling? If it's too painful for you—if I'm too heavy—"

She shook her head and the struggle within her concluded as she reached a decision. His presence inside her was an unfamiliar invasion that strained her muscles and bruised her body, but even though it hurt, she would not have changed a single thing about what was happening.

"Liam, stay just as you are," she told him in a low rasp that still managed to sound shy and hesitant.

To his surprise Felicity raised her legs, taking him farther inside her body, and coating him with her slick heat. She began breathing a little quicker, and he saw her eyes widen as he filled her. And then suddenly she rewarded his patience by pushing against him. Her movements were awkward and unskilled, until Liam placed a hand on her hip, encouraging her to move with him in an easy rhythm.

Feeling an uncontrollable desire sweep through her, Felicity abandoned all reason, all sense of self, and rode the wave as it quickened, going faster and faster until finally, in an explosion of silken fire, they fell together, their passion sated.

* * * *

It was well past the witching hour when Rian quietly entered the townhouse. He had thoroughly enjoyed himself once he received word that the most recent Mr. and Mrs. Connor had arrived safely at the same destination some hours earlier. In the meantime, Isabel had apparently grown bored and departed without saying a word to anyone. He was certain that none of the other guests noticed anything different about her behavior, but Rian could sense something was amiss. He did not know what exactly, but he felt certain she was still smarting from her encounter with Catherine.

Slipping quietly into the library, he was about to pour himself a nightcap when he spied a glass, its contents untouched, on the mantel. There was no sense in wasting perfectly good brandy. Raising the glass to the ceiling, Rian silently toasted the happy couple before tossing the contents down his throat. Welcoming the smooth burn that suffused him, he sat down on the nearest chair and pulled off his boots. He did not want to risk waking anyone as he made his way upstairs.

The door to his room creaked as he pushed it open, but he was confident the noise would not be noted by the occupants of the master bedroom. Still, he couldn't help wincing as another round of protesting hinges came with the door's closure. Placing his boots by the chair, he removed his coat and laid it on the seat. The waistcoat followed, and he was pulling the fine linen shirt free of his breeches when a sound made the hair on the nape of his neck rise. Turning his head, Rian saw he was not alone.

Pale moonlight spilled through the window, giving him enough light to pad softly toward the bed and find a naked Isabel fast asleep there, her dark luxurious hair spread out across the pillow. Rian sighed. In repose she looked as beautiful as anything painted by one of the Masters, but then he felt his brows pull together, wondering how she had managed to get into the house, and more particularly his room. Without Mrs. Hatch knowing. There was no excuse she could have fabricated that would have made the housekeeper offer her a bed on this of all nights, so he was certain the housekeeper had no idea there was an extra guest sleeping beneath their roof.

Isabel murmured as she dreamed, and then, kicking the sheet down, she rolled over so Rian could admire the length of her back and the soft roundness of her buttocks. He stared at her, knowing how easy it would be to simply slip between the sheets alongside her. And then, almost before the thought had time to fully develop, that odd feeling of guilt washed over him. With steely resolve he told himself, not this time, not tonight, and most certainly not in this house.

Looking down at the creamy body that was both a temptation and an invitation, Rian told himself it was over. He had no intention of being intimate with Isabel again, and was surprised that he felt no remorse or regret at his decision. Still, his body had betrayed him once before and he saw no need to test his resolution. Almost as if a weight had been lifted, he felt a sense of relief that was quite liberating. Moving stealthily he retraced his steps back to the door. Tonight he would sleep in the adjacent bedroom.

It was not until he was settled in the other bed and about to drift off to sleep that he remembered he had not brought his coat and boots with him. Isabel would surely see them when she awoke, and know he had seen her, and had left. It would be interesting to hear what excuse she came up with to explain her presence.

Chapter 6

The chime of the clock striking the hour seemed to be particularly booming, until Rian realized he was hungover. A parting gift from the numerous glasses of wine he had consumed the night before. Sitting on the edge of the bed, he hoped the man pounding on the drum inside his skull would leave him alone—and soon. He rubbed his bleary eyes with the heel of each hand, and then looked at his surroundings. The bedroom was unfamiliar, and he couldn't recall why he'd decided to sleep here instead of the room he'd been using. The answer came to him as he made use of the chamber pot.

Getting dressed was made more challenging by his throbbing head, and the fact the room insisted on spinning. But he managed, even though it took two attempts to button his shirt properly. Unfortunately the room still refused to cooperate. How the devil was he supposed to get through the door if it wouldn't stay still? He closed his eyes and took a few deep breaths to steady himself. When he opened them again the room had decided to behave itself. The same could not be said about the man inside his head. Doing his best to ignore the pounding at his temples, Rian made his way through the door and down the hall. He stopped, surprised to see the door to his original bedroom standing wide open. Peering inside he was even more surprised to discover the bed was neatly made. There was no sign of Isabel, but his coat and boots remained exactly where he had placed them in the wee hours of the night.

"Have you lost something, Master Rian?" Mrs. Hatch watched him from across the hall, a smile tugging at the corners of her mouth.

"I'm not sure," he murmured hesitantly.

"I think you must have been making quite merry last night," she admonished with a gentle chuckle. "Although what the bed did to displease you I cannot say."

"The bed?"

She moved past him into the room. "Well, you obviously started to get undressed," she said, pointing to his clothing on the chair and the boots still standing at attention, "but for some reason you decided to sleep in the other room. Did the bed look lumpy?" she chuckled.

"Can't say," Rian muttered with a shake of his head that he instantly regretted. The man with the drum was enjoying himself immensely.

Seeing him wince, and noting the sharp furrow of his brow, the housekeeper became sympathetic. "There, there, Master Rian, why don't you sit down here, and I'll get you something that will make you feel better in no time." She guided him to a chair before going to pull on the bell cord by the fireplace. The maid who answered was given a set of explicit instructions as the housekeeper went to the washstand and poured some cold water into the basin. After wetting a cloth, she wrung it out before approaching Rian once more. "Lean your head back, and close your eyes," she instructed, placing the damp cloth across his forehead as he complied. "This should help," she said.

The cool cloth felt wonderful, and Rian could already feel the ache in his temples easing, but expecting to see Isabel come walking through the open door at any moment kept him tense. Beneath half-closed lids he gazed at the pristine bed, finding it hard to picture Lady Howard carefully straightening the sheets and plumping the pillows to hide any evidence of her stay. He almost jumped out of his skin when Mrs. Hatch asked, "Did you know Lady Howard was here?"

"Here?" he spluttered in a voice that was too loud. Regulating his tone he asked, "When was she here?"

Mrs. Hatch gave him a curious look before proceeding. "She came last night to deliver Master Liam and Miss Felicity's wedding gift in person. And she also left a note for you. Did you not read it?"

At that point the maid returned with a tall glass filled with an opaque liquid and a dish containing an egg. The housekeeper quickly broke the raw egg into the glass, stirring it briskly before handing it to Rian. He looked dubiously at the contents before Mrs. Hatch's raised brow gave him no option but to drink it down with a grimace.

"I didn't find any note," he said, handing back the empty glass and wiping the back of his hand across his mouth. "What was the hour?"

"I don't remember exactly," Mrs. Hatch apologized, "but it was before Master Liam and Miss Felicity arrived. She was most particular that I put her gift in the morning room so the happy couple would be sure to see it when they came down for breakfast. She said she would leave your note on the mantel in the library."

The only thing he'd seen on the mantel had been the glass of brandy. "Did you see her leave it?" Rian asked.

"No. She was already gone when I returned from placing her gift." The housekeeper's brows pulled together. "She must have just missed Master Liam and Miss Felicity, for they arrived at that time. I'm sorry to say I forgot all about her until just now."

"Do not concern yourself, Mrs. Hatch; I am sure it was of no consequence."

At least now he knew how Isabel had made it to the upper floor of the house without the housekeeper being aware of it. A quick glance in each room would have led her to the one she was looking for, but puzzling over how she had managed to slip out unobserved made him frown. "I'm sorry, Mrs. Hatch, what did you say?"

"I was asking if you could have a word with George. I don't want to bother Master Liam with it. Not today of all days."

George was the only other servant with permission to be abroad last night. "George? What's wrong with George?"

"It seems he forgot to secure the front door," Mrs. Hatch told him. "Anyone could have slipped in and murdered us in our beds."

Suddenly everything became crystal clear. Knowing he had sent George to bed before slipping home the bolt on the front door himself, Rian could not now reprimand the man. "The fault is mine, Mrs. Hatch. I assured George I would lock up, but too much wine must have made me forget." He gave her his best sheepish smile. "My sincere apologies to you and all the staff. I promise it won't happen again."

"Well, best we say no more about it then. I'll have a bath made up for you if you would like."

"That, Mrs. Hatch, would be a godsend."

He concluded that Isabel must have woken before any of the staff were about, and seeing he had chosen to sleep elsewhere, left before anyone else knew of her nocturnal visit. He could only speculate that she'd decided remaking the bed would add credibility to her denial if her whereabouts of the past night were ever questioned. Far better to claim Rian was delusional than admit he had deliberately chosen not to sleep with her.

* * * *

It would have taken an expert to realize just how furious Isabel really was beneath her seemingly calm exterior. Almost two weeks had passed since Liam and Felicity's wedding, and still no word from Rian. It was insufferable! She heard, from Charlotte Maitling herself that the newlyweds continued to remain in town. A great many invitations to Yuletide festivities begged their presence, with an equal number asking them to be available to celebrate the New Year. Liam and Felicity had been delighted to accept most of them. But the absence of Rian at all but the smaller, more intimate family gatherings had not gone unnoticed. In a strange way this had been Isabel's saving grace. She would have been at a loss to explain her absence from Rian's arm had he attended some of the larger celebratory functions. As it was, the gossips were already in a feeding frenzy over the obvious rift in their relationship.

"Well I must admit, darling, you certainly had me fooled," Charlotte Maitling told her. "I've never seen your interest so firmly fixed, although I can understand why."

Isabel gave the older woman a hard look.

"He is quite the handsome brute," Charlotte continued, ignoring Isabel's expression. "I was absolutely positive you were about to tell me he'd made an offer for your hand. Still, not to be, I suppose," she added with a smile that bore more than a hint of malicious mischief.

"If you must know, I got tired of him," Isabel explained. "Sometimes a woman needs more than a handsome face and well-endowed physique."

Charlotte's laugh had more in common with a tavern wench's than that of a member of the aristocracy who enjoyed the privilege of conversing with royalty. "Oh Isabel, now I know you're lying!" she exclaimed gleefully.

Isabel had pouted sulkily for the rest of Lady Maitling's visit. Her temper did not improve when John Fletcher, her eyes and ears about town, informed her that, due to Liam and Felicity's extended stay in London, Rian had accepted the hospitality of Charles and Emily Pelham to afford the newlyweds some privacy. It was insulting enough that he had spurned her on the night of the wedding, refusing to even acknowledge she'd been in the house—much less his bed. Isabel thought Rian at the very least would want to know where she had vanished to, but he gave every indication of having not the slightest concern. And now he was compounding her humiliation by remaining in town and preferring the company of two decrepit fossils to the warmth of her perfumed silk sheets. It was no wonder she was beside herself.

Deciding that the first step to winning Rian back was to discover as much as she possibly could about her rival, Isabel had turned to John, seeking information. But all she had so far was Catherine's name, as supplied by the avaricious footman. Still, she had used it to great effect as Liam's reaction had proved. He did not possess any talent for hiding his emotions, and the mention of Catherine's name had clearly unnerved him. It had been a small victory, but now Isabel was getting frustrated at the lack of progress by her agent. She forced herself to push her doubts aside. John had always come through for her in the past. Now, as if aware of her concern, he had sent a note requesting an appointment.

John Fletcher's relationship with Isabel meant he never needed an appointment to see her, so the formality of his request told her that he would not be alone. He was bringing a 'person of interest.' She was mildly intrigued and, though she did not like surprises, she knew that nothing would be gained at being fretful beforehand. Smoothing an imaginary wrinkle from the front of her dress, she entered the drawing room where the two men waited for her. After a brief salutation to John, she turned her attention to his companion. Cost was not a factor in the man's wardrobe choice, Isabel noted, but rich fabrics could only disguise wasted flesh so much. The once handsome face now bore all the marks of a dissolute lifestyle, and she did not try to hide her disappointment as she raised a questioning eyebrow. Stepping forward, John Fletcher made the introductions.

"Lady Isabel Howard, please allow me to present Mr. Phillip Davenport."

Chapter 7

Catherine bloomed at Oakhaven. Allowed to take the matter of her recovery into her own hands, she became a model patient. She obeyed every instruction sent from Mrs. Hatch, and her health quickly began to reap the benefits. Her own naturally robust constitution factored a great deal into her progress, and Catherine was clever enough to heed the rhythm of her body. Making certain she did not overtax her resources, she grew stronger and was soon exploring her new world from top to bottom, inside and out.

As neither Rian nor Liam had left any instructions regarding her position at Oakhaven, Catherine quickly made friends with everyone. Whether in the main house or the grounds, she treated all as equals and addressed each person who crossed her path with polite respect. In the beginning Cook had insisted she take her meals in the formal dining room where the family ate, but after two days Catherine begged to be permitted to eat with the rest of the staff in the friendly, informal atmosphere of the kitchen. Permission was granted, but only after she gave her solemn word she would resume taking her meals with the family once they returned.

Left to her own devices, she explored the house. Out of respect for Rian and his brother she did not venture into any of the family rooms, but considered the rest of the house fair game. In no time at all, from attic to basement, she had familiarized herself with the layout of each floor.

There were a number of rooms that were not used, and she found the furnishings draped with heavy, protective coverings. It made sense when she was told that for a long time Liam had been the sole occupant of Oakhaven. While she stood on the threshold of one such chamber, an echo of familiarity swept over Catherine, as if she had known shrouded rooms like this before, only she could not remember when or where. The closed rooms at Oakhaven did not carry the shame of neglect, however. It was as if they knew the lack of use was a temporary situation, and a quick turn with a broom and a polishing cloth was all that would be required to make them hospitable again. Whatever memory skittered through her mind told her that what she had witnessed in the past was a more permanent abandonment.

Catherine had been delighted by the library, and the number of books and periodicals filling the shelves amazed her. Some of the titles she recognized as duplicates from the townhouse, and she shook her head at the extravagance of the same book being in two different libraries. It did not, however, curb her enthusiasm. With slippers kicked off and legs curled beneath her, she could often be found in an overstuffed chair enjoying one of the fine works that had been left unattended for too long. Some of what she read stirred the echo of a memory, allowing her to recite passages she inexplicably knew by heart. Tilly watched in amazement at the animation in Catherine's face as she described characters and story lines from memory. They had both laughed, convinced this was a positive start to a full recovery.

Winter descended on them in all its chilling, regal glory, but it did little to diminish the outdoor grandeur of the estate, which was just as beautiful and awe inspiring as the interior of the great house. With her feet now healed she was able to wear boots, so when the weather cooperated Catherine was able to persuade Tilly to let her explore the grounds. Walking would help rebuild her strength, and it did not matter that the trees were bare or the flower beds empty beneath a blanket of fallen snow.

The day she discovered the stables brought forth an infectious joy others found hard to resist. Tilly, who loudly admitted to being deathly afraid of horses to anyone within earshot, reluctantly resigned herself to accompanying Catherine. But only with the clear understanding that she would not be made to actually go anywhere near one of the terrifying beasts. The younger girl was astute enough to know that if she refused to accompany her patient, then Catherine would simply go on her own.

Catherine was disappointed, however, to learn that orders had already been given to the head groomsman, and riding was out of the question. Rian must have suspected that she would venture out of the house, and knew it was only a matter of time before she found her way to the stables. Irritated by what she considered his overprotectiveness, she began to wonder why Rian would assume she'd even want to ride. What if she was like Tilly, and scared to death of horses? Perhaps Rian was simply erring on the side of caution, but no matter his reason, the stern look on the stablemaster's face told her he would not be persuaded to break the orders he had received.

"And don't you go trying to get one of my lads to saddle up for you," he told her. "A pretty face like yours could get them to turn cartwheels, but if I'm not mistaken, you'd feel bad knowing I'd have no choice but to let them go for their disobedience."

Catherine was horrified. She never wanted to be the reason anyone lost their livelihood or position. And it wasn't as if Rian had said she could *never* go riding; she could ride with a companion he deemed suitable. Until then she had to be content to meet the stable's residents with her feet firmly on the ground.

"Do you remember if you ever had a horse of your own, Miss?" Tilly asked one afternoon as she nervously watched Catherine lead a big hunter out of his stall and into the yard for one of the grooms.

"I don't know, Tilly, but I think I must have," Catherine said, stroking the horse's muzzle. She moved to the animal's side, laying her head against the glossy coat and inhaling the unique equine scent. A fierce, searing joy came over her, infusing her heart and mind with a sense of completeness as she passed her hand gently down the horse's neck. As if recognizing a kindred spirit, the horse, perfectly at ease with her touch, chuffed in approval.

"'Course she's 'ad 'orses!" grumbled a man irritably. "Can't touch an 'orse like she does lessen you growed up with 'em." He pointed a gnarled finger in Catherine's direction. "Mark my words, Missus; I knows 'orse people and you're 'orsey right enough!"

"I'm 'orsey!" Catherine declared, giving Tilly a beaming smile. "Who would have known!"

As her body healed, so did her emotional well-being. Snippets of memories returned, but the process was slow and Catherine did not know if what she was remembering was an event from her childhood or something more recent. Of course she knew anything that involved Rian and the members of the household was recent, and she could now recall quite clearly standing on the docks that fateful morning when Rian had rescued her. Though thoroughly ashamed of the fact, she could also admit that it had been her intention to jump into the river. But the identity of the one who had driven her to such desperation still eluded her.

With steadfast certainty she knew Rian was not responsible for the assault on her, and she wanted very much to express her gratitude to him. Without his intervention she would have easily succumbed to a watery grave, and she secretly hoped the wedding party would return soon. But there were other reasons she wanted Rian back. An image suddenly filled her mind. A picture of Rian as she saw him in her dreams, reaching for her, wanting her. These were not the same dreams she had had of him before. These dreams had evolved, turning into fantasies that were erotic, sexually charged, and very vivid. And she welcomed them as would any young, healthy woman, even though they left her breathless, with her blood pounding, and a sweet, hot ache flowing through her.

"It's not possible. He doesn't think of me in that way!" she protested weakly to her dream self.

In the grey area of slumber, when she was dancing on the edge of her dreams and not yet fully awake, Catherine was forced to acknowledge a truth. Standing before the final barrier that separated a young girl's innocence from a woman's knowledge, she was left with no doubt that it was Rian Connor she wanted to help her complete the journey. She could not explain why it had to be him, not even to herself, but instinctively she felt he was the only man who could guide her through the labyrinth of her awakening desire.

Such thoughts did not bring her any comfort in the harsh light of day, and Catherine chided herself for having such ridiculous fantasies. Plagued by insecurities, she could not imagine a man like Rian Connor choosing to be with her. He was older, mature, and no doubt used to having his pick of beautiful, confident women. Women who could stand as his equal both in bed and out of it.

Women very much like Isabel Howard.

Seated at the kitchen table, Catherine listened in amazement as everyone gossiped openly about Rian's affair with Isabel. It was an unspoken rule that whatever was discussed amongst the staff, particularly if it involved any of the family, never went beyond the house. And it went without saying that absolutely nothing was repeated to strangers.

"It would be the ruin of a good man if she got her claws in him!" Tilly declared as she poured another mug of ale from the large brown jug on the table.

"Is that likely?" someone seated on the opposite side of the table asked.

"No." Tilly shook her head sagely. "I think Master Rian has his wits about him with that one."

"They say she has the morals of an alley cat."

"Is it true she's bedded half the royal family?"

"Aye, and not just the men either!"

This last was followed by a burst of raucous laughter.

"Is she as beautiful as they say?" one of the stable boys asked, his face beet red. "Have you ever seen her, Tilly?"

"Oh, aye, she's beautiful right enough. I caught a glimpse of her when she came to visit—" Tilly stopped abruptly, her face matching the inquisitive stable boy's as she swiveled her head to stare at Catherine seated at the far end of the table. "Oh, Miss Catherine, I'm so very sorry," she apologized.

"It's all right, Tilly. No harm done," Catherine said, smiling at them all as she stood. "For all we know I may have bedded members of the royal family as well!"

A howl of protests denying such behavior followed Catherine through the door, and it comforted her to know the staff believed her incapable of such depravity. Still, she had to wonder about Rian's choice of a lover. It seemed that Isabel found no favor with any member of staff in either household; however, she must possess some quality that intrigued him. Then again, what did Catherine know about men, and the attraction of one woman over another? Nothing. At least nothing she could remember.

Frowning as she pondered the question of men and choices, Catherine made her way to her room. Was physical beauty all that was needed to inflame a man's desire? A pleasing face could hide many a fault, but what if a woman was plain? If the symmetry of her face was not pleasing, could she hope to compensate with a shapely figure? And what if that figure was flawed in some way? Catherine now carried scars. Dr. McGregor had told her she would, and she had witnessed the sudden flare of pity in the eyes of both the housekeeper and her maid as they helped her bathe and dress. Was her body now so repulsive no man would ever want to touch her? No man would ever want to marry her? Would she never know the joy of bearing children?

Having reached her room, Catherine closed the door and turned the key in the lock. She leaned against it and shut her eyes for a moment or two, gathering her courage. Catching her lower lip in her teeth, she pushed away from the door and walked toward the large freestanding mirror. Earlier that morning with Tilly's help, she had tilted the reflective surface to an angle that would serve her purpose.

"You have put this off long enough," she whispered fiercely to her image. "It is time to see the truth with your own eyes." And slowly, with trembling fingers, she undid the buttons on her bodice, sliding the dress off her shoulders and letting it fall to the floor. Her petticoat and shift quickly followed, and Catherine stood before the looking glass completely naked. Afraid that she would lose her nerve, she turned around and pulled the thick braid over one shoulder so it hung in front of her. Twisting her head, she stared at herself in the mirror.

Her fingers trembled as she traced the livid scar as far as she was able to reach, her vision blurring from the silent tears coursing down her cheeks. Catherine could not fathom what transgression she was guilty of to have received such punishment. Her mind still would not allow her to reach through the fog and pull this one moment out of her past and examine it. Not knowing what else might have been taken from her, she told herself to be content with her dreams. It was possible that her dream world was as close as she would ever get to knowing Rian.

One final look at her scarred body and she shuddered. How could she expect any man to choose her over someone as perfectly beautiful as Isabel Howard?

Chapter 8

It was a week past New Year when Rian, Liam, and Felicity finally returned, and they immediately noticed the change in Catherine. She had shrieked with delight to see the carriage come down the driveway, and despite the cold, had run out to greet them. She waved and jumped up and down, almost startling the horses as the carriage came to a stop. Felicity hugged her, an expression of amazement on her face, and the two exchanged looks as if each was the other's long-lost sister. Liam, just as pleased with her noticeable improvement, opened his arms for a hug and kissed her on both cheeks.

"Good Lord, who is this imposter, and what has become of our Catherine?" he joked before turning and giving his brother a smug look. "I told you Oakhaven would be good for her."

"And you were right," Rian agreed without any outward sign of emotion.

Free of Liam's embrace, Catherine turned and hesitated. She was shy about greeting Rian, but she need not have worried. His arms loaded with packages, he acknowledged her with nothing but a brief nod before moving past her into the house. Deflated by the cold indifference of his greeting, Catherine consoled herself by hugging Mrs. Hatch so hard, the woman was in danger of having all the breath forced out of her.

"There, there, lass!" She beamed when Catherine finally let her go. "I told you I would be back."

And so Catherine spent the greater part of the day not with Felicity, but rather in the safety of the kitchen. Seated at the large kitchen table she listened to the warm, gossipy chatter about the wedding, and the difference between life at Oakhaven and life in the city. It seemed to

Catherine that country living was much preferred by the staff. A sentiment she wholeheartedly agreed with.

Now the family had returned, Catherine realized she had eaten her last meal in the kitchen. She was expected to take her meals once more in the large formal dining room, and it was with some trepidation she entered the room at the appropriate time. Perhaps she would not find it such an ordeal with Felicity and Liam for company, but she was unsure how anyone was expected to conduct a normal conversation seated at a table so big. It was a pleasant surprise to find it was not quite so intimidating a prospect as she had first thought. Felicity had decided that instead of being spread out down the length of the large table, they should all be grouped closer together at one end. It certainly made for a cozier arrangement, and Catherine was grateful to find that she was next to Felicity, but across from Rian.

Unfortunately the seating arrangement did little to dispel the awkwardness of the ordeal. For the most part conversation between herself and Felicity and Liam flowed easily enough, but when Catherine found herself addressing Rian, he continued to act much as he had on his arrival. He answered the few general questions she dared ask in a brusque tone, and asked none of her. After excusing herself as soon as she could, Catherine escaped to the safety of her room, where, alone in her bed, she realized the only sensible thing to do was to not think about Rian Connor. It was obvious the little regard he had held for her no longer existed, and she could only assume Lady Howard was the reason for the change in him. Her feelings hurt, she cried herself to sleep.

* * * *

It had been snowing every day for almost two weeks and even in a house as large as Oakhaven, where it was easy enough to get lost among the maze of corridors, Catherine thought she would go mad if she didn't get outside. Looking out of her bedroom window, she was grateful to see the sky had finally cleared and a pale wintry sun peeked through the clouds. It would be good to get outside, out of the house and away from Rian.

Conversing with him continued to be awkward, and he gave no indication that he wanted to rekindle the warmth that had flourished between them in London. She could not deny his manner was hurtful, and it only seemed to confirm her belief that his mistress was behind it. Catherine knew he had escorted Lady Isabel Howard to the wedding, and, though none said it, it made sense they must have seen each other while he remained in town.

Isabel's ugly words rang in her ears: *You're nothing but a trollop. A doxie who has managed to wheedle her way beneath this roof with some ridiculous tale of woe in order to gain sympathy, and the hope of bettering her situation.* Catherine was sure Lady Howard had successfully poisoned Rian against her. Nothing else made any sense.

A part of her wanted to confront Rian, and demand to be given the chance to defend herself. But she was terrified that he would simply laugh at her and walk away, and what would she do then? Her temper was unpredictable. The encounter with Isabel had shown her that. She had no way of being able to predict her reaction if she and Rian were ever alone together. Until she could be certain she would not make a complete fool of herself around him, she decided the only way to avoid an embarrassing confrontation was to avoid the man himself.

So she began playing a perverse game of hide-and-seek. If Rian entered a room, she would find a reason to leave. If she saw him in a hallway, she would duck into a room or alcove until she heard his footsteps pass by. But the longer the game continued the more attentive Rian became regarding her whereabouts. He seemed to know her destination and sought to be in the same room as she, as if by deliberate choice. But why he would do such a thing, she could not say.

The issue was further complicated by her desire to have Rian admit his reasons for bruising her feelings, and her yearning to throw herself into his arms in the fervent hope he would kiss her. With a shake of her head, Catherine scolded herself. She was being ridiculous. What she was feeling was nothing more than a young girl's first romantic passion, which, given her circumstances, was not so unexpected. He had saved her life. But when she lay in bed at night what she felt was so much more than girlish infatuation. The sensual, erotic dreams she experienced were very adult, and she wondered if her response to Rian's touch would, in reality, be the same as in her fantasies. In the pale light of day, would the desire she kept tightly leashed be loosed if he were to take her hand again? In her dreams she had no hesitation about wrapping herself around his muscular body, but then in her dreams he was more than eager to return her feelings.

Deciding she needed some crisp, cold air to clear her head, Catherine dressed warmly before making her way through the kitchen to see if Cook could spare a couple of apples or some carrots. She was long overdue for a visit to the stables, and she spent an hour visiting everyone, both those with two legs and those with four, and was delighted to hear that Will, the blushing stable hand who had wanted to know if Isabel was beautiful, had been given permission to court one of the housemaids. Catherine felt certain the peal of wedding bells would be heard before summer's end. But now that the family was back and settled into their appointed roles at Oakhaven, she found an odd disquiet pulling at her. She had no place. No duties or responsibilities. What was expected of her?

Eternally grateful for the easy relationship she was developing with Felicity, Catherine knew she could never ask for a kinder, better friend. And she was also happy that Liam was equally as accepting of her unexpected intrusion in their lives. They asked nothing of her, and the one time she expressed a desire to contribute in some way, both Felicity and Liam stared at her with matching horrified expressions. Her sole task, they assured her, was to get completely well again.

Making her way back to the main house from the stables, she was halted by the sight of two sets of footprints in the fresh snow. The direction they took sent them away from the stables, in the opposite direction she herself had so recently walked. Her first inclination was to believe Liam and Felicity had decided to steal a moment away from the house and enjoy the majesty of the outdoors, but she quickly scolded herself for her foolishness. Both sets of footprints were far too large to belong to a woman, and the shape of each was that of a man's boot.

It occurred to Catherine that if one set belonged to Liam, then the other most likely belonged to his brother, and for a brief moment she was mildly irritated. Until it occurred to her this could be an opportunity to turn the tables on Rian. Let him see how he liked having his day ruined by unwanted company. Following the footprints, she quickly found herself in a part of the grounds she had not yet explored. The snow was not too deep and the walk was a pleasant one, and, after climbing a small rise, Catherine came upon an unexpected sight. Nestled in the center of a group of majestic oak trees was a small chapel. The sight took her breath away and all thoughts of following Rian flew out of her head. This was obviously where the Connors came to worship, and it seemed the small church was now extending an invitation for her to do the same.

The building, elegant in its simplicity, had been constructed of stone to withstand the passage of time. Lifting the heavy iron ring that served as the doorhandle, Catherine was surprised when it swung open easily. Inside was a small stone font with a half-dozen plain wooden pews taking up the remaining space. Above the altar, flanked by two windows of clear glass, a stained-glass window captured her attention. It was quite an extravagance for a small family chapel, but it was the window's subject that made Catherine pause. A dove with an olive branch in its beak was caught by the rays of the winter sun, splashing the walls with bright spots of color.

"The promise of a new beginning," Catherine murmured. "How appropriate."

She knelt at the altar rail, the corners of her mouth lifting at the sight of the snowy white cloth covering the raised dais, and the arrangement of winter evergreens decorating the altar. Recognizing Felicity's touch, Catherine bent her head in prayer.

When her communication with God was over, she sat in the front pew, relishing the feeling of peace and tranquility that stole over her. Had attending church been a regular part of her past life? Catherine couldn't remember, but the sense of comfort that now settled about her made her believe it must have been. A sensation so profound could only come from a strong foundation. She couldn't speak for Liam, but she felt she already knew Felicity well enough to guess that, given a choice, her new friend would have much preferred to pledge herself in marriage in this small chapel. Perhaps their children would be christened and baptized here.

Having lost all sense of time, Catherine was startled by the sound of voices. She had left the chapel door open, and the cold air amplified the sound. Recognizing Rian and Liam, she went to the door with every intention of closing it, but the tone and volume of the conversation signaled the discussion was becoming heated. Catherine found herself caught in a terrible dilemma. She didn't want to be accused of eavesdropping, but alerting them to her presence might not be the best idea. And, if she was honest, there was a secret part of her that wanted to know more about them. The relationship between the brothers fascinated her. She was constantly surprised by their easy interaction with one another, given the difference in their temperaments. Guiltily she remained by the open door, standing quite still and shamelessly eavesdropping.

"You must make your peace," Liam urged in a voice filled with concern and exasperation.

"Why?" Rian's retort was laced with bitterness. "You know he was never much of a father to me. Where was he when I needed guidance or sought the benefit of his wisdom and experience? All I was to him was an heir to carry on his precious name. I can't do much about my birth, but I want nothing more to do with him."

The sound of a stinging slap had Catherine's hand flying to muffle the gasp that escaped her mouth.

"Now you listen to me." Liam's voice, thick with emotion, sounded rough and grating. "No man in the world could ever ask for a better brother, and I thank God every day of my life that he saw fit not only to give you to me in the first place, but to bring you back to me. You will never know a single moment's peace in your life until you come to terms with the fact that your leaving was in no way responsible for Father's death. It was not your fault then, and it is not your fault now."

Catherine's eyes opened wide. Rian thought he was responsible for his father's death? How could that be?

"He did love you, Rian," Liam continued. "He just didn't know how to show it. Never doubt for a single moment that he was proud of all you accomplished." The rough edge had vanished and the younger Connor now spoke in a softer tone.

"Did he know that we wrote to each other?" Rian asked, his own voice now the husky one.

"Aye. He never asked outright of course—you know that wasn't his way—but I think it comforted him greatly knowing we had each other."

"I don't ever want to lose that, Liam."

"And you never will."

She heard the crunch of snow as one of them moved. She suspected it was Rian and she could picture him running his fingers through his hair. It was a mannerism she had noticed he adopted whenever he needed to think.

The silence lasted so long Catherine wondered if both men had actually moved on, but they could not have departed so quietly. Any movement would have been betrayed by the crunch of snow beneath their boots. Finally she heard Liam's regulated tone again.

"Rian, if you cannot make your peace with Father, then at least speak with Mama. Ask her for guidance."

"And on what subject do I require guidance?" Rian asked, sounding humorous.

"Do you really need me to answer that?"

Catherine felt her brows pull together, at a loss to know what could be troubling Rian.

"Are you questioning my choice, Liam?" Rian asked.

"I would never presume," the younger Connor replied. "The question is, are you?" Hearing no verbal reply, Catherine could only assume Rian's expression was sufficient response, especially as Liam continued, "Then perhaps it is another question you should be asking."

"What other question is there?"

"How much you will risk to make Catherine aware of your desire for her?"

The air whooshed out of Catherine's lungs, and her knees nearly buckled. Blindly she reached for the nearest pew and lowered herself shakily onto the seat. To know she was the topic of the discussion was mortifying, and it caused a hot, burning sensation to flush her cheeks. What was that old saying about those who eavesdrop never hearing good about themselves? She was about to find out how much truth there was in it.

"I can't even begin to imagine what type of an ordeal she has been through," Rian said, "or how difficult it must be for her knowing she has no memory of it."

"Aye," Liam agreed, "but something lingers. You can see the shadow of it in her face." He paused before asking, "Do you suppose, if her memory does return, she will be able to come to terms with what happened?"

Rian made a sound that might have been a harsh laugh. "I have more confidence in her ability to face that particular horror than I do in her welcoming either my attention or affection."

"Give her time." Liam sounded sympathetic. "There is strength in Catherine that she has yet to discover."

Certain that her heart had stopped working, or at the very least had definitely skipped a beat, Catherine pressed her hand to her mouth. Now Rian's laugh was genuine and filled with warmth.

"I beg to differ, Liam. She may not know its full extent, but Catherine is aware of her strength. Don't forget, she bested Isabel."

"Aye, that she did." Liam's chuckle joined his brother's, but when he spoke again his tone was grave. "Be careful, brother. When you fall, you fall hard. You know no other way. Talk to Mama; she will set you on your path."

Chapter 9

Catherine felt terrible. Agonizing guilt overwhelmed her, and she sank to her knees asking God to forgive her transgression. The peace that had comforted her before was nowhere to be found, most likely because her mind was in such turmoil. This unexpected revelation of Rian's changed everything. How could he admit to Liam that he had feelings for her, but still treat her with apathy and indifference?

A voice spoke crossly in her head. *Foolish girl! How could you possibly know he's being indifferent when you have refused to spend even one minute in his company?*

But he hadn't seemed happy to see her when he first returned. He'd barely acknowledged her presence.

And what did you expect him to do? Take you in his arms and declare his undying love for you?

What of your own behavior? How is he supposed to know that you would encourage any affection on his part when all you do is run away from him?

It was a pivotal question, but Catherine had no answer. Realizing she had spent almost every waking moment telling herself that she meant nothing to him, she now could not help but wonder if Rian had indeed been trying to let her know he felt the opposite. His apparent indifference upon his return from the city had been hurtful, but instead of giving him the chance to explain his change of attitude, she had supplied the reason for it herself, thus denying him the opportunity to explain. Was it any wonder he now believed she would not welcome his attention?

Catherine chewed her lip as she pondered her problem, and then a glow swept through her. Of course, she would ask Felicity! As a married woman, one courted by Rian's brother, she would surely have some insight to share.

The decision made, Catherine closed her eyes, and waited for the anxious pounding of her heart to settle. She wanted to be sure enough time had passed for Rian to have concluded his visit to the graveyard, so the chance of their paths crossing would be slim. Despite her desire to explore this new revelation, she still wasn't sure she was ready to deal with Rian, face to face. At least, not just yet. A chill began to seep into her bones, telling her it was time to leave. She stepped out of the pew, genuflected, but as she turned away from the altar an involuntary gasp escaped her. Rian was seated in the last pew, watching her. Catherine might not think she was ready to face him, but it seemed fate had decided otherwise.

"Oh my goodness! You gave me a start," she babbled, placing a hand on her chest. "I did not hear you come in." She could feel the heat rise to her face, but hoped it would not be noticed in the chapel's dim light.

"My apologies," Rian said, getting to his feet. "You seemed deep in your devotions, and I did not wish to disturb you."

"Then permit me to offer the same courtesy," Catherine said, seizing the opening. "I will leave you to your solitude and prayers."

"I have already said my prayers." Placing his hand on the top of the adjacent pew, he effectively blocked her path. "And I have had enough solitude to last a lifetime."

Catherine wondered how it was possible for her heart to remain confined inside her chest when his gaze was so singularly focused. "I beg your pardon?" she murmured. Rian had spoken, but she had not heard his words.

"I asked if you would care to take a walk with me."

It crossed her mind to refuse him. Though there were no rules stopping her from being with him, Catherine wasn't certain she should accept his invitation. She wasn't ready for this.

Idiot! How many more chances do you suppose he will give you?

"Thank you. That would be…nice." The hesitancy in her response made it seem as if she was questioning his motives. It's only a walk, she told herself, allowing a thrill of hope to run through her.

But Rian had heard the wariness in her tone, and he frowned. "If you would rather not—" he began.

"No, a walk would most invigorating."

"Invigorating?"

"I'm fine, perfectly fine, and I can manage a walk." *Especially with you as my companion.*

Taking a deep breath, Catherine placed her hand on the arm he held out to her. A familiar throbbing ache rose, answering the question of how she would react at his touch. She wondered if she would always experience this sensation whenever she touched him. Opening her eyes she saw that Rian was looking at her intently, as if trying to read her thoughts, but then he covered her smaller hand with his and escorted her from the chapel.

Once outside, he steered her on a new path, one that led away from the great house. Their route skirted the thick tree line that acted as a natural boundary between the Connor and Pelham properties. Virginal snow crunched beneath their boots and their breath became puffs of white smoke on the frigid air. Rian made no attempt at conversation. He seemed content to enjoy the silence, and, for her part, Catherine was uncharacteristically struck dumb. Terrified she would say the wrong thing and make him regret his invitation, she remained mute. Rian was a grown man who had experienced the world, while she had lived a sheltered life. Or so she assumed. How on earth was she supposed to confess that she also was consumed with feelings for him? Feelings she desperately wanted to share.

* * * *

Outwardly Rian may have been a picture of calm steadiness as they walked, but inside he was a churning river of battered emotions. Kneeling at his mother's grave had brought no insight, until he entered the chapel, and was startled to find Catherine deep in prayer. His mother, it seemed, had been listening after all. Inviting Catherine to walk with him had been an act of pure impulse, and he'd fully expected her to refuse. But her acceptance now filled him with a cautious optimism. The last thing he wanted to do was to frighten her with a declaration of affection.

He estimated the difference in their age to be possibly as great as fifteen years, which meant nothing to him. Indeed, many would consider such a span an asset to a relationship, but Catherine might think him too old. A man in his midthirties might seem positively doddering to a girl perhaps not yet in her twenties. Everything about her made him believe she lacked any true worldly experience, and sadly, the one encounter she had known had been a brutal one. There was no way to know if she would ever allow him, or any other man for that matter, to show her that physical affection between a man and a woman wasn't supposed to be like that.

Movement at the wood's periphery caught his attention and he stopped walking. Turning to Catherine, he put a finger to his lips and then pointed. Just beyond the boundary of the trees stood a large stag. If Rian had not pointed him out to her, Catherine would never have noticed the creature against the camouflage of trees. Taking a few bold steps into the open, the magnificent animal stopped to survey his surroundings. Raising his head, he sniffed the air.

Clutching Rian's arm, Catherine stood on tiptoe. Unaware that her breath tickled Rian's cheek, she whispered, "Do you think he knows we are here?"

"I don't think so," he replied, feeling her press herself closer to his side.

The stag began pawing the ground, clearing away the newly fallen snow with his hoof and then he lifted his head, a signal to those behind him. More deer emerged from the cover of the trees and Catherine gave a little gasp before quickly covering her mouth with her hand. Like a good protector, the stag stood vigilant as the rest of his herd nibbled on the winter grass he had uncovered. Rian could almost feel the disappointment flowing through Catherine as the herd began to meld back into the trees, the stag being the last to vanish.

"They will return," Rian assured her, seeing the dejected look on her face. She brightened at once. "When? Tomorrow?"

"Possibly."

"May we return then and see if they do?" Her eagerness was infectious.

"If it would please you," Rian said.She turned her head and started to stamp her feet on the ground in order to get the blood moving again. Rian cursed under his breath as he suddenly realized how cold the air had turned. And how foolish it was for him to keep her out here.

"I must get you back before you take a chill," he said in an authoritative voice, reaching for her arm.

Like a recalcitrant child, Catherine took a step back, the look on her face clearly telling him she cared little for his tone. "I'm not going to take a chill," she told him testily. "I am dressed warmly and my health is very much improved. Something I'm surprised you're not already aware of." Was he no longer receiving reports on her health from Mrs. Hatch or Tilly?

"And whom was I supposed to ask?" Rian countered, answering her unasked question. "You?"

"Of course. How else do you suppose you will discover anything that is useful?"

"That would be difficult when you're always leaving the room," he pointed out.

He hadn't meant to embarrass her, but it appeared he had. Turning on her heel, Catherine stomped angrily along the path, leaving Rian to stare after her.

She was in the wrong and she knew it. The fault was not his. There was no reason to suppose the housekeeper or maid would continue to update him on her progress. Feeling Rian's eyes as he continued to stare after her, Catherine knew he was waiting for an apology. She sighed. It was the mature thing to do. It was the *right* thing to do.

"I'm sorry," she told him, when he caught up to her. "That was both rude and very unfair of me, and you didn't deserve either."

"No," Rian agreed amiably. "I did not."

This time he did not offer her his arm, and she was not bold enough to take it. Instead their journey continued without speaking and also without touching. They took a circuitous route and, after topping a small rise, Catherine found herself looking down at the rear of Oakhaven. The house looked like something out of a fairy tale nestled on a pillow of snow with more of the same covering the roof and leaving drifts in each of the windows. The late morning sun broke through the clouds highlighting the perfection of the grand building, making it sparkle like a precious gem.

"I have always preferred the view of the house from this situation," Rian murmured, apparently deciding to say nothing more about her outburst. He walked a few paces in front of her and then turned. Their progress was going to take them down a small incline. "The path can be a little treacherous," he explained, holding out his hand to her.

They had taken less than a half-dozen steps before his words proved prophetic; his foot slipped on a patch of ice hidden by a thin covering of snow. But even as he lost his balance he did not release his grip on Catherine. Instead, Rian pulled her closer to him, holding her tightly as they tumbled down the hill, landing with a resounding *whump* at the bottom of the slope. For a few moments neither of them did anything but steady their breathing. Rian had managed to ensure that he was the one who landed on his back, with Catherine atop him, and he could feel the pressure of her hands as she gripped the lapels of his coat.

Somehow her bonnet had fallen off during the course of their wild descent. Now her white-blond hair tumbled about her face. Keeping one arm firmly about her waist, Rian brushed the hair from her face with the other.

"Catherine, are you all right? Are you hurt anywhere?" he asked, his concern evident.

Slowly she opened her eyes. Brilliant and blue, they danced with a wild exhilaration as she stared down at him. "Do you think—is it possible—can we do that again?"

"I'm not sure my old bones could take another tumble like that," Rian told her with a grin.

"Pish. You're not *that* old!"

Her expression suddenly turned serious as she studied his face. Her gaze traced the creases in his forehead, the fine lines marking the corners of his eyes, the grooves bracketing his mouth. She seemed mesmerized by his high cheekbones, the strong jaw and stubborn chin with its hint of shadowy whiskers. Catherine had no way of knowing that the bright cornflower blue of her eyes had deepened, becoming a darker, richer color. But she felt the unexpected heat in her cheeks as her gaze was drawn to his mouth. Rian's lips were slightly parted, and she felt the warmth of his breath on her face and saw the even, white teeth behind the sensuous curve of his lips. It was temptation and distraction combined in one, and savoring the feel of his body as he held her, the delicious tightness of the arm that imprisoned her, she closed her eyes tightly...and kissed him.

To say Rian was surprised would have been a marked understatement. The softness of Catherine's lips as she pressed her firmly closed mouth against his amazed him. Unfortunately the kiss was over before he had time to appreciate it as she jerked her head away, burying her face in his shoulder, refusing to look at him.

In itself, her kiss told him nothing at all, but its execution told him everything he wanted to know. Reaching up with his free hand, he gently stroked her hair, waiting patiently for her to raise her head and look at him once more. After a few moments she did so, and Rian noted her face was now a delightful shade of pink.

"I-I don't know why I did that," she stammered.

"Yes, you do," Rian told her. "You did it because you wanted to."

"You must think me terribly forward."

"Must I?" Continuing to stroke her hair, he asked, "Would you be disappointed if I chose not to?"

"You're not shocked by what I did?"

"Shocked?" Rian arched a brow. "No, but I am surprised."

"Oh."

He didn't know it was possible for such a small word to carry so much anguish.

"Did you like kissing me?" He made no attempt to move, keeping his arm firmly around her waist, and enjoying the feel of her lying on top of him.

"Mmmm, well..." She wrinkled her nose. "It really wasn't how I thought it would be." Her head sought the comfort of his shoulder again, and she worried she had hurt his feelings by saying the wrong thing.

"Catherine, look at me." Rian's voice was a low, warm, seductive whisper in her ear. Hesitantly she obeyed, and now her heart began to pound wildly. She felt as if she were prey, only she had to wonder, how often did prey want to be caught by the hunter? "Have you ever been kissed?" Rian asked her.

"I don't know. Perhaps. I'm not sure."

"Well, is that how you think a kiss is supposed to feel?"

She had no idea, but as the question was being asked she reasoned perhaps there was more to kissing than the way she had pressed her mouth against Rian's. Although what else could possibly be involved she couldn't begin to imagine. With nothing else to go on, she nodded in answer to Rian's question, only to wince when he sighed in exasperation.

"Would you like me to kiss you?" he asked.

She didn't answer because she didn't trust her voice, but Rian read the response in her eyes easily enough. Framing her face with his hands, he pulled her down to him and gently covered her mouth with his. Catherine would never know how much self-control it took for him not to simply take her. Taste all that she had to give, and let himself become lost in her. Instead, he kept his kiss light, his tongue gently sweeping over her closed lips, and when he felt her beginning to surrender to him so he could taste the sweetness of her breath, he stopped and lifted his mouth from hers.

Her eyes had turned glassy, her voice husky with desire as she asked, "Is it always like that?"

"No, it usually gets better."

"It does?" She positively glowed at his nod. "Then...will you kiss me again?"

Burgeoning desire overcame any feelings of impropriety, and now it was Rian's turn to have breathing difficulties as he felt his heart lurch in his chest. "Yes, I will," he finally managed to say, but as Catherine closed her eyes and pursed her lips he continued, "but only when you are ready."

Her eyes flew open and she stared at him. A challenge flickered in the blue depths. It was enough for Rian to tell himself she would be all kinds of delicious trouble when she was riled.

"I'm ready now."

"No, you're not," Rian disagreed with a chuckle. Smoothing the hair from her cheek, he became serious. "When I kiss you again, Catherine, it will be because you will ask me to."

"But forgive me, did I not just do so?"

"Yes," he admitted, "but you're not ready to be kissed the way you should be. Not ready to be kissed the way I want to kiss you."

Confusion clouded her features. "And how is that?"

"The way a lover should kiss you."

"A lover?"

Rian prayed he had not overstepped the boundary between them.

But then Catherine's eyes became dreamy, and her voice wistful. "And when will I be ready for a lover?"

"You will know," he murmured, seeing the promise of what was to come shine in her eyes. "Trust me, you will know."

"And is it you who will assume such a role?"

Her question was something he would have expected from a more experienced woman. But there was no guile in her inquiry, only honest and open curiosity.

"Only if you ask it of me."

Rian's voice was almost unrecognizable to his own ears, and realizing they were both slipping toward a point where restraint was in danger of being surrendered, he gently rolled Catherine off him. Reluctantly he got to his feet, and holding out a hand, helped her stand. It occurred to him he could easily tumble her once more. Her face said she would offer no resistance because she wanted him as much as he wanted her.

It would all be so easy, so pleasurable, and so very wrong.

Letting go of her hand, he retrieved her bonnet from where it lay in the snow and handed it back to her. With emotions riding high, neither trusted themselves enough to link arms. So they continued their journey back to Oakhaven without touching, but now completely connected. And each relishing the small miracle they had been granted.

Chapter 10

With the Yuletide celebrations having come and gone amidst the usual amount of joyful revelry, there was a small pause in the winter social season, allowing everyone to catch their breath before commencing the next whirlwind round of parties and fashionable gatherings. Isabel sat in her drawing room mulling over the events of the past few weeks. Too much time had passed since she had last seen Rian, and she now realized how badly she had misjudged the situation between them.

Her initial fury over his apparent rejection of her had long since abated, and she was forced to admit to herself that she missed him desperately. Never in her life had she thought that one man could make her feel this way. She had clung stubbornly to the hope that Rian might yet come to her while he remained in town, but he had not. It would have been more bearable to discover he was enjoying the charms of another woman, but John had reported that her suspicions about Catherine were so far unfounded. There was nothing to substantiate the suggestion of a relationship developing between Rian and the girl. If anything the opposite seemed true.

The self-imposed delay of his return to Oakhaven gave all the appearance that Rian was not beguiled by Catherine, or, if he had been, the attraction had since waned.

Still, Isabel was not completely convinced. The girl may not have been able to seduce her way into Rian's bed yet, but something had sparked between them. Something strong enough to make Rian believe he no longer wanted *her*. She would stake her own blotted reputation on it. Pacing back and forth, she tapped a well-manicured nail against her teeth. Perhaps Catherine had heeded her warning after all, but she thought it doubtful. Experience had shown her that someone who had nothing rarely turned down the chance to take everything when it was offered. As frustrating as it was, Isabel seemed to be left with two options. She could wait for Rian to come to his senses, or hope that ignorance tipped the girl's hand into doing something foolish.

With a sigh, she turned her thoughts toward her previous meeting with Phillip Davenport. It had taken her only moments to recognize him for the cunning predator he was. As if clothing himself in fashionable silks could disguise the foulness of his true nature. She loathed him on sight but knew John would not ask her to meet with him were it not important. Putting aside her personal abhorrence, Isabel had listened as Phillip related the circumstances regarding the disappearance of his cousin, Catherine Davenport.

Despite his protests to the contrary, she knew immediately who had been responsible for the girl's desperate flight. And also whose hand had left the marks on Catherine's back. Under different circumstances Isabel would have applauded the fortitude it took to escape such a despicable monster, but of all the men in the city, Catherine had crossed paths with Rian. And Isabel still wasn't entirely convinced that the memory loss was genuine. Given the choice between a sadistic pig like Phillip Davenport and Rian Connor, well, there really was no choice.

She listened attentively as Phillip wove his web of lies, clucking sympathetically in all the right places. The timeline of Catherine's disappearance as well as the physical description he gave only confirmed that Rian had indeed rescued the missing cousin.

"Mr. Fletcher informs me you might possibly know the whereabouts of our dear Catherine," Phillip said, licking his lips as high spots of color danced in his cheeks. "I pray that this is so. My wife has been so worried she has taken to her bed." He paused as if to impress upon his audience the seriousness of his wife's ailment before continuing. "As I am sure you know, the city can be most unkind to a young woman who is wandering, friendless and alone. It is far too easy to fall victim to unprincipled rogues."

"Indeed, indeed," Isabel murmured. "I do not wish to offer false hope, Mr. Davenport, but it would be wrong of me not to share that I have recently become acquainted with a young woman who would seem to fit the description of your cousin." Phillip opened his mouth to speak, but Isabel's raised hand stopped him. "However, it would be wrong of me to make assumptions. I believe another visit with the young woman is necessary in order to be completely certain. Anything less would be a disservice to both of you." Rising from her seat, she gave him a dazzling smile. An indication their meeting was concluded.

"You understand my concern, Lady Howard," Phillip said. "In her present state of mind, who knows what my poor Catherine might say or do."

Hearing a thread of unease in his tone, Isabel wondered how high his agitation might climb if he knew she had already witnessed his handiwork. "Quite so, Mr. Davenport, and I will take that into consideration," she told him solicitously. "Once the issue of the girl's identity is no longer in question, then I will send word through my associate." She tipped her head in John's direction, and then turned her back, signaling their meeting was concluded.

When John returned she poured a generous snifter of brandy for each of them. "That man," she began, handing him a glass, "is a consummate liar."

"Quite so, but a liar with the skill to weave some truth amongst the lies."

Grudgingly, Isabel agreed. "Now, tell me all that I don't know about the loathsome piece of filth," she said, inviting John to sit.

For the next fifteen minutes she listened, making no comment as her informant apprised her of Phillip Davenport's diminishing fortunes and his penchant for brutality.

"I have seen his handiwork for myself," Isabel murmured. "There can be no doubt he is responsible for the girl's condition."

"Given what we know about him, I would imagine so," John agreed.

"I'm sure you know what I need of you."

"A trip north to discover all I can about the elusive Miss Davenport?" John said, finishing off his drink.

Isabel gave a little laugh. "It really is a pleasure doing business with you, John." She refilled his glass before going to the bureau where she kept a small lockbox. Unlocking it, Isabel withdrew a small brown purse that she handed to John. The weight in his palm was generous, signifying the importance of the matter. He looked at Isabel with a raised brow.

"A bonus for you," she said in answer to his unspoken inquiry. "I want to know *everything*, John." He finished his drink as Isabel resumed pacing before the large picture window. "And there is one other thing I need you to do." Her voice was soft, but the frigid tone made him pay attention.

"Yes?"

"Make certain that Phillip Davenport never comes near me again."

Isabel watched as the carriage pulled away from the door. Winter in the North Country was always so much crueler than in London. The cold held a deeper bite, but she had no doubt that John had already anticipated this. His fee was more than enough to cover the cost of a warm coat and heavy boots, should he need either. She did not regret the money. The information it would buy was well worth the price.

It started to snow again, and as Isabel raised her eyes to look at the grey sky, a slow smile crept across her face. A wedding was always cause for celebration, and for most families one gathering was enough to satisfy the obligation. But the Connors also held to traditions of their own making. Marriage into the family required a second joyful festivity to mark the occasion. One in which the new bride was presented to the tenants who worked the land. This second ball was a more informal gathering held at the family estate, and rumored to be a far more boisterous affair than the traditional ceremony enjoyed by the happy couple's relatives and peers. Though she found the idea quite vulgar, Isabel could understand the appeal. Rules of etiquette were relaxed, and no-one would be waiting to pounce if the newest Mrs. Connor forgot the correct way to address a viscount. Which no doubt explained why invitations were never issued beyond the immediate family. It would take very little effort on her part to find out precisely when this other gala was going to take place, and being the consummate actress she was, Isabel had every confidence that her unexpected arrival at Oakhaven would be forgiven.

Chapter 11

Isabel was correct in both her facts and timing. Preparations to introduce the new Mistress of Oakhaven were already underway. Both Liam and Felicity were looking forward to sharing this special moment with the people they owed a great part of their livelihood to. In her new role, it was Felicity's responsibility to make sure that each family who shared the evening with them went home with a well-filled basket, and so the kitchen had been in a near constant state of activity from the time the date had been set. In this veritable hive of industry, filled with the most delicious mix of aromas, the offer of an extra pair of hands was not about to be turned down. Which was how Catherine found herself up to her elbows in flour alongside Felicity, taking orders from Cook and Mrs. Hatch and loving every minute of it. But now there was no more dough to be kneaded, no more bread to be baked. Pies had been filled and topped with fancy crusts. Everything had been prepared as much as it could be, leaving Felicity and Catherine a few moments to enjoy a well-earned rest.

Like many brides, Felicity planned to don the dress she'd worn to become Liam's wife for special events, and this second celebration was such an occasion. Carefully Catherine ran her finger over the decorated bodice, delighted to be given the opportunity of seeing Felicity wear it.

"Will Liam also be wearing his wedding finery?" she asked.

"Yes," Felicity told her. "It's traditional for both of us to dress so."

"Are you wearing your wedding bonnet too?"

"No. Thankfully I can wear my hair how I choose, so I thought perhaps something simple with a jeweled comb might be enough?" She raised her hands above her head and with her fingers fashioned an imaginary coiffure.

"Oh, Felicity, you will look beautiful!" Catherine exclaimed. "Liam will want to marry you all over again."

"I think once was enough," Felicity said, fussing with the shoulder pleats of the decorative gown, "but I do regret that you were not able to be with us then."

"No matter, I am with you now," Catherine said, touched by her concern.

Liam had been apprehensive at having Catherine join the celebration and he shared his feelings with his wife and brother. "Are we really certain she's ready to be among so many people?"

"Liam, we cannot keep Catherine shut away for the rest of her life," Felicity told him. "Besides, those in attendance will not be the same gossips who took advantage of my parent's generosity at our wedding. Country folk are more honest, more genuine with their affections. I believe they will treat Catherine kindly, and she will feel more at ease amongst them."

Rian agreed with his sister-in-law, adding, "Why not let Catherine decide? If she chooses to join us, so much the better, but if not, let us agree now to not be concerned. We will accept her decision, and not try to change her mind."

Liam looked skeptical. Rian's recent display of nonchalance regarding Catherine had a hollow ring to it. He believed his brother concerned himself a great deal over anything that might make Catherine uneasy, but he nodded and gave his word. It was only later, in private, he noted to his wife, "Something has changed between those two."

"Changed? How?" Felicity paused as she brushed her hair, momentarily distracted by the reflection of her half-naked husband in the mirror.

"I don't know. Can't quite put my finger on it, but they seem calmer with each other, and...happy."

"So you noticed it too? I did not want to say anything because I thought I was being fanciful. Wishing for something that might not truly be happening." She swiveled on her seat, facing him. "Do you think Rian has told Catherine he has feelings for her?"

"Would she not have told you if he had?"

"Yes, I think she would." A small frown puckered Felicity's brow. "So what do you think is behind this change in attitude?"

"Absolutely no idea, but whatever it is, I welcome it."

It was as if someone had given both Catherine and Rian a good shake, or perhaps a quick tumble down a snow bank, resulting in a notable absence of tension between them. The awkwardness had vanished; conversations consisted of more than monosyllabic exchanges. Now, it seemed as if they actively sought each other's company, as if wanting to make amends for time already lost. The entire household heaved a collective sigh of relief, but Liam, always cautious, admitted to having some reservations. He hoped his brother wasn't subtly pushing Catherine in a direction she might not be ready to go.

He need not have worried. Rian shared the same concern, and for that reason he made certain that whenever he and Catherine were together, they were never completely alone. Since their walk in the snow he had made certain a third party was always present. He smiled to himself, wondering how many of the household staff questioned Mrs. Hatch's need for the library shelves to be dusted only when Rian and Catherine were present. If Catherine noticed their chaperones, and he was certain she was perceptive enough to do just that, she made no comment. Rian considered she might welcome the restraint that was enforced by the inclusion of another. It gave her time to be certain of her own feelings.

For Rian no such evaluation was needed, but a chaperone meant safety. He couldn't promise that, if tempted to kiss Catherine again, he would be able to command the same measure of self-control as before. Especially as he had already told her just how he intended to kiss her when it happened again. And it would happen again. So for that reason alone it was better to err on the side of caution.

And then, one morning Catherine had woken to find a note slipped under her door. Rian had left Oakhaven, but promised to return soon. She kept the note in her pocket, taking it out when she thought no one else was looking, and reading it several times a day. Until Felicity had found her, dejected and moping, hiding in the library.

"Don't fret. Rian promised he would be home soon," she told her with a sunny smile.

But now almost a full week had passed, and Catherine decided once Rian was back, they would have a frank discussion about the definition of the word "soon." Felicity's wedding gown was indeed beautiful, and Catherine couldn't help but express her admiration for the quality of the workmanship. Until it suddenly occurred to her that she had no idea what she was going to wear for the party. It was a question that had bedeviled women everywhere at some point or another in their lives. When she voiced her concern, she saw her friend frown.

"Surely there must be something in that trunk you brought with you?" Felicity asked.

"Yes, I think there are some dresses, but I have no idea if they would be suitable. I would value your opinion," Catherine added shyly.

Like a pair of excited schoolgirls they pulled out the dresses Rian had bought in London. Catherine thought all of them were wonderful but was dismayed to see Felicity discard them, one by one.

"Not even this?" Catherine said, holding out a beautiful gown of sea green silk, trimmed with ivory lace. "Don't you think the color is pretty?"

Felicity shook her head. "Oh, it's a beautiful dress, I grant you, but not what I had in mind."

"Let's not forget whom this celebration is for," Catherine joked. "I'm sure no one will pay any attention to what I am wearing." Asking for help in selecting a dress had resulted in complications she'd never anticipated.

Felicity's smooth forehead wrinkled. "Have you ever been to a ball before?"

"I don't think so," Catherine said matching her friend's frown. Though she could recall a vague sense of anticipated excitement whenever she thought about the music and dancing, it was more a sense of something she had been told, not an actual event she'd experienced. "No," she said with a decisive shake of her head. "I'm sure I have not."

"Then if this is to be your first ball, I want it to be special. Something you will always remember, and for that you need just the right gown. One that is stunning and beautiful and—"

"Hopefully like this."

They both turned at the sound of Rian's voice. He was leaning against the open doorway, holding a large box in his hands. Catherine smiled hesitantly, feeling her pulse begin to race as it always did whenever she saw him after any absence. The memory of his kiss burned in her mind, along with his words. It was a secret that she kept close, unwilling to share with anyone else.

"Rian! When did you get back and, more to the point, where on earth have you been?" Felicity asked, kissing him on the cheek.

Envy unexpectedly reared its head as Catherine witnessed the easy familiarity between Rian and his sister-in-law. She wished she could be so openly affectionate, but that was a privilege the wedding band on Felicity's hand gave her. Still, it was nice to see Rian smile at her before returning his attention to the other woman.

"In answer to the first part of your question, I returned only moments ago, and as for the second"—he looked over the top of Felicity's dark head—"I went to buy a gown for a beautiful woman." He handed over the box as Catherine blushed furiously. "I thought perhaps you might find an occasion to wear this."

Felicity gasped as she opened the delicate wrapping and viewed the contents. "Oh my goodness! Now this is just what I had in mind." She removed the gown from the box, holding it up for Catherine to see.

It was a glorious creation that shimmered in the light as Felicity gently shook out the folds. The ribbon and pearl embellishments at the elbows and neckline were exquisitely detailed, as was the intricate embroidery that decorated the bodice. "Rian, I will never cease to wonder at your knowledge of women's fashion," Felicity observed, smiling at him. "And this color will complement Catherine's complexion perfectly."

For Catherine, the whole world suddenly tilted sideways, and she found herself gasping for breath as a vicious wave of nausea rolled through her. She clutched at her throat, suddenly unable to draw a breath as the room took on the same shade of pink as the gown Felicity held before her. It was a familiar hue, one that Catherine knew only too well, but had forgotten until now. It was the color of pain.

Taking a step back in an effort to escape the hideous dress, Catherine caught her leg on the edge of a small side table. It fell over, breaking the carafe of fruit cordial she and Felicity had been enjoying as they went through her wardrobe. The pretty glass decanter shattered, spilling its contents on the floor, and Catherine stared aghast at the stain pooling at her feet. The deep raspberry color triggered something inside her, bringing with it a host of violent images. Frozen to the spot, a bewildered Felicity was staring incomprehensively at the look of absolute terror on Catherine's face. Unsure what to do, she reached out to her friend, but Rian quickly placed himself between the two women.

"Catherine?" She gave no sign of having heard him, so he repeated himself, adding an unexpected firmness to his tone. "Catherine, look at me."

Her blond head turned, and she stared up at him with eyes that were filled with so much fear, Rian knew whoever she saw, it was not he. And then the fear was replaced by something else. A resolve that turned the sunny blue of her eyes to the cold, hard color of slate. A surge of protectiveness roared through him, telling him to take her in his arms and hold her close, but reason warned that to do so would be a mistake. The lack of responsiveness in Catherine's eyes served as a warning. A promise that said whatever had caused such fear would not be allowed to do so again. Standing as still as he possibly could, Rian watched a flurry of emotions do battle across Catherine's face.

She moved her head just enough to allow her to look around Rian's broad shoulder to where Felicity stood with the offending garment still in her arms. A strangled cry escaped Catherine's lips, and she lunged forward, halted only as Rian caught her about the waist. If she did not recognize him, then the same was probably true of Felicity, and he could not allow Catherine to inflict any harm on the woman he now regarded as a sister.

"Felicity, the dress!" he barked. "Take it with you and go!"

Her face ashen, Felicity hurriedly gathered up the gown and stuffed it back in the box.

"Get out of here!" Rian snapped as Catherine struggled to free herself from his hold. With a stunned look on her face, Felicity did as he ordered.

Once the hateful costume was gone, Rian released his hold, and Catherine, momentarily surprised by her sudden freedom, whirled around to look at him. Her pulse fluttered wildly at the base of her throat. As if fearing a trap, she began to look about her for a means of escape, her eyes darting frantically about the room.

"Catherine?" This time Rian spoke softly, hoping to bring her back from whatever dark place she had gone.

The sound of his voice made her tilt her head to one side. Obviously, she heard him, but gave no sign he was familiar to her in any way. Moving cautiously Rian approached, hands held out with palms up. He spoke her name again. This time so quietly it was barely a whisper.

He was totally unprepared for the speed with which she moved. Darting toward the dresser, she picked up the heavy, silver backed hairbrush and threw it at him. Whether by accident or design, she managed to strike him above his left temple. A sharp burst of pain exploded in his head, and Rian felt the warm trickle of blood running down the side of his face. He was going to have one hell of a headache, but he would count himself lucky if this was his only injury when everything was over. Something told him it might not be. Incensed that her effort had not felled him, Catherine began screaming unintelligibly. Her hand fastened on a small, silver trinket box, but Rian grabbed her wrist and quickly pinned her arms to her sides, making her open her hand and drop the item on the floor. Catherine was nothing if not resourceful. If Rian insisted on imprisoning her arms, she would use her legs. She stomped down hard on his instep, making him snarl in pain before he let her go.

With his foot throbbing from the rude assault, Rian took a step back and steeled himself as Catherine attacked him again. Her hands balled into fists, she rained blow after blow on him, but he made no effort to protect himself. Absorbing every strike to his chest and arms, Rian passively accepted whatever punishment Catherine sought to impose on him.

The duration of her attack lasted no more than a few minutes, but to Rian it seemed as if time stood still. He dared not touch her until he felt her efforts weaken, and then he caught her as she fell against him, sobbing. Picking her up in his arms, he carried her to the bed. Lying with her gathered close to his body, he rocked her gently as she continued to weep. When she was able to finally lift her face, his shirt was wet with her hot, salty tears. Though they were now red rimmed and swollen, Rian was relieved to see her eyes had returned to their familiar blue color, and she recognized him once more. Whatever demon had tried to claim her had been sent back to the hell bitch that spawned it.

"Are you all right?" It was a stupid question, but he couldn't think of anything else to say as he pulled a handkerchief from his pocket and gently wiped her cheeks.

She shook her head. "I don't think I will ever be all right again. Not now…not now I know what was done to me."

"I'm so sorry," Rian apologized. The dress had been the catalyst, managing to somehow reopen the wound in Catherine's mind. "Can you tell me what happened?" he asked, understanding she needed to share the horrifying experience with someone, and recognizing there would be no better time than this. "What is wrong with the dress?"

"There's nothing wrong with the style," she explained hesitantly. "It's the color. I once had to wear a dress that exact shade."

Rian was stunned. The dressmaker had assured him that while fashionable in Europe, the color was only recently becoming popular in England. It was why he had chosen it for Catherine, believing it would be a new experience for her. There was no way he could have known how wrong he was. The way she spoke, the inflection in her voice, told Rian that nothing could ever atone for what had happened to her. Raising her hand to his mouth, he gently swept his lips over her knuckles. She flinched at his touch, but did not pull away.

"Do not blame yourself," she told him. "You could not have anticipated my reaction. I had no idea I was capable of such unruly behavior." Her voice cracked and she choked down a sob. She pulled her hand from his, and with trembling fingers traced the wound above his brow. The blood, which had stopped flowing, was now turning a dull rust color. "I'm so sorry. I didn't mean to hurt you."

Rian sat up, forcing Catherine to do the same. Taking her face in his hands, he leaned forward and pressed his lips to the tears on her cheeks. Then he kissed her wet lashes, her forehead, and her temples. His lips touched everywhere but her mouth. He would not be able to stop himself if he did that, and this was not the moment.

"I know you didn't mean it," he told her. "I don't know who you saw, but I know it wasn't me."

He leaned back against the headboard and pulled her to him, keeping his arms loose enough that she could pull away if she chose to. Instead she crawled up his body until her head was nestled just below his collar bone. She began to speak, her voice faltering at first, and then growing stronger as she continued. Now the words tumbled out of her, flowing like water over the edge of a dam. It was as if she was afraid to stop, knowing she could only tell this one time. And realizing this was the only way to heal the unspeakable wound she carried inside, Rian held her close. And prayed he would not betray his own feelings as he listened to the black nightmare that had splashed silk lined walls when last Catherine wore a pink dress.

"He must have untied me when he was done with the beating. He would have—would have raped me if I hadn't hit him with a candlestick. That was how I managed to escape," she concluded.

When she was done there was nothing but silence for a long time until Rian finally spoke. "Catherine, who did this to you?" His voice was calm, but fury rolled just beneath the surface.

"I don't know."

"Can you recall a face, or perhaps some feature that would help to identify him?"

She shook her head. "I know *what* was done, but I do not know who wielded the hand that beat me. Or *why.*" She pulled away from him and sat up. "And I still don't know who I am. Why can't I remember that, Rian? How is it I am able to recall such a terrible moment in my life, but nothing about my family?"

"You will. In time I promise you will," he assured her. "We just have to find the key that will unlock all the good things that have happened to you."

"What makes you think there are any?" she asked bitterly.

"Because destiny would not have sent you to me otherwise."

A gentle knock stopped any further conversation. Leaving Catherine on the bed, Rian went and opened the door. On the other side Felicity was almost beside herself with worry as she clutched the arm of an equally concerned Liam.

"I'm so sorry," Liam apologized as Felicity pushed past Rian and ran to Catherine's side. "I've never seen her so distraught."

"It was a frightening moment," Rian told him.

Not sure how to respond, Liam pointed to the wound on his brother's forehead. "That looks like it smarts."

"I've had worse."

Both men turned as the sound of renewed weeping came from across the room, where Felicity was offering her own comfort to Catherine.

"Best let them be," Liam said.

Nodding in agreement Rian followed his brother out of the room, closing the door gently behind him. He had spoken the truth. His head might be the only physical injury he suffered, but his heart had been torn apart by Catherine's words.

Chapter 12

The house was quiet and settled for the night when Rian stole down the hall to Catherine's room. Barefoot and wearing only his breeches and a half-buttoned shirt, he slipped through the door and stood quietly, waiting for his eyes to adjust to the dark. He had wanted to go to her before now, but Felicity had advised against it. As they no longer had any of Dr. MacGregor's draughts, Mrs. Hatch had made some of her own 'special' tea for Catherine.

No one knew exactly what was in Mrs. Hatch's soothing brew, and Rian knew better than to ask. He was just grateful for the calming effect it produced. In his mind's eye he saw himself as a child standing in the kitchen watching as the newly married, younger and slimmer housekeeper brewed her tea for his mother.

"Be careful now, young Master Rian," she told him, the seriousness of her expression matching his own as she handed him the tray on which she placed a cup filled with the hot liquid. "Mind you take a care not to spill it."

He could feel her eyes on him as he slowly made his way out of the kitchen with the precious elixir. It wasn't until he was older he realized she knew exactly how long the journey would take him, and timed it so the tea would have cooled sufficiently when he reached his destination. His mother trusted the young housekeeper implicitly, and Rian found no reason to do otherwise.

Now he made his way across the room to the bed and stared down at the sleeping figure. He forced himself to slow his breathing and with it the sudden acceleration of his heart. Catherine lay on her side, facing away from him. Her white-blond hair, braided into a thick rope, pooled behind her on the pillow. The anger he had felt at hearing her speak of her ordeal still simmered inside him. Had he not exercised absolute control of himself, his rage would have easily spiraled into an uncontrollable fury. Forcing himself to remain calm, for Catherine's sake, had produced an unexpected effect.

He had lived every moment of the terrifying trauma with her. Able to feel each blow of the whip as it bit into her skin. He suffered every punishing bruise inflicted by her tormentor's hand. And as she described it all in cold, dispassionate detail, the invisible silken cord that had first ensnared him, the one that relentlessly pulled him toward her, became an unbreakable rope that would forever join him to her.

His intent in entering her room was to offer reassurance. He had felt the shame flowing from her when her tale was done. Catherine believed herself somehow to blame, that in a perverse way she had brought this evil upon herself. Rian intended to let her know that she was to carry no guilt. That he would never turn her away.

"Rian...."

The sound of Catherine murmuring his name as she slept made him start, but only for a moment. Quietly he took the chair from the dresser, and set it next to her bed. For the longest time he did nothing but watch her sleep. His own heart beat fiercely in his chest, but the soothing measure of Catherine's breathing calmed him. He reached out to pick up the hand lying on top of the coverlet, holding it inside his own, his mouth turning upward at the memory of her snatching it from his grasp at their first meeting. It would be so easy to slip into the bed next to her. To feel the warmth of her body covered by nothing more than a fine linen shift, next to his. But this was not the time to think about passion. Though Rian knew he wanted to be her lover, he was mature enough to understand there existed the possibility Catherine might never welcome the physical attentions of a man. And while she had taken the initiative and kissed him, that was before she had remembered what had been done to her. It would be stupid to assume such chilling recall would have no effect, though he clung selfishly to the hope he'd been given. Catherine had reached out to him, and Rian would not betray her trust. When the time was right, and if she so desired it, she would come to him. Giving herself with no reservation. In turn, he would show her what it meant to be loved for who she was, completely and utterly.

As if reading his thoughts in her sleep, Catherine's hand moved, her fingers curling around his and Rian felt her squeeze gently as she murmured his name again.

"Shhhh," he whispered, brushing a loose curl from her cheek with his other hand. "Go back to sleep. Nothing will harm you."

She opened her eyes and gave him a sleepy look. "Are you truly here?" He bent his head and brushed his lips across the knuckles on her hand. "Stay with me," she asked in a voice that was sensuously sleep heavy.

"I will."

"Promise me...."

"I promise."

Her eyes closed and she smiled. Rian thought it the most beautiful thing he had ever seen. Watching her fall back asleep, he felt her hand go slack in his, and then she rolled onto her side. There was enough ambient light that he could see the angry red welt branding the pale ivory of her skin. Rising from his seat, he leaned far enough over that he could carefully press his lips to the scar, his tongue savoring the sweet taste of her skin.

"Rian...." Her whisper caressed him in the dark.

He lay down next to her, opening his arms as she turned and instinctively sought him. She placed her head on his chest, her arm around his waist. A tidal wave of long hidden emotions broke through the wall he had painstakingly erected, forcing him to deal with them in the only way he knew how. Surrendering, Rian closed his eyes and gave himself up to the maelstrom of mixed feelings that broke down his reserves, taking comfort in knowing he lay next to the only woman he wanted to share the rest of his life with.

* * * *

Opening her eyes slowly, Catherine sleepily reached out a hand and ran it over the rumpled coverings, feeling the warmth that lingered there. At first she had thought she was dreaming, in all truth one of her less erotic fantasies, but one that seemed more real because of it. Given everything that had happened, it was not beyond the realm of possibility for her mind to have fabricated the comfort she most desired. Especially after reliving the horror of her past. But last night she had not needed her dream world to conjure up a fantasy scenario. Rian had come to her, had lain by her side and held her as she slept, giving her the security she needed.

She focused on the heavy brocade curtains that were tied back from the canopy above the bed. The intricate woven pattern of flowers and birds seemed especially bright this morning. Catherine knew Rian would not return to her bed again, not in this way, but the thought did not dismay her. He had given her a secret gift, something only the two of them could share, and she was more than content to have it remain so. She had slept with him by her side.

Regretfully. she pushed back the covers and got out of bed. After stepping behind the decorated screen to perform her morning ablutions, she quickly dressed and began the task of repairing her hair. A guilty frown creased her face when she picked up the hairbrush. Turning it over she checked to see if it carried a mark from striking Rian's head. She was thankful to find it did not.

With each stroke of the brush Catherine called up another moment of that terrible night, and replayed it in her mind. Examining the event with an icy objectivity, she felt as if it had happened to someone else. She searched for clues, anything that would reveal the identity of her assailant. But none came. With her hair now fashioned in its customary thick braid, she stared at her reflection in the mirror for a long time. The face that looked back was becoming more familiar and as she stared, it seemed the look in her eyes promised two things. First, that the name she was searching for was still locked inside her head, but it would, in time, reveal itself. And second, that Rian would come to her again. Only this time he would not come to comfort her, but to satisfy this strange, wonderful ache she felt. An ache he also carried. And that made her smile in anticipation.

Chapter 13

Oakhaven's tenants and their families began to arrive later that morning. After a while it seemed to be nothing but one continuous stream of people passing through the massive front doors and into the house. The lofty ceilings soon echoed with conversation alongside children's laughter. Liam and Felicity were generous hosts, quickly putting their guests at ease by simply talking with them. Treating everyone with respect, they easily spoke of matters that were of concern to them all.

Almost at once Felicity found herself the center of attention amongst a group of married women determined to give her as much advice about husbands and children as they could. Seized by a number of husbands, Liam and Rian were equally engaged in lively banter, but theirs involved crops, cattle, and ale. No one it seemed was in the least hesitant about sharing an opinion.

Catherine had thought long and hard about whether or not to share in the festivities. In the end she decided the loss would be hers if she kept herself apart. Seeing the great ballroom populated by multiple groups of people, she nervously skirted one group after another, listening to snippets of conversation before moving on. She was about to leave one such small cluster when she suddenly found her hand enclosed inside that of another. A young woman, close to her own age, pulled Catherine farther into the circle.

"You'll hear better if you lean in," the girl advised with a smile. "Me mam tends to mumble sometimes."

No one questioned her presence amongst them, and slowly Catherine's nervousness faded. Still, it was a comfort to know that every time she looked across the room, she found Rian watching her.

In the late afternoon a welcome lull fell over the house. All of the children present, due to bribery in one form or another, were either napping or had at least been coerced into lying down to rest. Their parents and older siblings took advantage of this respite by either following suit or forming quieter gatherings with friends and neighbors. It was a chance to exchange more intimate news, and the new Mistress of Oakhaven had thoughtfully prepared some extra rooms for such a purpose.

Bringing a tea tray and Mrs. Hatch with her, Felicity found Catherine in her bedroom. The three women sat comfortably in front of the fire, enjoying the few moments of peace and quiet the day would offer.

"I thought perhaps I might wear the green dress after all," Catherine said conversationally, referring to her selection of a gown for the dinner and celebration that would follow.

"I think that would be a splendid choice," Felicity told her.

"Aye, lass, it will bring out the sparkle in your eyes," Mrs. Hatch agreed.

"What did you do with it?" Catherine asked softly, sipping her tea.

"Do with what, lass?"

"The other dress, the pink one." The sudden recollection of her snarling at Felicity made her flush uncomfortably.

"Master Rian burned it," Mrs. Hatch said somberly, recalling once more the look on his face as he stood before the massive stone hearth in the kitchen while the flames hungrily consumed the gown. She had never seen such fury in him.

With Catherine's permission, Rian had told his brother and sister-in-law what had triggered her violent outburst. The truth had been far worse than anything they had imagined. Mrs. Hatch, having played a pivotal role in her recovery since the beginning, was also included in this confidence, which left them all wondering how Catherine had managed to survive at all.

"I think the green will look very nice indeed," Felicity said, finishing her tea and giving Catherine a smile of such warmth that Catherine knew she was not only forgiven, but understood as well.

* * * *

It was a good choice, but the dress seemed to be in some confusion over what color it was supposed to be. Standing one way, it was the most wonderful shade of emerald green and then, as Catherine turned, it seemed to shimmer itself into an amazing blue.

"I have seen the seas of the Caribbean change color in just the same way," Rian said, coming up behind her and leaning down to whisper in her ear.

"How wonderful. It must be a sight to see," Catherine replied, her eyes shining as she turned around. "Perhaps I can persuade you to take me there one day."

Whatever response he was about to make, it was lost as a pair of identical twins accosted him, demanding his presence for the next dance. Laughing, Catherine clapped her hands, keeping time to the lively beat, and was impressed to discover Rian was quite an accomplished dancer. He would not be short of partners tonight, she told herself.

"Are you enjoying yourself?" Liam held out a cup of punch.

"Yes, very much so. Thank you for allowing me to share this with you." Standing on tiptoe, Catherine impulsively kissed his cheek, making him blush.

"Good God! What the hell is she doing here?"

Thinking he was angered by her impulsiveness, Catherine started to apologize, but then she followed his eyes. Despite the organized mayhem on the ballroom floor, Liam had been distracted by something on the other side of the room. His startled exclamation had turned the heads of those standing alongside him. Like Catherine, they followed his gaze to the open doorway across the room.

Dressed in a sumptuous gown of black and white, complemented by matching feathers adorning an impossibly elaborate hairstyle, Lady Isabel Howard stood in the entryway. It made no difference that the guests present were all farmers; an entrance was an entrance, and Isabel was an expert at making sure she always made a memorable one. She scanned the assembly looking for a familiar face when her eyes suddenly locked onto Catherine and Liam. With a slight nod of her head, Isabel acknowledged her host before fixing her gaze on Catherine, daring her to look away. She did not, and after a few moments Isabel gave her a small, but patronizing smile.

"Liam, did you see who has just arrived?" Felicity, breathless from the last dance, had reached the two of them. Her husband nodded grimly. "Has Rian?" she asked.

"I don't know where he is at the moment," Liam confessed, "but I would imagine not."

"Then I suggest you greet her first."

Apologizing to those nearby who had overheard his words, Liam kissed his wife on the cheek, and then made his way through the crowd to their uninvited guest.

"You didn't invite her?" Catherine asked Felicity.

"Good Lord no! Everyone knows this is a private affair. No one outside the immediate family is invited to attend."

"You invited me," Catherine pointed out.

"As I said, no-one outside the immediate family."

Warmed by Felicity's words, Catherine asked, "So what do you think has brought her here?"

"That is something I would very much like to know myself." At that moment the dance came to an end, and the musicians decided it was time to take a much deserved break. Catherine scanned the couples, hoping to see one of the twins Rian had been dancing with, but there were too many people milling about. She did, however, manage to see that Liam had now reached Isabel. "If she ruins this night for Liam, I swear I will never forgive the bitch!"

"Felicity! I had no idea you actually knew that word," Catherine said in an attempt to diffuse her friend's simmering anger.

"You'd be surprised how being married expands one's vocabulary. Conversation is more liberated," Felicity said as her eyes continued to dart around the room. "I just hope Liam can deal with her before—oh, too late!"

Rian had now joined his brother, and the two women watched as both men turned and walked out of the ballroom. With Isabel between them. Felicity knew her husband well enough to read the message being broadcast by the stiff set of his shoulders. It told her he was not at all pleased.

"I met her, you know," Catherine said matter-of-factly.

"Who? Isabel?" Felicity was astonished.

Catherine nodded.

"When?" Felicity asked.

Catherine gave a brief account of the meeting, and when she was done Felicity took her by the hand. "Come, let us find somewhere a little more private, and you can tell me everything you do not wish others to overhear." Then, as a way of sweetening the invitation, she added, "And I will tell you all I know about Lady Isabel Howard."

* * * *

"Lady Howard, welcome to Oakhaven," Liam said as he bent to kiss the back of Isabel's hand. "What brings you to our small part of the world tonight?"

"Oh Liam, why the formality?" In a display of teasing annoyance, she tapped him with her closed fan. It was something Liam was getting heartily sick of. "A little bird whispered in my ear that you were hosting a grand ball here at Oakhaven, so I decided to indulge my curiosity. I do hope you will forgive my impetuous nature."

"Impetuous?" Rian said raising a brow. "I think you mean impertinent, don't you?"

"Oh, come now, Rian, there's no need to be rude."

Knowing that Isabel could give lessons in rudeness, Rian shook his head. There would be no point in discussing the issue any further. Isabel was here and intent on staying, it seemed. And the look on Liam's face said he expected nothing less than his older brother's best behavior.

"Are you not even the tiniest bit pleased to see me?" their unexpected guest asked.

"Of course," Rian replied, "and we are very pleased to have you here." He would be the model of perfect behavior, making sure no one could fault him for his manners. But it wouldn't be for Liam. He was doing it for Felicity and Catherine.

"Let us find a place where we can talk in private," Liam said.

Isabel's nostrils flared slightly at the suggestion, but she smiled graciously and allowed herself to be led away from the ballroom and into an adjoining salon. She sat while Liam poured her a glass of sweet wine.

"Lady Howard—"

An arched brow reflected her displeasure at the use of her title.

"Forgive me, *Isabel*," Liam amended, "I'm sure both you and my brother have much to discuss. However, I would ask that you respect both my family and my guests while you enjoy our hospitality."

Isabel took a sip of her wine. Liam's warning was crystal clear. Do not upset his wife, brother or the lowliest farmhand. As long as they were under his roof certain courtesies would be extended, and there would be consequences if the same were not observed.

"I understand you perfectly," Isabel said, gracing him with her famous winning smile. It was a shame it did not reach her eyes. "And I promise to be on my best behavior."

Saying nothing more, Liam gave a slight bow, and then retreated, leaving her alone with Rian, who wasted no time in getting straight to the point.

"What the devil are you doing here, Isabel?" he asked bluntly. "You know perfectly well this is a family gathering."

"One of the things I've always admired about you, Rian, is your complete and utter disdain for useless conversation." He said nothing, but the look on his face implied he was in no mood to be toyed with. "Oh, don't be angry with me," Isabel continued, appearing genuinely contrite. "You have no idea how boring town has become. I was going out of my mind."

"And you thought a houseful of farmers and their wives would be more stimulating?" Rian snorted. "Forgive me if I find that somewhat hard to believe."

"But that's where you're wrong. I kept seeing the same faces, hearing the same gossip no matter what function I was attending."

"It didn't seem to bother you when we attended those same parties together."

"Well no…but that's because we were the subject of all the gossip."

Unable to help himself, Rian grinned. Isabel was completely shameless. She had no remorse about letting everyone know the world revolved around her, and if it didn't, it damn well should. It had been one of the many things he had enjoyed about her.

"Rian, please, I know you think things between us have changed—"

"There is nothing between us, Isabel," he interrupted firmly. "Not anymore."

She pouted prettily. "Yes, I realize that *now*, and I want to tell you how sorry I am for my behavior the night of Liam's wedding. It was very wrong of me." An admission of deplorable conduct along with an apology was something he had not been expecting. Was Isabel truly sorry? She looked almost shamefaced as she asked, "Did anyone else know I was ever there?"

Rian shook his head. "Not that I am aware of."

"Not even the formidable Mrs. Hatch?"

"She was under the impression you had departed after leaving your fictitious note for me."

"Ah yes, the note. I'd forgotten about that."

"I have to admire your ingenuity. It was clever of you to leave the front door open."

She sipped her wine as the hint of a smile flirted with the corners of her mouth. Rian said nothing. He understood she was trying to decide how to continue.

"May I speak plainly?"

"When have you ever not?"

Her mouth became a moue of frustration. "As I was saying, I realize the affection between us has changed, and I know that I have no future with you—at least not the one I had hoped for—but can we not remain friends?" Her voice trembled slightly. "I am not so proud I cannot admit to missing your company, Rian, as well as your conversation and wit. It would be just too awful to have to confess that I have fallen so far out of favor, you refuse to even speak to me." She paused. "Please don't send me away. I know I am here uninvited, but it would just be too humiliating to be dismissed, especially when I have only just arrived." He searched Isabel's face, looking for signs of trickery or false coquettishness, but all he could see was sincerity. "I promise I will be on my best behavior," she repeated earnestly.

"Your very best behavior," Rian added dryly, seeing her smile. Isabel never did like to lose. "I think it only fair to warn you that if, for one moment, I suspect you are about to embarrass my family or any of our guests, then I will take great pleasure in personally putting you over my shoulder and dumping you outside the door."

"Oh, stop being such a tease." With a wicked laugh, Isabel took his arm. "Can I at least claim one dance with you this evening?"

"I think that might be arranged." Rian sighed, leading her out of the salon and back into the ballroom.

"And do you think perhaps I might meet Catherine again?"

Her tone was all innocence and light on the surface, but Rian thought he detected the hidden snarl of a predatory hunter in her words. He stared at her, but Isabel's expression remained open, and seemingly without guile. Perhaps he had misjudged her.

"Only if Catherine wishes it," he said in reply to her question. *And I very much doubt that she will.*

"Of course," Isabel agreed, giving him a smile that had once brought two Dukes and a Crown Prince to their knees.

Chapter 14

Catherine took a large sip of the blackberry brandy Felicity had poured for her, and stared morosely at the flames dancing in the fireplace. It wasn't Felicity's fault. She had no idea of the recent events that had occurred between Catherine and Rian, or the depth of Catherine's feelings. If she had, she would have chosen her words with more discretion. Unable to help herself, Catherine listened as Felicity talked on. Having given her opinion of Isabel's dismal lack of morals, and total disregard for acceptable behavior, Felicity now took a path that had the potential for becoming decidedly uncomfortable, Isabel's many love affairs.

Even without Mrs. Hatch's confirmation, Isabel's disastrous London visit had left Catherine in no doubt that such an affair existed between the dark-haired beauty and Rian. The household staff spoke openly of their being lovers, and although Catherine had sat with the rest of them, listening as they discussed the matter, it was somehow more painful to hear Felicity speak of it in such a casual way.

"I'm sorry, what did you say?" Catherine snapped her head around, and waited for Felicity to repeat herself.

"I said that Liam and I were most pleased when Rian chose to end the affair. It was, after all, naught but a dalliance."

"Oh, when did he do that?" It was difficult to sound detached about something that could change her life.

Felicity thought for a moment. "It must have been around the time of our wedding. Either right before or soon after." She paused and looked at Catherine. "Is it important?"

"No, not at all," Catherine lied, shaking her head as a rush of inexplicable warmth suddenly enveloped her. To know that Rian no longer regarded Isabel with affection when they had kissed pleased her enormously.

But now Isabel was here, full of confidence and looking absolutely ravishing in a dress that made certain she was noticed by every set of male eyes. Of course, every set of female eyes noticed her too, but that reaction wasn't quite the same.

"Does she know that Rian is no longer in love with her?" she asked as Felicity replenished her glass of blackberry brandy.

The Mistress of Oakhaven snorted. "I don't think my brother-in-law was ever 'in love' with Isabel to begin with, but to answer your question, yes. It is my understanding that he has made it quite plain."

"So either she is choosing to ignore the fact, or she is hoping to rekindle his affection." Catherine took more than a sip this time, and spluttered as the brandy flowed through her. It did little to dispel the misery that now replaced the earlier glow she had been feeling. "And in that dress she's wearing, anything is possible."

Leaning forward Felicity said, "Well 'tis of no concern now, for I do believe Rian's affections are securely fixed in another direction." Her smile left Catherine in no doubt as to what—and whom—she was referring to.

"Oh no, please Felicity, whatever it is you're thinking, you're quite wrong." Self-preservation made Catherine utter the protest, knowing she would not be able to bear it if Isabel's presence gave Rian second thoughts about his feelings toward her. She could already feel doubt trying to slither its way inside her heart.

He came to your room. He stayed with you, again.

"I don't think so. In fact, I am positive I am not mistaken," Felicity said firmly as she took Catherine's hands in hers. "I do not claim to be knowledgeable in the ways of men—certainly not as knowledgeable as Lady Howard—but I am experienced enough to recognize when a fond regard has turned to something more."

"No, Felicity, you are mistaken I assure you. Any affection Rian may have for me is merely kindness, and nothing else."

"Is that what you think he feels for you, kindness?"

Pulling her hands free of Felicity's hold, Catherine stared down at the carpet. "Of course, what else could it be?" she mumbled.

"Catherine, darling, remember to whom you are speaking." Felicity put her hands on Catherine's shoulders giving her a not-so-gentle shake. "Why are you so determined to believe Rian bears no deep affection for you?"

She started as a thought occurred to her. "Oh, my dear, is it because you don't want him to? You don't like him?"

Catherine felt the sudden burn on her cheeks. Rian had kissed her, had told her he would do so again, and had secretly slipped into her room and held her through the night. But Felicity knew none of this, and, despite the fondness between them, Catherine was not ready to share such secrets with her. Felicity was married to Rian's brother, and her loyalties would be with him. What if, after this night, Rian had a change of heart? What if, even now, he was regretting everything he had said to her in the snow? What if he never meant any of it to begin with? He was a man who could change his mind as easily as he changed his shirt—or have it changed for him. Now all her insecurities came tumbling out, neatly wrapped in a brightly colored package of black and white silk.

"Catherine." Felicity's tone was gentle. "Do you think we have not noticed the recent change in attitude between you and Rian? Noticed and rejoiced in it. What makes you think he will reverse his position?"

"Because *she* is here!" Catherine wailed miserably, pointing a finger at the closed library door.

"And that should tell you—"

"They have unfinished business with each other."

"—she's the one who is insecure."

Catherine started to say something, and then stopped, frowning, as she pondered Felicity's words. The blackberry brandy was beginning to take effect, and her thinking was becoming fuzzy. "Why do you think Lady Howard is here?"

"Oh, I don't know, perhaps she's going to try to persuade Cook to part with her recipe for apple tart."

"Really?" Catherine raised her brows in surprise. Cook did make very good pies, and her apple tart was exceptional.

Felicity let loose an exasperated laugh. "No, you silly goose, of course not! Isabel detests the country. The only reason she is here is to try to win Rian back. If there was the slightest chance of his returning to the city, she would simply wait for him to come to her. Deep down she knows her cause is lost. What you are seeing is the act of a desperate woman."

"Do you think so?" Catherine asked, clutching at the faint glimmer of hope.

"Oh yes. I am most certain of it."

Picking up her glass, Catherine took a more ladylike sip. It really was excellent brandy, and she told herself to compliment Mrs. Hatch the next time she saw her. She was about to ask another question when there came a light knock on the door, and Liam entered the room.

"Is everything all right?" he asked with only the smallest amount of concern detectable in his voice.

"Of course," his wife reassured him. "Should I be asking the same of you regarding our uninvited guest?"

Liam sighed. "I have Lady Howard's word she will be on her best behavior." His wife snorted and her expression told him not to be disappointed when that did not happen. Stepping forward, he took her hands in his and kissed her lightly on the lips before asking, "Catherine, may I steal my wife away?"

"Of course you may," she said, assuming a false brightness. "If you will forgive me, I think I will stay here for a little longer." Concern pulled Felicity's brows together, making Catherine add, "'Tis nothing more than tiredness. I am not used to so much excitement."

"Are you sure?" Felicity hesitated, unconvinced.

"Quite sure. I promise I will sit here for just a little while longer, and then, with your permission, I think I will retire."

"Of course," Liam said, overruling whatever protest his wife was about to make.

Catherine made a show of good-naturedly shooing them both from the room, but once the door was secured she allowed utter despair to wash over her. Felicity's words, well-meaning though they were, made little difference. The truth of the matter was undeniable. Isabel was here and she was not about to be ignored. It didn't matter that Catherine had kissed Rian or that he had kissed her back. That was all in the past. Isabel was far more accomplished in the art of seduction, and she already knew how to kiss Rian as well as what would tempt him.

Besides, Catherine did not believe Isabel was at all desperate. It might have been different if Rian had actually stated out loud his affection for her, but the words had not been spoken, and now, as Catherine questioned everything that had happened between them, her mind became a jumble of disconnected thoughts.

Would Rian turn from her?

Had he pursued her simply because she was here?

Were his promises made in haste, and now ones he no longer wanted to keep?

Isabel looked as beautiful as ever. It would be hard for any man not to be drawn to her, and Rian was no callow youth. He was a grown man with appetites and needs.

Needs Catherine had no idea if she could satisfy.

She didn't realize she was crying until she felt a tear splash on the back of her hand, and she swiped a palm across her cheek in anger. Damn it all to hell! She couldn't control what Rian was feeling; she could barely control her own desires. Glancing at the half-empty glass on the table she immediately looked around for the brandy. It sat on a shelf where Felicity had placed it, practically begging to be taken down. Catherine stared at the dark colored liquid. The decanter was almost full, and its contents were very good. With just the right amount of sweetness to bring out the flavor of the alcohol, why it hardly seemed like drinking at all. Suddenly the decision to drown her sorrows in blackberry brandy seemed the best idea she'd had in a long time. It had been her father's way of blunting the sharp edges of the world, to escape the truths he could not face, so why not follow his example?

What an excellent idea, a voice in her head whispered. She did not even realize that the recollection of her father was another step in the recovery of her memory.

* * * *

Rian was impressed. Isabel had been better than her word. Making pleasant conversation with everyone she met, she was the perfect guest. Delighting all and being delightful in return. He sighed, knowing he would never understand the complexities of the fairer sex. Standing to one side, he watched as Isabel listened in complete fascination while a mournful farmer shared his woes regarding milking cows with infected teats.

"Sounds absolutely ghastly," she empathized as Rian came to her rescue, and led her to the floor for their promised dance. They danced more than once, the twins suddenly turning shy now Isabel was among them. Rian was so busy making sure Isabel did not cause any mischief, he lost track of Catherine. Felicity told him in passing that Catherine had mentioned being tired, and had most likely already retired.

At the stroke of midnight the new Mistress of Oakhaven was presented to the head of each family that lived on the estate. Looking as proud as any peacock, Liam took his wife around the room and formally introduced her. It was a wonderful, time-honored ritual that the newest Mrs. Connor was very pleased to continue. The general gaiety of the evening continued for another hour or so and then it came time for their guests to leave. The weather, though cold, was clear enough that traveling could be safely accomplished but even so, accommodation was offered for any not wishing to journey at so late an hour.

As part of her final duty of the evening, Felicity made certain every woman left with her allotted basket of food to get the family through the next day or two. Tucked between the loaves of bread, wheels of cheese and all manner of leftover dainties, was an extra gift. Using one of her original wedding petticoats, Felicity and her mother had made silk pouches. Inside each was a gold coin. A gift in case of hard times. This, too, was a Connor tradition.

Finally the last family left. The sound of their hearty farewells and good wishes carried on the still night air. Rian and Liam made sure that the men folk had extra wood for their fires, along with some liquid warmth to guard against the cold. When the family returned to the ballroom, the house seemed eerily quiet after being filled with so many voices. The only sound heard now was the low murmur of Mrs. Hatch issuing instructions to those clearing the room. Rian, humming out loud, grabbed the housekeeper's hands and, taking her in his arms, swirled her around the ballroom, much to the delight of the kitchen maids and footmen who clapped their hands to keep time.

"Get away with you, Master Rian!" Mrs. Hatch exclaimed, flapping her apron at him when he finally let her go. Her face, however, was pleasantly flushed by his attention and the laughter in her voice matched the joy in her eyes.

"I still don't know why you won't marry me, Mrs. Hatch," he said, leaning down to kiss her cheek. "But I pray that all your dreams come true."

She reached up and held her palm to his cheek. "They already have, lad," she told him affectionately. "You're back where you belong."

Felicity, accepting Rian's offer of help, decided it was time to get her husband to bed. Liam hadn't started drinking until after the presentation ceremony. Oh, he'd taken a sip or two throughout the evening, but once his wife had been presented, he found himself in the middle of a group of tenants who insisted on helping him celebrate the success of the night with some very fine liquid refreshment.

"Have you sheen Ishbel?" he slurred, as Rian put an arm about his shoulder.

"Your guest has already been shown to her room," Mrs. Hatch informed him.

"Ah well, g'night then." Liam called out to anyone who might be listening. "It was a wunnerful shella-shella-shellabrashun!"

After helping deposit his brother on his bed, and leaving him to the care of his wife, Rian decided to check on Catherine. Acutely aware that her disappearance had coincided with Isabel's arrival, he wanted to reassure himself it was just that. A coincidence and nothing more sinister. He knocked gently on the bedroom door, and receiving no answer, assumed she must already be asleep. Quietly he slipped inside, only to find the room empty. The bed, which had been turned down earlier, remained undisturbed; the plain cotton shift Catherine wore to bed waiting for her. He picked it up, holding it to his face and inhaling her scent before laying it carefully back down. A sinking feeling began to roll in the pit of his stomach as he frowned, wondering where she could be at so late an hour.

Suddenly his face lit up. Felicity had told him they had been talking in the library earlier. Next to the stables it was Catherine's favorite place, and it would not have surprised him if she had abandoned the overall merriment for a chance to lose herself in the pages of a book. He retraced his steps to the lower floor of the house, not seeing the shapely figure standing in the shadows, watching him.

Chapter 15

"Catherine?"

The library was in almost total darkness with the only light coming from the embers of a dying fire. Rian strained to hear a response to his inquiry, but none came.

Although he believed it to be a waste of time, he nevertheless called out again, a little louder this time while he tried to imagine where else she might be.

"Catherine?"

Silence. And then, as he turned to go, there came a soft *whump* from across the room. Being careful not to bump into any furniture, Rian followed the noise and discovered Catherine lying peacefully on the carpet next to one of the overstuffed chairs. Noticing the empty decanter on the floor next to her, he wasn't sure if what he'd heard was the empty carafe falling from her hand, or her body as she slipped from the chair to her now recumbent position. It was a lucky thing the glass decanter had not broken, but then it hadn't had far to fall.

He bent on one knee and leaned over the horizontal body, brushing an errant curl from Catherine's forehead as he gazed down at her. Her eyes were closed, her lips slightly parted. Rian wondered just how much of the decanter's contents she'd consumed.

"Catherine, wake up." He put a hand on her shoulder and gave a gentle shake.

His efforts were met with an irritated mutter as she tried to dislodge his hand. Undeterred, Rian continued shaking, an amused grin on his face, until finally Catherine opened her eyes. It took some effort, and was accompanied by a lot of blinking, but eventually she focused on him. The semi-glazed expression told Rian Catherine had gone beyond tipsy, and was, in fact, quite inebriated. Picking up the empty decanter from the floor, he sniffed the neck cautiously. The aroma of sweet brandy tickled his nose.

"How much of this did you drink?" he asked, trying to sound stern as he helped her to a sitting position.

She peered at the decanter as if she'd never seen it before. The crease between her brows deepened, and then recognition made her open her eyes wide. "All of it," she answered, punctuating her remark with the most spectacular belch. "'Scuse me!" She put a hand over her mouth, trying to stifle the sudden fit of giggles that quickly followed her impressive burp. Rian picked up the empty decanter and put it on the table as the giggles gave way to hiccups. "It was very good—hic!—but s'all gone—hic!" Her voice matched her expression. Both were wistful until the solution to the problem presented itself. "Let's get—hic!—s'more!"

Assuming she had found an ally, Catherine tried to get to her feet, but in doing so lost her balance and fell back into the chair. Her giggles became peals of laughter, interspersed with hiccups.

"I can't—hic!—get up!" she blurted.

"Allow me to assist you," Rian said, taking hold of her arms and helping her to her feet. She swayed unsteadily against him.

"You drunk I'm think, don't you?"

"No," Rian told her, doing his best to be serious, "I *know* you're drunk." Holding her firmly, he relished the feel of her in his arms, drunk or sober. "Did you enjoy yourself at the party?" he asked.

"Yes, very much." Swaying alarmingly, she began looking around as if she had lost something. Rian tightened his hold about her waist. "It was nice—hic!—until *she* came."

"Who?"

"Her!" She poked him hard in the chest with a finger, and Rian knew all too well whom Catherine was referring to. "Your lover!" she stated in an exaggerated whisper as she held up the same finger and now stared at it, as if trying to recall what she'd been using it for only moments before. The effort made her slightly cross-eyed.

"Isabel is not my lover."

"Liar," she contradicted, good-naturedly.

All interest in her finger now lost, Catherine leaned forward and rested her head against Rian's chest as her hiccups finally ended. He moved his hand gently across her back, his palm making wide circles. He had dreamed of a moment like this, only in his fantasy he didn't remember Mrs. Hatch's excellent brandy playing such a pivotal role. He sighed softly. Catherine's head was going to hurt like hell in the morning.

"I wish I was your lover," she mumbled.

The blood rushed through him, pounding in his ears and making him think he had misheard, even though he knew he had not. She was drunk and it was doubtful she would remember much of anything in the morning, including this conversation between them, but alcohol did have a way of relaxing a person's inhibitions, allowing them to reveal things they never would when sober. Rian swallowed a couple of times. He knew, given her current state of intoxication, it was unfair of him, but he asked the question anyway.

"Are you certain that is what you want?"

Catherine raised her head from his breastbone and gazed at him. Her expression was a mix of unfulfilled lust and naive wantonness. Saying nothing, she carefully took the same finger she had poked him with, and placed it over his mouth, tracing the curve of his lips with her finger. She narrowed her eyes in concentration.

He opened his mouth slightly and she pulled gently on his lower lip, letting her wayward finger trace the soft warmth inside. He couldn't stop the groan that escaped him as she then put the same finger on her own bottom lip, sliding it back and forth. She had no idea what she was doing to him, but the sudden swelling in his breeches threatened to show her if he didn't regain some measure of restraint. Taking her finger from her mouth, Catherine looked up at Rian and smiled. It was a sultry smile filled with the promise of sex, yet still managing to stay deceptively innocent.

"You haven't kissed me." Now she sounded more petulant than drunk.

"I didn't know you wanted me to."

"You said I would know…that I would ask you."

He nodded "I remember."

"Well, I'm asking."

She tipped her head back and he could see the pulse throbbing at the base of her throat. Dear God, did she have any idea what she was doing? The brandy had done its job well, perhaps a little too well, and Catherine's inhibitions had gone far beyond relaxed. They had been totally stripped away, giving Rian a glimpse of the woman that lay beneath. Someone he had seen once before when she had been delirious. All she needed was his touch to awaken her.

Rian could feel his own blood racing, pounding in his temples as he repositioned his hold around her waist while his other hand moved from her back to stroke the smooth column of her neck. He was rewarded with a throaty sound that reminded him of a purr, but not the kind the barn cats made. This belonged to a much larger cousin.

Catherine suddenly snapped her head up, loosening some curls from what had started out as a most becoming coiffure. The escaping ringlets danced enticingly across her cheek and forehead, teasing him. Rian found her disheveled appearance utterly alluring. She placed her hands on his upper arms to steady herself.

"You came to me…to my bedroom," she whispered, huskily.

"Catherine, I—"

His explanation was lost as without warning she threw herself at him. Standing on tiptoe she flung her arms around his neck and pressed her mouth to his as she sought to fulfill her own desire. It was a repeat of the shared moment in the snow, only this time Rian was not so certain he was going to let her go without educating her a little.

Although he was sure she must have received her fair share of kisses in her past, it was obvious she had never been kissed by anyone possessing a modicum of skill. And certainly never by a grown man. Gently he unlocked her hands from around his neck and moved her away from him. Disappointment covered her face like a veil.

"Oh." She paused, swaying gently from side to side. "I knew you didn't want to kiss me."

"You couldn't be more wrong," Rian said. "I'm going to kiss you, but I'm going to do it properly."

She looked up at him with fire dancing in her eyes as he sat down in the chair she had recently vacated and pulled her onto his lap.

Her nervousness broke through the alcohol-tinged euphoria as she asked, "What should I do?"

"Enjoy it."

Any conscious thought Catherine may have had was lost as Rian covered her mouth with his. She had forgotten how soft his lips were, and she gave an involuntary gasp as she felt his tongue trace the corners of her mouth. It was all the invitation he needed, and he seized the opportunity to explore her mouth. Catherine moved her hands so she could grip the front of his jacket and Rian held her fast, cupping the back of her head so she could not pull away. His tongue began a slow slide in and out of her mouth, tasting and teasing and, like a man dying of thirst, he drank his fill of her.

With his need temporarily satisfied, Rian lifted his mouth from hers. He kept his face only inches away as he watched for her reaction. Catherine kept her eyes closed. Her breath had an uneven hitch to it as she tried to absorb the sensations released in her. The flame that had been ignited exploded and it ran, course unchecked, through her body. Slowly she opened her eyes and looked at him. Lust had darkened the normal cornflower blue to a rich shade of indigo, and the glazed look Catherine now wore owed nothing to the housekeeper's excellent wine.

"You were right," she told him, her voice quavering with need. "It does get better."

Rian groaned. Leaning forward he tipped his head and traced the hollow at the base of her throat with his tongue. She threw her head back as he continued to burn her skin with his mouth, while his fingers stroked the flesh above her bodice. Feeling his hair sweep silkily over her cleavage, Catherine took his face in her hands.

"Do you want me?" she asked, staring at him with wide eyes.

He stared back, wondering how much of her question was her own desire, and how much was the brandy. "What do you mean?"

She made a tutting sound. "I am not so naïve that I don't know what happens between a man and a woman when they are lovers."

"And this is what you want? To have me as your lover?" It was a dangerous question to ask in the dark, and Rian knew it. But it did not stop him from delivering it in a seductive whisper.

Catherine said nothing, but her eyes were large and luminous as she offered herself to him. His fingers continued to stroke her flesh, dipping far enough inside her bodice to make her shudder as a thrill of sexual anticipation ran through her.

"Do you want me?" she repeated, her voice trembling as her hunger began to rise. Dear God in heaven, he wanted nothing more! But... "Not like this," Rian said, firmly.

It was not the answer she had been expecting. "I don't understand."

Taking her hands in his, Rian spoke. "Well, for one thing I would prefer you to be sober. That way I will know that it is truly me you want in your bed."

"Why would you think I want anyone else?"

The question, Rian thought, was more for Catherine to answer than himself. Uncertainty made her catch her lower lip between her teeth, and he felt the heat in his groin flare.

"I'm trusting that you will," he said, speaking slowly, "but I need to be sure your decision will bring no regrets."

She turned her head away and he sensed the change in her immediately. This was more than disappointment. Rian had failed in some way, and now he could sense the wall Catherine was erecting with frightening speed. It was a wall that threatened to keep him out. And then it hit him, and he silently cursed himself for the fool he was. He had been thinking of her as any other young woman on the verge of realizing her own sexuality. But Catherine wasn't just another virgin waiting to cross the threshold into womanhood. The violence and brutality forced upon her had tainted the pleasure she ought to have derived from such an act, and he had been so consumed with his own need to possess her, he had forgotten that fact. She had not. She could not.

She had offered herself to him out of need, but the wrong kind of need. Catherine was misguidedly trying to prove something to herself. Hoping that Rian would take what she was so willing to give in the mistaken belief it would make her whole again. Help her feel no different from any other beautiful woman. But his rejection told her she was tainted and undesirable, and before he could say anything she scrambled awkwardly off his lap.

"I'm sorry." In her haste to put distance between them, she stumbled. "Too much wine has made me forward. I beg of you to forgive my vulgar behavior."

"What are you sorry for?" Rian demanded in a low voice as he jumped up from the chair and caught hold of her arm. "Kissing me or wanting to give yourself to me?" He took her nod as an affirmative to both parts of his question. "Well, I'm not," he growled more at himself than her, pulling her into his arms.

This time the kiss was not soft or gentle, but filled with the raw hunger she had awakened in him. As he plundered her mouth, Rian pulled her against him so she could feel his hardness. He was rewarded when she snaked her arms about his neck, burying her fingers in his hair, and answering him with her own fierce yearning.

When they finally broke apart Catherine pushed herself out of his arms, keeping her hands stretched out before her as if warding him off. He smiled. He would yield to her request for now, but they both knew it would take more than that to keep him from her. She struggled to catch her breath, and the scent of restless longing filled the empty space between them. Rian took a step forward but the look on her face stopped him.

"No...don't..." Her breaths were nothing but ragged gasps, and he worried she might faint from the effort it was taking to draw in air. He should have thought to loosen the laces on her gown.

"Catherine." For the first time in his life he was unsure of what to say. He raked his fingers through his hair, already missing the feel of her hands.

God, you have no idea what you are doing to me, how much I want you, how much I need you!

Her expression told him the words had not remained in his head, but had been spoken aloud. She stared at him, and any doubt she had vanished. An innate awareness stole over her, one that all women possess the moment they realize they hold the heart of a man in the palm of their hand. The dark tint of her eyes mesmerized him, and Rian wondered how long it would be before she invited him to drown in their depths.

She came toward him and put her hand against his face. The new growth of beard scraped her palm, making her smile as she stroked his jaw. Reaching up she pressed her lips against his rough cheek. "Then make it soon," she told him thickly, and with a soft whisper of her skirts, she was gone before he could stop her.

Chapter 16

Rian had already removed his boots, waistcoat, and shirt before a polite cough warned him he was not alone. Warily he turned around, not needing to be told who was reclining on his couch. In an eerie repeat of Liam and Felicity's wedding night, he once again found Isabel in his room. Sitting up she yawned, rubbing her eyes as if she had fallen asleep waiting for him to return.

"Now is not the time, Isabel, and I'm in no mood for your games." He surprised even himself with the roughness of his voice.

Undeterred by his brusqueness, she asked, "Is that any way to greet a friend who has been waiting patiently for a private moment alone with you?"

Rian stared at her. Coming to his room was a mistake, her first of the evening, but he reminded himself that her behavior up until this point had been exemplary. That she wanted something from him went without saying. The sensible part of him said he should ask her to leave without hearing another word, but the euphoria still rolling through him made him generous enough to give her the benefit of the doubt. Besides, being agreeable was surely the quickest way to hasten her from his room.

"What can I do for you, Isabel?" he asked.

"I want to ask your forgiveness for my past behavior. Assure me we can remain friends or, failing that, at least be civil to each other when we meet."

"Hasn't my behavior tonight been demonstration enough regarding my civility?" His eyes narrowed slightly as doubt marred her features. It made him sigh. "I have no wish to be your enemy, Isabel. I see no reason why we cannot remain friends."

The look of uncertainty was replaced with one of relief. "Then will you share a toast with me?" She gestured to the bottle and two glasses on a small table in front of the couch.

More alcohol was the last thing Rian wanted at this moment. He had done more than his own fair share of imbibing throughout the evening, but this was Isabel, and refusing would be churlish. "Of course," he said, watching as she filled the two glasses. "French brandy?"

She laughed softly. "I recall you having quite a fondness for it when we first met." She gently clinked the rim of her glass to his. "I trust it still remains a favorite."

"What would you like to toast to?"

Tipping her head to one side, she seemed momentarily lost in thought. "To not standing in the way of fate," she murmured quietly.

Rian looked at her quizzically. She didn't sound smug, and yet there was something in her voice that made him wary. But the arch of her brow as he hesitated made him think perhaps he was being overly suspicious. He was tired and possibly seeing things that were not there.

"To fate," he said, raising his glass and swallowing the liquid. It slid down the back of his throat smoothly but came with an unexpected bite he didn't recall any brandy, French or otherwise, having. Heat flared down his sternum before exploding in a ball of fire in his belly. He staggered back a step.

"Oh dear, Rian, I should have warned you. This has a particular potency with a kick like a horse." Setting down her glass, Isabel quickly took his arm, managing to get him to the bed just as his legs gave out.

"Isabel...what...the...hell..." It was all he could manage as the room started to spin and he spiraled down into unconsciousness.

Picking up her own glass, Isabel sipped the contents delicately before addressing the now insensible figure sprawled face down across the bed. "I suppose I should have mentioned the 'kick' was a little something I made sure was in your glass alone."

With a practiced hand she began to undress him. She savored each piece of clothing she removed as if she was unwrapping a treasured gift, though moving an inert body, especially one as large as Rian's, was no easy task for a small woman. It took more than a little effort on Isabel's part, but determination provided the strength she needed.

"Don't worry, darling, the apothecary assured me when you wake in the morning you'll have a hazy recollection at best, if you remember anything at all," Isabel gasped as she rolled Rian onto his back.

Now she stripped off her own clothes, making sure each article was deliberately placed in such a way the 'spontaneous' abandonment would be seen at once by anyone entering the room. To a particular set of eyes the effect would be devastating, although how she would lure Catherine to Rian's room was a problem Isabel hadn't quite solved. Yet. But that was something to deal with later. Right now she had another, more pressing matter to attend to.

Unpinning her hair from its elaborate coiffure, Isabel carefully ran her fingers through the thick locks until she was satisfied with the tousled appearance. She climbed on the bed, and smoothed her hands over Rian's torso, feeling the firm muscles in his chest and arms before letting her fingers drift across his taut belly. With a sigh she followed the line of dark hair that ran from his navel down to the thick nest below, and then she reached down and stroked the heavy length of him. Feeling the flesh begin to stiffen beneath her practiced hand, Isabel smiled wickedly.

The apothecary had been worth every coin he demanded, but it was unfortunate this particular potion would work one time only. Rian had never left her bed after satisfying her only once. Still, when he awoke in the morning and saw her lying beside him, she was certain she could convince him to provide a repeat performance.

* * * *

Rian knew he was dreaming.

A part of his brain simply shut down and told him to stop trying to fight what was happening because it was only a dream. It was a highly erotic and very arousing dream, but that's all it was.

All it could be.

He couldn't have protested even if he wanted to. His limbs felt heavy, unable to move. Even his eyelids refused to obey his command to open.

Why do you want to open your eyes? You're sleeping.

Without hesitation he surrendered to the physical demands of his body and let the sensations he was feeling guide him. Heat sparked in his groin, and he felt himself getting harder as the blaze fanned out across his belly and down his thighs. He moaned softly and ran his tongue over parched lips.

It's only a dream.

The cool sheet slid over his skin, caressing his legs, his buttocks, his shoulders, only—when had he taken off his clothes? He didn't remember removing them, but there was no mistake about it. He *was* naked.

Carla Susan Smith

The hand around his cock applied a firm pressure, slow and rhythmic, moving up and down the length. A tunnel of fingers progressing with a surety that came from experience, before giving way to the smooth heat of a palm.

Ah, but whose palm? Whose hand?

He tried to reach out and offer encouragement, but his arms were leaden, and lay unresponsive by his side.

It's only a dream.

The phantom hand became insistent, and more demanding. Other fingers stroked the inside of his thigh before moving to the outside of his leg. A nail raked across his hip bone, continuing to score a path along his lower belly. His muscles began to quiver and jump with each sensation as the fingers gently teased the thick curly hair. He moaned again and tried to move his legs, but like his arms, they would not obey his command. *Don't fight it,* his brain told him. *Enjoy, it's only a dream...*

He suddenly jolted as warm wetness enclosed his throbbing organ and he felt the delicate scrape of teeth over engorged flesh. A tongue licked lazily up and down the length of him, and a hand cupped his balls, squeezing gently to heighten his desire.

Whose hand? Whose mouth?

The tempo of his breathing changed, coming more rapidly with each new sensation as his seducer brought him closer to his release. Lips sucked along his shaft and the tip of a tongue toyed with the dimple in the head of his cock. And then he felt the warmth of a mouth again. The delicate scrape of teeth, not to hurt but to arouse, as the sucking pull threatened to wring him dry.

It's only a dream.

There came a certain measure of relief at the feel of full breasts with hard, swollen nipples, pillowing against him. At least he knew his tormentor was a woman. Rian groaned. The pressure of her mouth was becoming almost unbearable and he knew that if she didn't stop he would not be able to control himself.

Oh God, don't stop!

Relentlessly she moved her demanding, glorious mouth up and down his swollen flesh, nipping and teasing him with her teeth, licking and sucking as she continued to cup his balls in her hand, increasing the pressure as she squeezed.

Dear God, it's only a dream.

Rian moaned and the intensity of the sound leaving his mouth caused his fantasy lover to pause, and raise her head. His cock, suddenly shocked to be in the cooler air, bobbed in protest. He was close to his climax, so close that he bit his lower lip in an effort to prolong the sexual torture. Never before had he wanted to be gratified as much as at this moment, and never before had he wanted so badly to find a way to make the sweet agony continue. He felt the bed shift as his hips were straddled, and a wave of long hair whispered erotically across his chest as she leaned forward to pull his nipple between her teeth. Teasing and suckling, she rubbed her core up and down his shaft.

A dream, just a dream...

Rian felt the heat of her, and it only served to inflame his own need. Then, just when his agony had reached its apex, she reached down and greedily impaled herself on him. He gasped as she moved her hips, riding him with muscles that clenched and squeezed, until finally, with a cry that came from the depth of his being, he called out her name as he exploded and felt himself wash through her.

"Catherine!"

It was only a dream...wasn't it?

Lying by Rian's side, her breath coming in shallow gasps, jealousy twisted Isabel's features into a mask of ugly bitterness as she realized that the sooner Catherine was returned to the loving arms of her cousin, the better.

Chapter 17

Catherine opened her eyes and winced. Her head was pounding, and lifting it from the pillow required too much effort. Closing her eyes again, she allowed a pitiful moan to escape her lips as she tried not to move. Her head was one enormous throbbing ache and it was difficult to determine where the pain began, or where it ended. Even her eyelashes hurt. Carefully she raised one arm and covered her eyes, wondering why the pale wintry light that filled the room seemed so much brighter than usual. What had happened to make her feel this awful?

Slowly it came back to her, *blackberry brandy.*

And that wasn't all.

Everything came at her in a rush, and Catherine made herself sit up. Gritting her teeth, she waited for the sudden dizziness to pass before carefully swinging her legs over the side of the bed. Gingerly, she made her way to the table where a jug of water always sat. She was halfway through her third glass when her body told her she needed to make use of the chamber pot. As she turned she caught a glimpse of herself in the mirror. It was enough to make her stop, appalled at the sight that stared back at her.

Oh my God, what a mess!

She had made an attempt to undress, but without help it had not gone well. Her bodice was partially unlaced, leaving her gown to slip crookedly off one shoulder. She had, however, successfully managed to untie her petticoats because they now lay in an untidy heap in the middle of the floor. Her shoes had been placed carefully on the dresser along with one stocking. For some unfathomable reason she still wore the other one. Why she would have only removed one was beyond her, but after carefully raising her skirt and looking at her legs the proof was undeniable. A sudden recollection of attempting to balance unsuccessfully on one leg flashed through her mind, and she realized that taking off the one stocking had used up the sum of her coordination.

Catherine sighed. Her hair tumbled about her shoulders and down her back in an unruly mess that gave the indisputable impression she had spent at least part of the night slumbering in a hedgerow. She took a step forward in order to examine her riotous appearance more closely, but the sudden wave of nausea that threatened changed her mind. She grabbed the wash basin just in time.

A short while later, her stomach having given up the last of the brandy, Catherine sat at her dressing table. Tilly had removed the basin and replaced it with another, and also brought fresh water so Catherine was able to wash her face and hands. The cool liquid had been a refreshing tonic and now she felt almost human again. The somber color choice of her dress was an accurate reflection of her fragile state.

Catherine passed the brush through her hair, but no matter how careful she was, the throbbing in her temples did not recede. Her scalp screamed when the bristles struggled with a tangled knot. Grimly she persevered, squeezing her eyes tightly shut at each stab of pain, until her hair was smooth and she was able to tie it back with a simple ribbon. Anything more elaborate was beyond her present capabilities. Her toilette completed, Catherine examined her image in the looking glass, surprised by what she saw. "You actually look much better than you have any right to," she told her reflection sternly, amazed that the effects of the night before were not more evident. Staring at the face that looked back at her, however, she noticed a change. There was a subtle, but nevertheless noticeable, difference. Something that owed nothing to the brandy she had consumed, and yet was an indirect result of it.

Her lips were swollen, and placing her fingertips against her mouth, she felt it was bruised. It was a good hurt, and she recalled in vivid detail the feel of Rian's mouth on hers. Closing her eyes she relived every moment that had occurred in the library. She savored the feel of being held in his arms, the warmth of his breath as he nuzzled the curve where her neck and shoulder met. His tongue tasting the hollow at the base of her throat, fingers gliding over the surface of her skin as they caressed the swell of her bosom before dipping just inside her bodice to trace the valley between her breasts. And then there was the quick savage hotness of his tongue in her mouth. The thrusting demands distracting her as his hands roamed freely across her body, staking his claim before pulling her tightly to him, molding her against him so she could feel his need.

She opened her eyes and stared at her reflection. Leaning forward she once more traced the fullness of her lips, shivering now with delicious anticipation. When Rian kissed her again, he would not stop there. The next time he would keep the promise his body had given her. Startled to see her eyes glazing over, Catherine took several deep, calming breaths. The pounding in her head, momentarily forgotten, now returned. Not as fiercely as when she first awoke, but still there nonetheless. Identifying it as her first and decidedly last hangover, she made her way downstairs to find some help for her aching head.

* * * *

Felicity was alone in the dining room when Catherine entered and took a seat across the table from her.

"Ah, how are you feeling?" the mistress of Oakhaven asked, buttering a piece of toast. The wounded expression on Catherine's face was answer enough. "Oh dear, perhaps this will help." Pouring a cup of hot tea, Felicity handed it to her.

"Thank you." Catherine sipped the beverage carefully, wondering if it had always tasted so good. Tea, she decided, was definitely the nectar of the gods.

"Are you quite all right?" Felicity asked gently.

Catherine gave her a tentative smile. "Yes, everything is wonderful. Well everything except my head."

"What happened to your head?" Felicity looked puzzled.

"Don't look so innocent. You're the one who introduced me to Mrs. Hatch's brandy." Catherine refilled her cup. If she made a conscious effort, she could stir the hot brew without allowing the spoon to clink too loudly against the side of the cup.

"I poured you half a glass!" Felicity exclaimed in her own defense. "How much did you drink?"

"All of it." Catherine admitted in a small voice.

Felicity drew her brows together. "Well even so, I wouldn't have thought half a glass so very terrible."

"I suppose not," Catherine agreed, "but I drank what was in the decanter."

Felicity's eyes became very large as she stared at the slight figure seated across from her. And then, before she could stop herself, she laughed out loud. Unfortunately the sound made Catherine wince and put a hand to her forehead.

"Oh my dear, I am so sorry." Getting up from her seat, Felicity came around the table and gave her a sympathetic hug. "It never occurred to me that you would drink all of it."

At that moment Liam shuffled in to join them. It was easy to see from the pallor of his face and bloodshot eyes that he was suffering far worse than Catherine. Felicity gave him a sweet smile.

"And just how are you feeling this morning, my love?" she cooed at him.

"Bloody awful," he replied succinctly.

"You have only yourself to blame, my darling. I do not rebuke you for wanting to enjoy yourself, but no one in his right mind would try to match Farmer Youngman drink for drink." There was a definite twinkle in her eyes as she added. "His reputation is well known among the staff at Pelham."

"Then you know I had no choice, pet," Liam said as he leaned down and kissed his wife on the cheek before sinking into the chair next to her. "He challenged me, and I had to defend the Connor name."

Felicity's derisive snort told him that his explanation would garner no sympathy from his wife, but because he was her husband, and they were newly married, she decided to let him know he was not alone in his misery. The twinkle in her eyes turned positively wicked.

"Catherine sampled Mrs. Hatch's blackberry brandy, and she liked it so much, she polished off the whole decanter," she told him, gleefully.

"Good Lord, really?" Liam's estimation of Catherine rose considerably.

"Yes, but I fear it was not something to celebrate. I feel awful," she admitted from across the table.

"Ah well, that makes two of us." He gave her a weak smile. "It's good to know I'm not suffering alone."

"But I think you look far worse than I do," Catherine observed bluntly.

"True, true, but you weren't drinking with Farmer Youngman," Liam said with a groan.

A half-smile suddenly lit up Catherine's face. "No, but I know how to make us both feel better."

Excusing herself she left the room, returning a short while later carrying a tray. Placing it on the table, she removed some drinking glasses, a pitcher of cold water, an assortment of small jars, and a pestle and mortar. Felicity and Liam watched curiously as Catherine carefully measured and spooned various powders from the collection of jars, added a few dried leaves and, using the pestle and mortar, crushed them together.

"What are you making?" Felicity asked her, interest stirring as she finished her breakfast.

"Oh, it's my own recipe, but I guarantee it will cure the very worst hangover."

"Ah. So you've made it before?"

"Goodness yes, more times than I can remember." Catherine gave a small laugh and then knotted her eyebrows together at the sudden stab of pain that came with her mirth.

Liam gave a start and his face took on an odd expression as he looked at his wife, who squeezed his hand under the table, an indication he should remain quiet.

"I know you told me, but I've since forgotten," Felicity said keeping her tone nonchalant. "Who did you make this for?"

Concentrating on spooning an equal amount of powder into each glass, Catherine's answer was automatic. "My papa."

"Of course," Felicity continued, "and your papa's name is Charles, is it not?"

A wrinkle appeared on Catherine's brow as she poured a measured amount of water into both glasses. "Charles? No silly, I thought I told you. His name is William. William Davenport."

Liam thought his delicate wife might break his fingers she squeezed so hard. They both watched as Catherine now stirred both concoctions vigorously, making the mixture turn milky. She handed a glass to Liam.

"It's best if you drink it down all at once," she instructed, demonstrating with the other glass. Liam made a valiant effort, but could only manage to consume half the contents before the taste proved too much.

"Gah! This stuff is horrible!" he declared to no one in particular.

The curving smile on Catherine's face froze in place as she found herself caught in Felicity's strange stare. "I swear I haven't poisoned your husband."

"No, I know you haven't."

"Then why are you staring at me like that?"

"It's just that...what you said—"

Catherine's sudden shriek as she dropped the glass made Felicity jump. Liam closed his eyes as the high pitched sound pierced his brain.

"I remembered!" Catherine exclaimed, whirling around to look at Felicity. "Oh, how clever of you! You made me remember my father. William Davenport, and my mother's name is, no *was*, Sarah, and I am—I am Catherine Davenport." The last came out in a rush, words tumbling over themselves in their eagerness to be heard.

"Yes, I suspect you are." Tears of joy rolled down Felicity's cheeks as she kissed and hugged Liam, both hangover and feeble excuse forgiven.

Feeling her legs begin to shake, Catherine sat down on her chair. A look of stunned wonderment was on her face as she marveled at the door in her mind that had just swung open. She repeated her name over and over again, running it across her tongue as if it were a delicious confection. Her eyes shimmered and she knew she had to find Rian and share this with him. It was too important to keep to herself.

"Where are you going?" Liam asked as she stood up.

"To find your brother," Catherine announced happily, her head feeling infinitely better.

"Well, you can give him the rest of this." He held the half-full glass of Catherine's hangover cure.

"Does he need it?" Felicity asked.

"Oh yes," Liam assured her, managing to wink. "He bested Farmer Youngman."

They both watched as Catherine fairly skipped out of the room, passing Mrs. Hatch as she did so.

"Wonderful news, Mrs. Hatch," Liam said. "Catherine just remembered her name."

The housekeeper clapped her hands to her face, and beamed. "Oh, how wonderful, how simply wonderful."

"Isn't it?" Felicity said, thinking the day couldn't get any better. "I feel certain this is the breakthrough we have been waiting for."

For a moment they all paused to reflect on how such a revelation would affect not only Catherine, but all of them as well.

Felicity broke their reverie by asking, "Is there something I can do for you, Mrs. Hatch?"

"My apologies, Miss Felicity, I was wondering if you might have seen Lady Howard this morning?"

"Isabel?" She turned to look at Liam, who shook his head. "No, we haven't seen her. Why do you ask?"

Bright spots of color appeared on the housekeeper's cheeks. "It's just that her room is empty"—the spots of color deepened—"and her bed does not appear to have been slept in." Mrs. Hatch wrung her hands together. "But her coachman is having a late breakfast in the kitchen, so it would seem she has not left the house."

Both Liam and Felicity looked at each other before staring at the open door that Catherine had joyously passed through just moments ago. In his haste to get to his feet, Liam knocked over his chair.

"Dear God, no, Rian. Please don't let it be so!"

Chapter 18

When Rian first opened his eyes the vicious pain that gripped his head made him think he was having a seizure. Unlike Catherine, however, after opening his eyes and blinking a couple of times, he could not remember what he had done that would result in this torture. His mind was a complete blank. A big, empty nothing. He had been drunk before, but this was the first time he'd woken with absolutely no memory of how he had reached such a state.

He tried to rise, but his arm was strangely numb and lifeless. Turning his head, he understood why. Isabel was lying on it. Without thinking he gave a sudden start, yanking the offending limb out from under her, and yelping at the stabbing jolt that resulted as the blood began to circulate. Isabel rolled over and looked up at him.

"Good morning, my love," she purred in a voice that he had heard on too many similar occasions. It sent an unpleasant shudder through him.

Coherent speech deserted him, and Rian remained slack-jawed as he tried desperately to recall the events of the night before. Why was Isabel in his bed? Fully anticipating the agony it would produce, Rian shook his head. It was as if he hoped the pain would help focus his thoughts. It did not.

"Isabel," he croaked hoarsely, "what are you doing here? What happened?"

"I would have thought that was obvious." She stretched, arching her back and letting the sheet fall to her waist.

Rian stared in panicked confusion. His brain insisted there was something wrong, something very wrong about what he was seeing, and his mood shifted accordingly. Bewilderment and frustration became tinged with anger.

Sensing his mood shift, Isabel slipped into the role she had rehearsed. An expert card player, she prided herself on reading people and knew that Rian would immediately be on his guard if she became emotional in any way. Weeping hysterically or spluttering indignant protests was not the way to get him to respond favorably to her. No, the best approach to ensure she got what she wanted was to remain calm, and appear to be just as baffled by his confused state as he was. No matter how much it chafed her to do so.

"Rian, whatever is the matter?" Pulling the sheet back around her, she allowed a frown of worry to crease her brow.

"I seem to be having some difficulty remembering exactly what happened last night...between us."

"That's not a very complimentary thing to say to a woman," she chided gently before changing her tone, and becoming concerned. "Oh my goodness. You really don't remember, do you?" He shook his head and stared at her, and she saw the confusion growing in his eyes. "Why don't you tell me exactly what you do remember."

Rian concentrated hard as memories began to resurface. The celebration... Catherine in a beautiful blue-green dress...dancing with the Habersham twins...Isabel's arrival...downing tankards with Farmer Youngman and Liam...Catherine in the library...in his arms...kissing him...wanting him...

A sudden heat flared through him and he found no difficulty in bringing to mind what had taken place in the library. He could plainly feel Catherine's mouth moving beneath his. Taste the lingering flavor of blackberry brandy on her lips. Feel her soft and pliant body responding eagerly to his touch. Not wanting Isabel to notice his sudden aroused state, Rian shifted and casually moved the sheet across his lap. God, why couldn't he have woken up to find Catherine in his bed? He would be neither confused nor disappointed.

He forced himself to concentrate. It was beginning to come back to him. Now he recalled Isabel being in his room, and sharing a toast with her, but a toast to what? And that was all. Everything else was a dark void he could not penetrate. Turning his head, Rian told Isabel all he could remember except his encounter with Catherine in the library. He was not sharing that with anyone, least of all Isabel.

"Please believe me when I say I do not doubt your recollection," she said after listening attentively, "but I must confess you became quite insistent about my not leaving." She looked up at him coyly from beneath her lashes.

"I'm sorry, Isabel, I truly do not remember."

"This has never happened to me before." Cleverly she let him hear the hurt in her voice as she pulled the sheet a little tighter around her. "I'm sure I would find it all quite amusing if it were happening to someone else."

There was a detached memory that darted just out of Rian's reach, something he couldn't quite put his finger on, but something he was sure was the key.

It was only a dream...wasn't it?

Swinging his legs over the side of the bed, he put his head in his hands and groaned. A door in his mind swung open and a familiar lingering sensation told him exactly what had taken place. It was as effective as having a pail of cold water poured over him.

What he had thought was nothing more than erotic fantasy had, in fact, been very real. But reality or fantasy, something about the coupling didn't feel right. There was a taint to the memory that made it seem unnatural somehow. An intense feeling of helplessness that made Rian question his own willingness as a participant. Was such a thing possible? Could a man be a reluctant contributor to such an act? His erection, aroused by memories of Catherine, now seemed to be mocking him, proclaiming it was quite capable of acting independently.

He shook his head, welcoming the vicious pain behind his eyes. How could it be that his body was telling him he had physically made love to Isabel when his mind could not consciously remember doing so? And why was it that his mouth tasted not of Isabel, but was filled with the lingering flavor of Catherine?

"Some cold water might help," Isabel suggested solicitously.

Rian nodded once and, pulling on his robe, he disappeared into the small adjoining room where he normally performed his ablutions, grateful for the privacy it offered.

Isabel watched as the door closed behind him, all signs of concern replaced by the anger puckering her features. Rian had not been as deft with the sheet as he had hoped. Noticing his semi-erect state, feminine intuition told her she was not the reason for it. Damn him! This was not going to be as simple as she had first thought. She would need to be very careful and make sure Rian found no reason to distrust her. It would seem that in order to achieve that end, she needed to become the model of agreeability.

Damn him and that stupid milkmaid!

Whatever spell the girl wove was a powerful aphrodisiac indeed. Phillip Davenport had been almost apoplectic because she had slipped from his grasp, and now Rian, the man Isabel was sure she would wed, had become dangerously infatuated with her. She had to discredit the milkmaid, but how?

Suddenly, she sat bolt upright in the bed. She was going about this all wrong. Instead of discrediting Catherine in Rian's eyes, she needed to change tactics and make sure the milkmaid no longer wanted *him*. If the hold she had on Rian was as strong as Isabel was beginning to suspect, then it would stand to reason that her rejection would be crushing. Rian would be forced to seek solace elsewhere. And where better than in the arms of someone he already felt comfortable with? Someone who would lend a sympathetic ear as well as a welcoming pillow? If Isabel could remain trustworthy to him, then surely Rian would accept her support and understanding to ease him through his dejection.

The only question now was how to convince Catherine that Rian was not the man for her. Isabel smiled. She was the answer, right here, in his bed. No woman liked to think she had been duped, and recalling the look on Catherine's face last night, Isabel could read the girl like an open book. All that was needed was for poor, naïve Catherine to discover the man of her dreams had spent the night in the arms of another woman.

She sank back amongst the pillows, tapping her teeth with a well-manicured nail as she wrestled with the best way to deliver such news with maximum impact. Of course it would have to be revealed in such a way that Rian would never suspect its origin. Ordinarily a servant coming into the room and seeing her in Rian's bed would be enough to set the wheels of the gossip mill turning, but she could not guarantee that such an interaction would occur. From various conversations she had overheard last night, all the servants at Oakhaven were already ridiculously fond of Catherine. It was possible, in order to protect her, they might not say anything at all. Practically unheard of, but still a possibility.

There had to be a way. Somehow she needed to let her rival know that Rian had not spent the night alone. In the same house, under the same roof that protected Catherine as she no doubt dreamed about her lover, Isabel had shared his bed. Scenario after scenario played through her mind and each one she rejected as either being impossible, implausible or just too ridiculous for words. She gave a start when Rian's voice broke through her musings.

"You seem lost in thought, Isabel. What occupies your mind?"

Consumed with her own thoughts, she hadn't heard the soft pad of his feet on the floor. She looked up to see him standing naked in the middle of the room, wiping himself down with a towel as droplets of water pooled onto the carpet.

"I'm worried about you, Rian," she lied smoothly. "To have no memory of an event is not a normal happenstance. Perhaps you consumed more alcohol than you realized. After all, you did say you and Liam were matching that rather large farmer drink for drink." Even she was amazed at how convincingly sincere she sounded.

Rian stared at her and wondered if he was being a little too judgmental. He had been fully prepared to deal with a pouting, sulky Isabel whose feelings were hurt by what he had said. Instead he found a woman who seemed to be genuinely worried over his predicament. It was a side of her he had not seen before. He was about to comment on this change when a light knock at the door interrupted him. Securing the towel around his waist he turned in time to see the bedroom door swing open, and miss the malicious smile gleefully adorning Isabel's face.

* * * *

Standing outside the bedroom door, Catherine had a sudden twinge of doubt. A moment of uncertainty that made her question her decision. She raised her hand to knock and then dropped it back to her side, reconsidering the idea of sharing her news with Rian. Young ladies did not invite themselves into a man's bedroom for any reason. Well, she was young and she was fairly certain she was a lady, but then again the invitation factor had already been breached. Rian had not only invited himself into her room; he had already lain on her bed. Admittedly he had been above the covers and she beneath them, but she had done nothing to make him leave. In truth she hadn't wanted to.

And then there was last night.

For a moment she paused as his voice filled her head, whispering her name over again, the way he had in the library. She remembered the look on his face as he told her he wanted her, how much he needed her. With a shake of her head, Catherine told herself that whatever the rules of good behavior demanded, they didn't apply under these circumstances. She and Rian had already shared so much, she doubted going to his room was something he would be shocked by. The news she had to impart was so wonderful, he would not even protest at her waking him. If anything, he would probably be disappointed if he found out she'd made him wait. Summoning up her courage she knocked lightly and then, before her nerve failed her, she opened the door and walked in.

The sight of Rian standing in the middle of the room with only a towel wrapped about his waist, wet hair clinging to his neck and shoulders, sent an unexpected shiver of delight down her spine. She could feel the color rise as she visualized how he would look without the towel. Staring hungrily at his broad, well-muscled chest glistening with droplets of water, Catherine felt her pulse begin to quicken and she found it hard to breathe. Broken rules or not, she was being very bold, and she forced herself to raise her eyes and look at his face, only to be taken aback by his expression.

Her first thought was embarrassment. Rian was giving every indication of being flustered that she had caught him almost naked, but the man Catherine knew would not be self-conscious about his state of undress. Not even being completely naked would cause the acute discomfort that now marked his features. Somehow she had unknowingly made a huge mistake by entering his room. She just didn't know why.

"Liam thought this might help your head," she murmured apologetically, gratefully using her hangover tonic as the reason for her intrusion.

"Thank you."

He stepped forward and took the glass from her hand, placing it on a table while keeping a tight hold on his covering with the other. To Catherine's ears his voice seemed strained. Was this the same man who had, to all intents and purposes, made love to her last night? Something had changed. There was a feeling of *wrongness* between them, and it made her think Rian was remorseful about his actions in the library. Anxiety flooded her, loosening her tongue and making her babble.

"The drink is my own cure for a hangover. It's something I've made many times in the past, too many if the truth be told, only I just remem—" She broke off as her glance dropped to the clothing strewn about the floor.

The untidy heap of black and white silk took her by surprise. The fabric and color scheme was familiar, but her mind was having difficulty processing where she had seen it. With a fixed stare, her eyes followed the natural progression from dress to petticoats, corset to stockings, and finally to the delicate lacy shift. Obviously there had been no difficulties with undressing in this room, and the clothing screamed at her to acknowledge what it meant. She opened her eyes wide in shock and looked at Rian's face, imploring him to vehemently deny what her mind was telling her. This had to be a jest, in poor taste, yes, but a jest none the less. But as she waited for the denial he could not provide, her heart stuttered and twisted cruelly in her breast.

A movement at the edge of her peripheral vision made Catherine turn her head and she found herself looking at the large four poster bed. Her eyes widened even further, this time in stunned disbelief as she saw Isabel sitting up with only a sheet wrapped around her. A blind man would have been able to see she was completely naked beneath it. Isabel gave her a smile that seemed to be awkward discomfort, but Catherine easily read the cruel taunt of triumph hiding behind the façade.

The breath left her body as she looked away from Isabel and back to Rian, who still said nothing. Whether remaining mute was a conscious choice Catherine couldn't say, but his expression spoke volumes. For the second time in recent memory she felt her world shift sideways. Only this time she wasn't as certain it would resume its appointed path.

An emotional vortex was gaining momentum inside her. Anger, betrayal and confusion all jumbled together. Everything rushed to the surface and part of her wanted to reach out and physically strike Rian. How could he do this to her? Had last night meant nothing? His words, his kisses, the way his hands had made her body yearn for him. All the things that she'd never felt before, but wanted desperately to feel again. Rian had awakened appetites that she had never known, and all his unspoken promises were now just meaningless words.

Lies, all lies!

"Catherine—" Rian began, his voice breaking on her name.

She blinked at him, her face taking on a tranquil almost somnolent quality, and he watched as she closed herself off to him. The woman who stood before him had been transformed, but it had happened so quickly he could not have prevented it even if it had been in his power to do so. This Catherine who now looked at him was a stranger. She was not the same person he had spoken to in the chapel or kissed in the snow and most definitely not the woman he had taken in his arms last night. As the tension in the room began to build, Isabel decided to remind them of the reason for their strained behavior by coughing politely.

"Your guest," Catherine said, shooting Isabel a glacial look before piercing Rian with the same degree of warmth, "would probably like some refreshment." She spoke with exaggerated politeness. "I'll see that a tray is sent up."

As she turned to go, Rian caught her arm. "Catherine—"

She stopped him without saying a word. The temporary mask of ice shifted just enough to let him see the pain and abject misery in her eyes that threatened to spill over and drown her. It was almost too much for him to bear. She had gone beyond being distressed. Catherine was now in a place where her trust of him had shattered so completely, Rian didn't know if the fragile links could ever be repaired.

"Please let go of me." She spoke so softly he almost didn't hear her. He didn't want to let go of her, terrified that if he did the steel cord binding them, the one he could now feel twisting and tightening behind his rib cage, would snap and she would be lost to him irrevocably. "*Please?*" Her whisper was tremulous, and reluctantly he did as she asked. His chest constricted, making him lightheaded as he became trapped inside her gaze. Her eyes were the coldest he had ever seen. "Nothing happened between us last night, or at any other time. Do you understand? Nothing."

The words fell from her lips with quiet finality before she walked away from him, closing the door behind her.

Chapter 19

Isabel held her breath, waiting for Rian to make the first move. Only a moment or two had passed but they moved with agonizing slowness. Keeping her face a carefully controlled picture of concern, she couldn't believe her good fortune. Catherine's unexpected appearance had been a gift, a treasure far beyond Isabel's wildest expectations. Finally Rian stopped staring down at the floor and lifted his head to look at her.

"Rian, I am so sorry," she said softly, her voice carrying just the right degree of pathos. "I had no idea Catherine would come into your room uninvited—"

Her words were rudely cut off as the bedroom door opened once more. This time a little more forcefully as a highly agitated Liam burst into the room. He dismissed her with a single glance, but his opinion made no difference to Isabel. That he had seen her was enough.

"Catherine was here?" Liam barked at his brother. Rian jerked his head in the affirmative. "Where is she now?"

"I don't know," Rian said, his entire being now suffused with shame.

"You damnable fool!" Liam snapped before turning on his heel and slamming the door behind him as he left.

After carefully wrapping the sheet around her, Isabel came to him. "Rian, I am so sorry, I had no idea. After last night…" Her voice trailed off.

"Don't blame yourself, Isabel. That burden is mine to bear, and mine alone." His voice matched his expression, and both were grim. Begging her pardon, he retreated to the relative safety of the washroom, and the door click closed behind him.

Isabel hugged herself triumphantly, allowing a jubilant smile to lift her lips. She couldn't have planned this any better. The events of the morning were totally unexpected, but so completely satisfying, she could only congratulate herself on her good fortune. Watching both Catherine and Rian intently during the encounter, she'd quickly realized the depth of feeling between them was stronger than she had anticipated. It was a lucky thing for her such feelings had not yet been acted on, or her plan to resume her role as Rian's lover would in all probability fail. Had Catherine already given herself to him, Isabel suspected no temptation she could offer would induce Rian to return to her bed.

But Catherine was young and, luckily for Isabel, inexperienced in the ways of men. She shared her feelings with the world, wearing her emotions on her sleeve with an almost childlike innocence. Isabel had known from the first time they'd met in the townhouse that Catherine was desperately in love with Rian, even if, at that time, she herself was not aware of it. The cut she now felt at finding another woman in his bed had quickly turned into a gaping, bleeding wound. His betrayal was unforgivable.

As for Rian, he was a matter she could deal with. All she had to do was be patient and wait until this temporary madness passed. It did not matter that his regard for her had never been as strong as what he felt for Catherine. What was important was the role she would play now. Isabel would be the one to restore order to his life and give him a sense of purpose. If the physical chemistry between them was strong enough, and she knew it was, then an emotional bonding would surely follow. All in all, it was an extremely gratifying situation to be in.

The faint sound of splashing water coming from behind the closed door refocused her attention, and Isabel knew the next few moments were crucial. It would determine whether or not her heart's desire would be fulfilled.

Coming back into the bedroom, Rian found Isabel struggling with the back of her gown. He went to help her. She thanked him with a small smile saying, "Dressing a woman is not a skill most men possess. Though they seem to have no trouble in removing a woman's clothes, the opposite action is not something they are adept at."

"Most men are not adept at dressing themselves. It is fortunate I can boast some practice with both." His efficiency tying her laces supported his claim.

Sitting down at the dresser, Isabel attempted to repair her hair but finally gave up. Instead she finger-combed the raven locks, securing the heavy tresses at the nape of her neck with the length of ribbon Rian normally used to tie back his own. He made no comment about her thievery, concentrating on dressing himself. Surreptitiously Isabel watched him in the mirror, waiting for the exact right moment to speak.

"Rian—"

"Isabel—"

"No, please allow me," she begged. "There is something I need to say before my courage fails." He raised a brow, acquiescing to her plea as she turned on her seat to face him. "Last night was a mistake, as was the night I slipped into your house after your brother's wedding. I know I have already told you this, but it is important that you hear it again. I make no secret that my hope was to rekindle a change in your affection toward me, but now I see that you are resolute. I accept that nothing I can do will change your feelings. Another has claimed your affection, but it isn't just my pride that is wounded. I do care a great deal about you."

She turned her head to the side, and Rian thought he heard her gulp down a sob before she was able to look at him once more. Her lower lip was trembling, and for the second time in less than an hour, Rian was looking at a woman on the verge of tears. This time the eyes were a brilliant emerald green instead of cornflower blue. He sighed unhappily as Isabel continued.

"It's not easy for me to let you go, and though I have lost you as a lover, I don't want to also lose your friendship. Lord knows you are one of the few men who has always treated me as an equal, and asked nothing of me. I don't have many friends of either sex that I trust. But I count you among the few."

She was begging his forgiveness, and pleading for his understanding. Rian came over and gently pulled her to her feet before taking her in his arms. Still reeling from the impact of Catherine's words, he did not have the strength, or will, to fight with another woman, no matter who it was or which of them was at fault.

"I wish it could have been different between us," he said softly before letting her go. Seeing her head jerk, he lifted her chin, noting the tears spilling down her cheeks. Pretending to make an effort to regain her composure, Isabel was disappointed that Rian was proving to be no different from the rest of his sex. Ridiculously easy to manipulate. Thankfully he had other attributes that she had not yet tired of. Giving an audible sigh, she dabbed at her eyes with a lace handkerchief. "I think it would be best if I left now," she whispered.

"Can I help in any way?" Rian offered.

"No, thank you. I must do this by myself."

"Of course."

She walked to the door. Everything was all falling into place perfectly. It really wasn't fair. She held a winning hand while Rian didn't even know the cards he had been dealt. "Please give my apologies to Liam and

Felicity," she said, her voice reflecting the proper amount of sincerity and regret. "It really was a lovely celebration."

She looked away, unsure how much longer she could disguise her true emotions, and then, as she opened the door, Isabel played her trump card.

"Rian...?"

"Yes?"

This was the hardest part. Conveying the right amount of compassion so he would believe her. "I am confident that Miss Davenport will forgive you. She's young. All she needs is time."

* * * *

Rian was sitting on the chaise in his mother's—now Catherine's—room with his head in his hands, miserable and wretched when Liam found him. Pulling up a chair, he sat and waited until his brother looked up.

"Have you seen her?" Rian asked, his voice lifeless.

Liam shook his head. "I do not think she can presently tolerate any member of our sex, but I do know where she is, and you can take comfort knowing Felicity is with her."

A spark ignited. "I must go to her. I need to explain—" He half rose out of his seat, but Liam's restraining hand held him back.

"Did you not hear me, man? What possible explanation can you give that would justify the presence of Isabel in your bed, and you half naked?" The misery on Liam's face said he suffered for his brother. "Where are the words that will explain that?"

"Damn it, I don't know!" Rian brought a fist crashing down on the small painted table before him, but the delicate spindle legs were not made for such abuse and the wood splintered.

"My wife was fond of that piece," Liam sighed. "Tell me what happened, brother. How did this come about?"

Rian looked at his sibling. It was a look quite unlike anything Liam had seen before, and he raised a quizzical eyebrow.

"I don't think I know what happened," Rian started. "Well, of course I *know* what happened, but it feels like it happened to someone else."

"You aren't making any sense," Liam rebuked gently.

"Believe me, no one knows better than I how ridiculous I sound, but Liam, I swear I don't remember taking Isabel to my bed." Rian ran his fingers through his thick hair, his frustration evident.

Narrowing his eyes, his brother studied him. He had never seen Rian like this. He was shaken, and badly. The torment he was putting himself through was of monumental proportions and it carried with it something Liam had never thought possible. His brother, always so confident and self-assured, was now plagued by uncertainty and doubt.

"Tell me precisely the last thing you do remember, and leave nothing out. Even the smallest detail might prove significant."

Rian grimaced. "Do you think I am on the first step to the madhouse?"

"No, far from it." Liam's response was confident and reassuring. "But I do believe that something seems quite odd, and if Isabel is involved in any way, then it bears examining."

"Where do you want me to begin?"

"Tell me everything that happened after we said good night."

And so Rian relayed all that he could remember from the night before. He omitted nothing, giving a self-conscious smile as he described Catherine's somewhat inebriated state and the liberties he'd allowed himself to take with her because of it. While his brother did not censure him for his behavior, the look in his eye said neither did he approve of it. However, Liam's mood noticeably darkened as he listened to Rian's account of finding Isabel in his room, and what he could recall taking place between them.

Liam suddenly stood up, pushed back the chair, and headed for the door. "You say you shared a toast?"

Rian nodded, a vertical line forming between his brows as he followed his brother out of Catherine's room. "I can't for the life of me tell you what we were drinking to, but I do know whatever it was had one hell of a kick!"

"Possibly too much kick for brandy alone?" Liam suggested.

Reaching Rian's room, Liam began looking around, searching for something. He peered behind the dresser and under the bed, even going so far as to shake out the heavy bed curtains. Hearing his brother curse, Rian gave him a questioning look.

"She must have taken it with her," Liam told him.

"Taken what?"

"I was hoping to find either the bottle or the glasses, but I think Isabel must have taken them with her. Now why do you suppose she would do that?"

"I have no idea," Rian replied as Liam's suspicions began to sink in. "Do you really think she would do such a thing?" His brother simply shook his head in disgust. "But, in God's name, for what reason?" A strange feeling of revulsion crept over him.

It's only a dream.

Unaware of his sibling's discomfort, Liam gave him a glum look. "I've told you before, Rian, Isabel doesn't like to lose. Ever."

"But we can't know for certain that she is guilty of anything wrong."

"No," Liam agreed, "we can't. But when was the last time you drank *anything* that knocked you out so completely?"

"I don't recall it ever happening before," Rian admitted, "but without the bottle, it's all just supposition."

"True, but it does raise a lot of questions, doesn't it? I mean don't you find it just a little odd that Isabel would show up so unexpectedly last night?"

Rian sighed and scrubbed a hand wearily across his face. His legs felt stiff from sitting too long and he paced. Stopping by the window, his eyes fixed on some distant point. "She's not going to let me see her, is she?"

Knowing he was no longer talking about Isabel, Liam shook his head. "I don't think so, not just yet. You must understand, Rian, from what you told me about your flirtation in the library, Catherine feels confused and betrayed."

"And you don't blame her," Rian finished for him.

"She needs time, that's all. A little time and she will forgive you. I am sure of it."

"Really?" He gave a snort of derision. "I wish I had your confidence. What in God's name possessed her to come into my room in the first place? What was so important it could not wait?"

"You don't know then? Catherine didn't tell you?"

Rian shook his head. "No, I think she was trying to, but then she saw Isabel and, well—" He spread his hands in a gesture of futility.

"Felicity managed to trick Catherine into remembering her family name."

"Are you serious?" Rian grabbed his brother's shoulders in a sudden rush of excitement. "How?"

Liam explained the earlier incident in the dining room. "I have no idea what prompted Felicity to ask the question. It was all very natural and unforced, so perhaps that is why Catherine was able to remember."

"And what is her name?"

Liam looked slightly abashed. The most important point of the tale and he was forgetting to reveal it. "My apologies, it's Davenport. Her name is Catherine Davenport."

The smile on his face froze as he watched Rian stagger back. "What is it? Is there something wrong?"

"Oh yes, Liam, something is very wrong," he said, grabbing his brother firmly by the arm. "If Catherine only just remembered her name a few hours ago, how is that Isabel already knew it?"

Chapter 20

The entire day passed with no sign of Catherine. It was as if she had disappeared off the face of the earth, or at least from Oakhaven. Rian spent most of his time roaming aimlessly about the house and grounds, hoping she might have decided to leave whatever sanctuary she had found, and their paths would cross. If so he would seize the opportunity to speak with her. Hold her to him if that's what it took to make her listen.

His first stop was the stables. What better way for Catherine to clear her head than to go for a ride? Once she had satisfied him she was well enough to mount a horse, Catherine had proved she was not only 'orsey,' but quite fearless in the saddle. Rian had been amazed by her skill, and her talent for dealing with even the most high-strung animal earned his admiration. That was a gift that could not be taught.

But with all the horses accounted for, Rian's presence only made the stable hands nervous and their charges restless. Never before had almost every horse needed to be exercised at the same time. Churlishly he left the stables, making his way to the edge of the woods where Catherine and he had seen the deer. Nothing stirred amongst the trees, so he turned back and made his way to the chapel. He paused at the door, his head resting against the seasoned wood and his fingers on the iron ring handle. He prayed she would be inside, but the small building was empty. Dejectedly Rian sank into a pew. He wanted to tell her he was sorry, to try to explain what had happened with Isabel, but his tongue tripped over his answers to her imagined accusations, and the conversation remained in his head.

It was close to midnight when Liam found him sitting at the desk in the study, an almost empty bottle of brandy before him. This was not Mrs. Hatch's homemade brew, but a more potent version imported from across the channel. It seemed a little bizarre knowing Isabel had used a similar brew to possibly drug him.

Startled by his haggard appearance, Liam asked, "Rian, man, what are you doing? Have you eaten anything?"

"Let me be," Rian growled.

Ignoring him, Liam pulled up a chair on the opposite side of the desk. "Is it helping?" he asked, pointing to the nearly empty bottle.

"It blunts the edges," Rian told him.

"Good, then pour me a glass."

Rian raised a brow and stared at his brother for a moment before getting another glass and pouring him a generous measure. He pushed the drink across the desktop toward him, asking, "What's biting you?"

"Probably the same thing that's sunk its teeth in your throat," Liam replied, taking a healthy swallow.

"Catherine?"

Liam nodded. "Yes, though in a far less direct manner." He took another mouthful, and swirled his glass, watching the candlelight reflect off the liquid. "My wife has spent most of the day consoling her."

"And you are feeling slighted?" Rian asked.

"Mmmm, a little I'll admit." Liam drained his drink and pushed the glass back to Rian, gesturing for a refill. "I feel like I am being punished for—"

"—my mistake," Rian interjected, frowning. "I would never have thought Felicity was that judgmental." He sounded disappointed.

"I was going to say for being male, and a Connor."

"Ah well, in that case I think we will need another bottle." Rian poured more brandy. "This won't be enough."

"For what?"

"To get drunk."

"I have no intention of getting drunk," Liam told him gravely. "I did that last night."

Rian pointed a finger at the glass in his brother's hand. "Then what are you doing?"

"Preventing you from getting drunk."

"Do you think it will work?"

Liam shrugged. "You tell me."

Rian's laugh was bitter and hollow sounding. "I know it won't."

"Ah, well."

Liam gulped down the brandy. The smooth taste coated his tongue and trailed a fiery path down his throat, making him splutter a little. Rian smiled to himself. His brother really wasn't that much of a drinker. Not enough practice, he supposed.

"What are you really doing, Liam?" he asked.

"I want to help you, if you're not too stubborn to accept my offer."

"I don't think there's anything you can say that would help me."

"I could tell you where Catherine has been all day."

Interest made the tawny flecks in Rian's eyes burn a little brighter. "Where?" he demanded, leaning forward.

"In Mrs. Hatch's rooms." Across the desk, Liam smiled slyly. "Didn't think to look there, did you?"

Rian shook his head. Because he had seen the housekeeper earlier, and she had not said anything, he had assumed, wrongly it now seemed, that Catherine was not with her. He should have asked. Mrs. Hatch would have told him the truth, but that would have also meant running the risk of seeing how much he had disappointed her. Burdening himself with Liam's censure was hard enough; Rian could not carry the weight of her condemnation also. "No, I did not," he admitted. "Was it your first thought?"

"Good God, no!"

Both of them smiled wryly at the idea of any man crossing the threshold of the housekeeper's room with or without an invitation.

"Who told you?" Rian asked.

"I managed to catch a few moments alone with Felicity."

"Catherine couldn't be in better hands."

"Unless she was in yours," Liam contradicted softly. "She needs your help."

Leaning his head against the back of the chair, Rian closed his eyes. He was still for so long Liam thought he might have drifted off to sleep. Finally he spoke. "What kind of help?"

"Looking into Catherine's past. Finding out what you can about her, where she's from, who her people are. It will be easier now that we have a name."

Rian opened his eyes. Obviously his younger brother had been occupied with this thought for most of the day. "Where do you propose I begin?"

Resting both arms on the desk's smooth surface, Liam asked, "Have you ever listened to Catherine talk when she gets excited?" The question was enough to make Rian raise a brow. When had his little brother witnessed Catherine in a state of excitement, and what had he done to put her there? Ignoring the unasked question on his brother's face, Liam continued. "Engage her in a topic of conversation that truly holds her interest, and you will hear the pattern of her speech change."

"I will?"

"Look, it's obvious Catherine had a governess or another influence that taught her how to behave as befits a proper young lady, but when she gets enthusiastic about something she sometimes slips up."

"Slips up how?"

"Her pronunciation is less precise," Liam said, warming to his subject. "And she uses phrases that have an almost lyrical quality to them."

"Really?" Rian asked, intrigued by his brother's keen observation, along with his even keener ear.

"Yes, really," Liam muttered irritably. "Honestly, Rian, all you have to do is listen to her."

"Well, there's listening and *listening*."

He was suddenly taken back to the library. Catherine had been drunk, and he had assumed the pleasing lilt he could hear in her voice was a result of the alcohol, but if he had been paying attention he would have realized that she was speaking to him with her true voice. The same voice that had murmured his name as she slept. He pushed the image out of his mind and forced himself to concentrate on what Liam was saying.

"...so I think that might be a good place to start."

"What might be?"

The younger Connor swore under his breath. "God's truth, man! Have you not been listening?"

"Of course, wasn't that the point you were making? Listening? Now, where might be a good place to start?" Rian asked again.

Slightly mollified, the younger Connor huffed. "I was thinking that Catherine might come from up north, and given her occasional lapse, perhaps one of the border counties."

"You don't think it possible she could have picked up the accent from someone she met?"

"Possible," Liam agreed reluctantly, "but I don't think so."

Rian put an elbow on the desk and cupped his chin in his hand as he gave his brother a thoughtful look. "Did you work this all out by yourself?"

Liam blushed. "Um, actually no. My wife deserves the credit. I'm simply the messenger."

"Just as well," Rian said, still finding the wherewithal to tease his sibling, "or else you might find yourself needing to explain how it is you know Catherine's speech changes when she gets excited."

Liam's blush expanded to reach the roots of his hair.

"Now, how would I begin?" Rian said, serious once more.

Liam pulled a piece of paper from an inside pocket and pushed it across the desk toward him. "Here's the name and address of a man I know who might be able to help."

Rian looked at the information. "He's in the city."

Liam nodded. "Obviously it will be much easier to conduct the search for information from there."

"Then I'd best leave first thing."

Liam was relieved. Armed with a purpose, his brother was once again the man he knew, shaking off the miserable wretch who had been masquerading in his place since early that morning. "Do you want to speak with Catherine before you leave?"

"More than I want to draw my next breath," Rian said, "but I doubt she feels the same."

"I could ask Felicity to intercede on your behalf...." Liam trailed off.

"Thank you, but no." Rian's voice was firm. "When Catherine talks with me again, it will not be because she feels obligated to do so."

Liam tipped his head, thankful that his brother had said *when* and not if. It was a step in the right direction. "What about Isabel? If you are returning to the city, do you intend to call on her?" It was a question that had to be asked.

"Right now, I'm not sure."

"Be careful, brother. No matter what she says, Isabel is at best... unpredictable."

Rian's expression told Liam that he would heed the warning in his words. He would not do anything impulsive or foolish. "It would be a one-sided conversation, and not a long one at that," he said grimly.

"Oh, why is that?" Liam suddenly felt his mouth go dry.

"I am confident Isabel and Catherine have never met, other than that one time at the townhouse."

"And yet she knew her full name, which can only mean—"

"—that someone must have told her," Rian finished for him. "Someone else is looking for Catherine, and I think it's time I found out just who that person is."

Rian's expression required no explanation, and it sent an icy chill racing down his brother's back. That Isabel had ulterior motives went without question, but just how far she would go to get her own way had yet to be determined.

* * * *

Catherine had not returned to her own room. Instead she spent the night in the housekeeper's cozy suite, dozing fitfully on Mrs. Hatch's bed. It would have been little comfort to her to know that Rian had also found sleep elusive. Hearing a familiar sound, she sat up, waiting to see if it was repeated. She was not disappointed, and throwing off the blanket, Catherine hurried to the window. It was a testament to the favor the housekeeper found in the eyes of the family that she had been allowed to select her own suite of rooms. Preferring the front of the house, Mrs. Hatch was afforded a clear view of the long driveway leading to and from Oakhaven, as well as any activity at the front of the house. As she looked out, Catherine's heart sank and a ragged ache squeezed her tightly as despair washed through her.

It was the sound of horses snorting and moving impatiently in their traces that had brought her to the window, as if they wanted her to know someone was getting ready to depart. The carriage in the driveway below was surrounded by a flurry of activity, and Catherine did not need to be told who was leaving so early. Still, her heart jumped into her throat as she watched Rian walk out of the house. All he needed to do was turn and tilt his head and he would see her.

"Look up here," she whispered, her hand pressed against the frigid pane of glass.

"Please, look up and see me."

But Rian did not raise his head, disappearing instead into the carriage. Catherine watched as it pulled away from the house and continued down the driveway. She did not turn away until the sound of movement behind her said she was not alone. Mrs. Hatch stood in the open doorway.

"He has gone?" Catherine asked, as if a denial from the housekeeper would make the carriage's progress an event in her imagination.

"Aye lass, that he has."

"Where to?"

"I believe Master Rian said he had business to attend to in the city. He'll be back in a few days I'm sure."

"Oh, I see." Her voice proclaimed she didn't see at all. Turning back to the window, Catherine rested her forehead against the cool glass.

The motherly figure stood behind her, and put an arm about her shoulders, giving her much needed comfort. "It'll be alright Miss Catherine," Mrs. Hatch soothed. "Master Rian will return, and then you can sort through this difficulty between you."

Catherine stiffened inside the housekeeper's embrace. "What makes you think any difficulty exists between us?"

Mrs. Hatch turned Catherine gently until she was facing her. "There must be, lass, else why would you be crying so hard at his leaving?"

Chapter 21

Rian had been in the city for almost two weeks before he decided he could control his temper well enough to pay Isabel a visit. He was not foolish enough to believe she didn't already know exactly when he had left Oakhaven, or how long he had been in residence at the townhouse. That she had made no effort to communicate with him was telling. It seemed she was keeping her own counsel. A wise move on her part, but perhaps she was merely waiting for him to decide how he wanted to proceed. Rian's own silence was deliberate. The last encounter between them was still profoundly disturbing to him. Besides, he'd been busy.

Stuart Collins was the name Liam had given him and, after their initial meeting, he had felt guardedly optimistic. Rian had taken an instant liking to the young man, and felt that he would have done so even without his brother's endorsement. Stuart's dogged determination and quiet intelligence inspired confidence. If anyone could discover the truth about Catherine, then it would be this serious-minded young man. After giving Stuart what little information he had regarding Catherine, all Rian could do now was wait.

Patience was not a trait that came easily to Rian, so he occupied his time with other matters. Plans for the future.

Despite Liam and Felicity's protests to the contrary, Rian knew he could not continue to intrude on their lives indefinitely. It was time he used his talents and wealth in the pursuit of a useful and satisfying endeavor. His future beckoned and though recent events might say otherwise, he was not ready to abandon the hope that it would include Catherine. And so he turned to Liam's man of business to see what advice he could offer.

Matthew Turner was a mournful looking man, and Rian's first impression was that he would be more at ease in a pulpit delivering the Sunday sermon than deciding whether the fields of industry or agriculture would be a better investment. Thankfully the woeful looking exterior hid a razor-sharp mind. One that had guided Liam through many important financial transactions, thereby increasing the Connor fortune substantially. Discussing investments for Rian's financial security had become a challenge that both men took delight in pursuing, with much good-natured wrangling involved.

"Tell me, Matthew," Rian said one evening over a late supper, "how is it that you have never amassed a sizeable fortune for yourself?" He paused, spooning more potatoes on his plate as he looked at his companion across the table. "You certainly have a keen enough mind to pursue such an ambition."

"It's really very simple, Mr. Connor," the older man said, waving his fork at him. "I am far more clever with my client's money than my own." For a moment he looked quite crestfallen, and then he brightened. "Taking a chance with your fortune is much more satisfying, and the risk substantially smaller!"

"Well, I would think that any man who takes such pleasure in speculating with my capital ought to be able to address me by my first name," Rian grumbled.

"Oh, good heavens, Mr. Connor." The broker looked horrified. "And have me forget my place? That would never do." They both laughed good-naturedly over the differences between them that nevertheless did not prevent the forging of a friendship that would last a lifetime. Even though Matthew never called Rian by his first name.

But now it was time to visit Isabel. He was meeting Stuart Collins later that afternoon. The young man had news and Rian had the feeling a great many things would change after today. He had kept his distance from his ex-lover for long enough. It was best to get this meeting with Isabel over.

A footman, wearing the elegant Howard livery, showed him into the same salon where he had waited before. He stared at the couch, remembering the last time he had seen it and what had taken place. He could not undo the past. It was what it was, but to prove it had no hold over him, Rian deliberately sat on the couch to wait for the lady of the house.

"Hello Rian, what a lovely surprise." Isabel's voice was soft and pleasing to the ear. She smiled as she came toward him, giving absolutely no indication that anything was amiss between them. It was as if the incident at Oakhaven had never happened.

He got to his feet, taking the outstretched hand she offered. She was dressed for riding, and he apologized. "Forgive me; am I keeping you from something?"

"Of course not, the horse will not mind waiting."

He gave a knowing smile. He already knew neither horse nor riding companions waited for Lady Howard, but he decided not to remark on it. Wearing such an outfit was merely a pretense, but perhaps Isabel wanted him to think she had resumed her busy social life and moved on. It might help to convince him her offer of friendship had been sincere. She sat on the couch, acknowledging his choice to sit next to her with a raised brow. The last time they had sat together on this particular piece of furniture, Rian had made love to her. But then she hadn't been wearing quite so many clothes.

"What brings you to see me," she asked. "Although as always, you need no reason to call."

"A particular question has been plaguing me of late, and it seems, my dear, you are the only one who can provide me with the answer."

Isabel tipped her head and looked at him. Things had definitely changed between them. There was no playful banter. Instead Rian's direct manner was a clear indication some weighty matter now occupied his thoughts. Quietly she reminded herself to be agreeable and reasonable. At least until she got what she wanted.

"Of course, if I can be of any help," she said, smiling at him as she tapped the toe of her riding boot with the crop she held.

"Had you ever met Catherine before I introduced you at our townhouse?"

Isabel cursed silently. Although it was inevitable Rian would still harbor some residual feelings for the milkmaid, it was galling to have every conversation center on the dim-witted girl. She had been hoping his obsession might be waning, but not just yet apparently.

John Fletcher had told her Rian was in the city an hour after his arrival, and she had taken this as a sign that her plan was already reaping success. It had taken a great deal of discipline to not send a note, and she had been thrilled that he had finally taken the initiative to call on her. Hoping to find him gloomy and dejected, in need of the type of distraction she was so accomplished at providing, it was frustrating to find him not in the least despondent.

"Catherine?" Isabel frowned as if pondering his question before favoring him with a sympathetic expression. "Oh, I'm so sorry, are things between you still…uncertain?" Rian gave her a steely look as Isabel tutted compassionately while pretending to search her memory. Her acting skills truly were sublime. "No, I don't believe we had ever been introduced before," she continued. "If you recall, she did not recognize the names of any of our mutual acquaintances. Of course it's always possible that our paths may have crossed at some minor function. It can be so difficult keeping track of everyone you meet." She gave him a dazzling smile. "Why? Did she say she had met me?"

"No, she did not." His expression turned grim. "You may not be aware of this, but Catherine suffered a distressing experience that resulted in a significant memory loss for her."

"Oh my goodness, how dreadful. What kind of experience?" Isabel's tone made him wary, confirming that she knew more than she was admitting. Could this have anything to do with the ill-feeling between the two women?

"The details are unimportant," Rian said, ignoring her question, "but what I find interesting is that you knew Catherine's name...even before I did." The smile on his face was chilling. "Now how can that be, Isabel, especially if, as you claim, you've never met before?"

"Why, Rian, I'm not sure I understand what it is you are trying to say to me." Realizing that she was going to step into quicksand if she wasn't careful, Isabel was still confident she could bluff her way through Rian's suspicions. *Agreeable and reasonable*, she reminded herself. "It must stand to reason that as I *do* know Catherine's name, then *obviously* I must have met her, although how escapes me for the present. Perhaps someone pointed her out to me, although I fail to see why you are attaching so much importance to such an insignificant detail."

"It's important to me, Isabel. Who else could have told you about Catherine?" His voice dropped and turned menacing. "What is it you're keeping from me?"

Her laugh was a token of bravado that did not fool him. "Why, Rian, it sounds almost as if you believe I am guilty of some deceit." The uneasy look in her eyes belied her confident tone. Their conversation was not evolving as she intended.

His voice now almost a low growl, Rian spoke again, spacing his words with the utmost care. "I will not ask you again, Isabel. Who is the person that furnished you with Catherine's name?"

"I don't know what you're talking about." She stared at him, daring him to call her a liar, or possibly threaten to beat the answer out of her. "You make it sound as if I am being deliberately evasive."

Her protest and false innocence jarred his nerves, and Rian watched as she glanced away. He knew she was weighing her options, trying to come to a decision. Then her eyes hardened and the way she pressed her lips into a tight line told him Isabel was not going to reveal the identity of her source to him. So be it.

Before she could take another breath he was looming over her, his hands effectively trapping her as they gripped the high back of the couch either side of her head. Isabel pressed herself further back although there was nowhere else she could go. She had not realized Rian could move so quickly, and with his face only inches away, his presence dwarfed her.

"I don't know what game you're playing, Isabel, or on whose instructions, but I will not be a part of it, and neither will Catherine." His voice was deadly calm. "I still do not know how you managed to be in my bed at Oakhaven, but, no matter what you may tell yourself, we both know I would never invite you there. You have proven yourself a liar, Isabel, the one thing I abhor more than anything else." He moved a hand from the back of the couch and grasped her face with his fingers, applying enough pressure to let her know she could not escape him. "Stay away from me, and stay away from Catherine. I will not be held responsible for the consequences if you don't."

There was no mistaking the violence behind his threat as he removed his hand and left Isabel trembling. Rian had almost reached the front door when her howl of rage stopped him. Any pretense at being reasonable or agreeable had vanished completely.

"What can you possibly want with that sop-faced girl? She's nobody, the daughter of a drunk who wasted his fortune and her future on whores and gambling!"

Rian turned slowly and looked back across the foyer at her. Isabel's words, a revelation she knew far more about Catherine than she would admit, now stood between them. An impenetrable barrier that could never be breached. Realizing she had said too much, Isabel clapped a hand to her mouth, and for the briefest of moments Rian considered putting his hands around her slender neck and forcing her to tell him, in exact detail, what she knew, along with the identity of her source. But she wasn't worth the effort. Whatever knowledge his former lover possessed, he was confident Stuart Collins would soon learn the same, if he had not done so already. He watched as frustrated rage distorted the exotic features to the point Rian almost didn't recognize the woman he had once cared for. How had she been able to hide this side of her nature from him?

"You ask what I want with Catherine?" His voice, cold and sharp as ice, carried easily across the distance between them. "I want to make her my wife, if she will have me."

Isabel's shriek of fury reached him even through the closed door.

Chapter 22

Rian dismissed the carriage, needing the bracing bite of cold air to clear the stench of female anger clinging to him. Striding along the paved streets he wondered how his relationship with Isabel had deteriorated to such a point. How had he not seen what she was really like? At Oakhaven he had been so emotionally distraught, he'd simply accepted her concern, sensitivity, and even her empathy at face value. He shook his head. It was all a sham. A façade that only proved how little he really knew her. The only thing he could be certain of now was that Isabel's rage was something he needed to be careful of. As Liam had pointed out, she was a woman who didn't like to lose at anything. A troubled frown creased his brow. He would have to make sure Catherine was kept safe. Whether she would accept his help or treat it as interference mattered not. He would keep her safe.

Stuart Collins was warming himself in front of a cheerful fire when Rian entered the room. Shaking his hand the young man looked at him curiously, noting the chill of his grip, and the fact Rian was without hat, scarf, or gloves. The weather had not yet warmed sufficiently to be walking with only a topcoat to ward off the elements.

"You have news for me?" Rian asked, offering Stuart a seat, and trying not to sound overly excited.

"Yes sir, I do." He handed Rian the thick sheaf of papers he had brought with him. "My report is quite detailed, and I would be more than happy to let you read it at your leisure."

"Are you engaged elsewhere this afternoon?"

Stuart shook his head. "No. I am quite at your disposal."

"Then would you mind staying while I read? I may have some questions."

"Of course."

Gesturing to the decanter and glasses, Rian said, "Please help yourself." Stuart's refusal, stating he did not drink alcohol whilst working, only enhanced Rian's respect for him. He rang for coffee.

For the next twenty minutes the only sounds to be heard came from wood crackling in the fireplace, and the crisp rustle of parchment as Rian turned the pages of the report. He read it through once and then read it again to make sure he had not missed anything. Catherine's life lay before him, carefully documented in the investigator's neat hand. Rian now knew everything about her from her birth, to the loss of each parent, and the circumstances that had resulted in her fall into poverty. A part of him had hoped that Isabel's words had been nothing more than spiteful ranting, but whoever her informer was, he had not been wrong about the gambling and the whores. The fortune that ought to have been Catherine's had been lost.

And it changed nothing for him.

"You have been most thorough, Mr. Collins," Rian told him.

"Thank you, sir. My task was made easier with the provision of the young lady's family name, and you pointed me northwards, which proved to be the right direction."

"The credit for that we owe to my sister-in-law, an extremely clever woman," Rian observed. Stuart nodded respectfully.

"I do have one question for you, Mr. Collins. I see nothing in your report that would explain what brought Miss Davenport here. I understand the reason she had to leave her home, but why come so far south? The woman I have observed would, I believe, have chosen to remain close to surroundings she was familiar with. Can you offer any insight?"

"That is something that would require additional investigation, I believe." He hesitated before saying, "I was unsure how much more you might want to know."

"You think to uncover information that will be distasteful?"

Stuart gave Rian an appraising look. "Sometimes perceptions can change, especially when secrets are revealed."

"So you believe there are secrets to find?"

Stuart gave him a wry smile. "Mr. Connor, there are *always* secrets. The flow of information regarding Miss Davenport comes to an abrupt end after her father's death. In my experience this tells me that whatever else took place—and mark my words, something did—it is neither common knowledge, nor is it obtainable through normal channels of inquiry."

"Ah." Rian brushed his forefinger across his mouth in thoughtful contemplation.

"Is there any record of her being married?" he asked. Even though he did not believe Catherine had ever been wed, it would be foolish to overlook the obvious. "Or betrothed, perhaps?"

"Either is possible," Stuart admitted with some reluctance, "but if she is married, I can find no record of it. Of course the possibility of a clandestine union cannot be discounted, but the validity of such a joining would have to be examined. I cannot find her name recorded in any local parish for such an event although, to be frank, I have not checked every church as yet." Stuart paused and looked at Rian. "But I promise I will."

"If she was betrothed, it could be that she found the match not to her liking," Rian observed. "With her father dead, she might have decided to take her chances by striking out on her own."

"An ill-advised recourse."

"No doubt," Rian agreed, "but who would there be to offer advice?"

"Who indeed?" Stuart mused.

"What if her betrothed was already in London?"

"No," Stuart said, folding his hands together. "I do not think that is the case. Miss Davenport was either sent here, or came of her own choosing, for reasons unknown. But not, I believe, because of matrimony."

"You seem very sure."

He shrugged and looked slightly apologetic. "A feeling, Mr. Connor, nothing more."

"And do such feelings ever prove to be false?"

Stuart's mouth twitched in amusement. "Hardly ever."

"So, in order to find out what brought Miss Davenport here, more information is needed." Stuart nodded. "Information that cannot be discerned via your normal methods." Rian got up and poured himself a brandy, and decided not to ask the clever young man how he intended to circumvent normal methods. "A task requiring both a personal touch and a journey north perhaps?"

"Only if you want to be absolutely certain."

"And are you willing to undertake such a journey?"

The young man sitting in the chair seemed to ponder the question. He looked thoughtfully at Rian, who became puzzled by his hesitation.

"If it's a matter of your fee—" Rian began, but Stuart cut him off with a shake of his head.

"No, you have been more than generous already."

"But I am sensing a certain reluctance. Why?"

"I will make the journey if that is your wish," Stuart explained, not in the least embarrassed at being asked to explain himself. "But I believe my time would be better spent here."

"You have doubts regarding the success of such a venture?" Rian inquired with some measure of surprise.

The other man made a negative motion with his head. "No, not at all. I am confident such an undertaking would prove to be most useful." He paused for a moment before continuing. "But I was thinking perhaps there might be someone better suited for this task."

"Better suited? Whom?"

"Why...yourself."

Rian was not surprised by the suggestion, and in truth he had considered making the journey. Considered and rejected the idea. "Ah, but I lack your expertise, Mr. Collins."

"You know how to listen, don't you?"

"Not according to my brother." Stuart gave him a quizzical look that Rian brushed off with a wave of his hand. "I'm curious to know why you think I should do this myself."

"Forgive me for being forward, but your interest is personal, and your knowledge of the young lady is singular. A knowledge I lack. It would give you the advantage of recognizing if a falsehood was being uttered or something being withheld."

There was a moment of silence as Rian digested his words before he tossed back the contents of his glass, his decision made. "And how is it you think your time here could be better spent?"

"As I said, I have not yet checked all the church records." Stuart Collins hesitated a moment before adding softly, "I can furnish you with a starting point, if you so wish."

Rian smiled at him. "That would be most helpful."

Chapter 23

The big hunter snorted and pawed impatiently at the ground. The day was too cold to be standing still for any length of time, and the horse had decided its rider had spent long enough staring at the house before them. An impatient shake of the head made the bridle clink noisily, and was rewarded by a slight pressure from the rider's knees urging the big animal forward.

A house known by a single name was not unusual. To the best of Rian's knowledge, Oakhaven had never been known by anything else. The why was no mystery. The circle of oaks on the estate had been compelling enough to not only name the property, but also persuade an ancestor it was the perfect place for worship. But why someone would refer to this building before him as The Hall was beyond his understanding. Perhaps it was a secret jest between designer, builder, and owner, for someone was surely in a fine humor when they christened this particular edifice. The Hall was a woefully inadequate appellation when considering the size of the building.

Rian guessed there were the same number of rooms as at Oakhaven, plus half as many again. He allowed a small grin to lift his mouth, realizing that it was no wonder Catherine did not find her current surroundings at all intimidating. But, as magnificent as The Hall was, an air of sadness seemed to wrap itself about the building. Some structures could remain empty for years, decades even, and show no ill effects from the passing of time, while others seemed to require continuous habitation to prevent bricks and mortar from crumbling. It had nothing to do with the quality of materials used. Some houses were just that, houses, while others were homes. It made no difference the size of the structure; some buildings did not fare well when left empty. Catherine's home was such a place.

When originally completed, it must have been a glorious sight to see. A magnificent house reflecting the pride of the family that enjoyed its comfort. Now it was sad to see neglect and decay eating away at the house and grounds, something that he suspected had begun while Catherine was still living here.

As Stuart Collins had predicted, with a name and a starting point, it had not been that difficult a matter to locate the seat of the Davenport family. Initially he had met with some resistance regarding his inquiries about the family. The local population in this part of the country were typically closemouthed when it came to outsiders, but then a rumor had been circulated that perhaps his interest might be in the purchase of The Hall, and so they'd opened up to him. As much as such taciturn people were willing to do. As for the rumor, Rian had no idea where it had originated, but he thought it prudent to neither confirm nor deny the speculation. And now here he was, an outsider on a borrowed horse, seeing with his own eyes the house where Catherine had been born, had grown up, and had been forced to leave.

Cutting across the hills and approaching the property from the rear, he had been astonished to see the focal point of what had once been beautifully landscaped grounds was an impressive fountain. Elaborate marble fish, almost as tall as himself, stood on their tails forming a circle. Their open mouths would have gushed forth sprays of water beneath which a smaller circle of frolicking water nymphs played. The center of the pool boasted a quartet of much larger fish in the reverse position. Tails in the air, they spewed water not from open mouths, but from the point where all four tails met. Sadly the weathered condition of the statuary, along with the vegetation and sour smelling brackish water, told Rian the fountain had not functioned for many years.

"I wager it was something to see, eh?" Rian murmured. The horse snorted and twitched his ears in agreement.

The late morning sun was pale and watery, but managed to reflect off the windows on the upper portion of the house. Rian's gaze wandered and he found himself staring at the glass, trying to guess which window might open into Catherine's room. Something told him she would have preferred the view the rear of the house afforded.

Spring had not yet been able to persuade winter to fully release its grip on this part of the country; hence the cold air and snow that still lay on the surrounding hills. The rugged wildness of the land appealed to him, and, knowing Catherine's love of the outdoors, Rian could not imagine her willingly leaving all of this behind. The turn of fate responsible for the loss of her home had been a cruel one.

He nudged the horse forward, continuing his inspection until he rounded the building and came to the front of the house. A multi-columned façade acted as a graceful curtain to frame the main doors. Rian was admiring the intricately carved details when the clip-clop of hooves made him look over his shoulder. With a keen eye for horseflesh, he admired the big black stallion making its way toward him. He also approved of the ease with which the rider handled the animal. His touch was strong enough to let the animal know who was in charge, but subtle enough that he did not quell the horse's spirit. Enjoying the graceful fluidity of movement presented by both beast and rider, Rian waited for them to reach him.

"Good morning," the man called out, bringing his horse to a stop.

Rian tipped his head, but the sudden eruption of nickering as the horses greeted each other prevented him from speaking. "It would appear they know each other," he said once the equine salutation had subsided.

"Most likely they are commiserating with each other at having to be out in the cold," the stranger said with a good-natured laugh. "If I might be so bold as to ask, are you interested in the house or just lost?"

"A little of both I think," Rian answered.

The man's presence came as no surprise to Rian. He had been expecting company ever since he'd first stepped onto Davenport land. Having declined the offer of an escort for his trip this morning, he had the distinct impression that word had been delivered to someone in authority the moment he set out. Now it would seem authority had answered.

The man had a pleasant, nonthreatening voice. One that bore no trace of any local accent, which told Rian he had also benefited from an above average education. And of course the horse was proof of its owner's wealth. But up close Rian was surprised to find his companion was younger than he had first thought. Not long out of his teens he guessed, which put him closer to Catherine's age than his own.

"Well, in either case allow me to introduce myself." The stranger removed his hat, revealing a shock of bright red hair. "Edward Barclay at your service."

Rian gave him a speculative look. Edward? Catherine's instructor in profanity? Surely not.

"So, are you at all interested in the house?" A slight smile played about the corners of Edward Barclay's mouth as he gestured to the brick edifice now standing behind them.

"I confess I am," Rian answered, not in the least offended by the inquisitive nature of the question. News of a stranger had already traveled quickly throughout the village and surrounding countryside and his companion was simply being neighborly while appeasing his own curiosity. Still, Rian did not want to reveal any connection to Catherine until he knew a little more about youthful looking Mr. Barclay. He introduced himself before saying, "I hear in the village it might be available for purchase."

Interest sparked in Edward's eyes, and Rian was suddenly grateful for his own accent. It would tell the educated Mr. Barclay that he was not from this part of the country, and was, therefore, ignorant of any relevant details about The Hall's former occupants. Any questions he might have would be regarded as nothing more than idle curiosity.

"Yes indeed, it might be," Edward Barclay answered in response to his question.

"How is it that such a grand house now stands empty?" Rian asked. "Do you know the history or the family?"

"Lord yes, I grew up on the neighboring estate." Rian felt his heart quicken as Edward pointed in the general direction of the tree line beyond the magnificent building. "Perhaps you would do me the honor of joining me for lunch? I could answer any questions you might have in far more comfortable surroundings."

* * * *

An excellent lunch complemented by a good wine dispelled any lingering doubts Rian may have had regarding the region's hospitality. Refilling his glass, Edward settled comfortably in the companion chair to the one Rian now occupied before a blazing fire in the salon. Several dogs, a mix of varying breeds and sizes, also wandered in and joined them, each settling quietly on the floor in its own appointed place.

"So what can I tell you about The Hall?" Edward asked.

"Has it been empty long?"

"Not long, no," Edward said with a small shake of his head. "Less than a year actually."

Rian grunted. "Then I must presume willful neglect is the reason for its condition."

"Sadly, that is a truth I cannot deny. The Hall seems to have been in a constant state of disrepair ever since I was a boy."

Rian smiled to himself. If it was Edward Barclay's wish to discourage him from making a purchase, he was starting off on the right foot. He had the feeling, however, that the young man was as truthful in all his dealings. "What happened to the family? I understand they share their name with the town. It would be a shame to have one exist without the other."

"That would have happened anyway," Edward explained, "with no son to continue the lineage."

"So, no children then?"

"No, there is a daughter."

"Ah, I suppose she has since married and moved away as daughters do." Rian could feel his heart begin to beat a little faster in his chest.

"I cannot speak with any certainty regarding a marriage, but it is my understanding she no longer resides within the county."

"Do you know where she went?"

Edward Barclay reached down to scratch the ear of a particularly elderly hound that lay at his feet. If Rian had to guess he would say, from the affection being shown, that man and dog had grown up together.

"Forgive me, Mr. Connor, but I don't think you're being completely honest with me regarding your interest." Edward leaned forward, his expression mildly curious. "Tell me what it is you really want to know, and I will see if I can assist you."

The open countenance made Rian take a chance. He spoke candidly. "You are very astute, and I apologize for any perceived subterfuge on my part. In truth, I am looking for any information related to Catherine Davenport."

"Cat!" Edward's brows rose toward his hairline. "Forgive me," he apologized, "it is a private, childhood name." His manner changed, the pleasant openness becoming more guarded as his eyes narrowed. "What is your interest in Cat—Miss Davenport?"

It occurred to Rian he might have made a mistake in revealing his true interest, but there was no turning back now. "If we are speaking about the same young woman, then she is presently a guest in my brother's home—"

"*If* she is the same young woman?" Edward interrupted, looking puzzled. "Why would you question her identity, and why has she not told you of her family herself?"

Rian spread his hands, palms upward, and shrugged. "She is not able to."

"Why? What has happened?"

Both Edward's tone and body language had become openly hostile, and Rian heard the threat implied in his question. He wasn't sure if he should be amused or offended at the enmity being directed toward him. In response to the change in their master's tone, a couple of the younger dogs growled softly.

"Calm yourself, young man," Rian directed, "I have done nothing to Miss Davenport, and I assure you our paths crossed quite by chance." He waited until he was certain both Edward and the dogs were going to allow him to explain. "Miss Davenport has been the victim of an unfortunate accident which resulted in some memory loss. I was hoping to aid in her recovery by providing some details of her past."

It wasn't the whole truth, but it wasn't an outright lie either. There were some things that were not his place to tell Edward Barclay. No matter how far back his friendship with 'Cat' might stretch.

"Is she well?" Genuine concern now swept the hostile attitude aside, making Rian wonder just how deep the childhood friendship went.

"Yes, physically she is well, and Liam and Felicity are taking great care of her. My brother and his wife," Rian added, anticipating Edward's question. He sipped his wine. It really was an excellent vintage. "So what are you willing to share with me about Catherine?"

"That depends on what she has already told you."

"Well, apart from her name, she hasn't been able to tell us very much of anything," Rian admitted before a mischievous grin lit up his face. "But she has confessed to being taught some rather vulgar phrases by someone named Edward."

The young lord's face colored, almost matching his hair perfectly. "Oh lord, she remembered *that*?" The statement-question was delivered with a blend of horror and pride.

"Well, she couldn't recall when the lesson had taken place, only that it had, along with the first name of her instructor."

"And what exactly did she say?" Edward asked slyly.

Rian repeated the salty phrase word for word. There was a moment of total silence and then, unable to help themselves, both men burst into uproarious laughter. The dogs that had been growling only moments before now gave startled whines at being disturbed by such raucous noise.

"I'm so s-s-sorry!" Edward said, shaking his head with enough vigor it looked like his head was on fire. "But I can just picture her saying that, and no doubt looking very serious too!"

"Unfortunately at the time she had her back to me so I cannot vouch for her expression, but it did not seem an appropriate moment to tell her that what she was proposing was anatomically impossible."

"It's not really her fault you know," Edward explained, now he had managed to get himself under some semblance of control. "I misheard one of our stewards cussing, and it wasn't until my own father heard me say that exact thing that he took me to one side and told me how I had totally mucked up the wording. Of course I got my ears boxed soundly when Papa realized I had shared this with Cat." He chuckled at the memory. "I told myself I'd correct her whenever I heard her say it again, but she never did," he finished quietly. Rubbing his chin, he smiled at Rian and continued. "I wish my father were here because he could tell you so much more than I can. Especially about Cat's own papa, his younger days when he and my father were friends. Unfortunately that's no longer possible."

Rian had offered his condolences on first entering the house after seeing the wreath on the door, and the covered mirrors, but he had not asked whom the family was in mourning for. "Anything you can tell me will be helpful," he offered encouragingly. "I will leave with more knowledge than I arrived with."

"As long as you understand that most of what I am going to relate is knowledge of a secondhand nature. Either my parents told me, or else I overheard servants gossiping." He gave a wry smile. "I have discovered that sometimes my cook and groom know more about what is going on inside my own house than I do."

"A similar fact was recently brought to my own attention," Rian shared.

Edward gave him a rueful grin. "The downfall of the Davenports has become common knowledge in these parts I'm sorry to say."

Chapter 24

Taking a sip of his wine, he began to speak and Rian sat motionless, his own glass forgotten, as he listened attentively, immersing himself in the details of Catherine's life. The mundane information, family names, dates of birth etc. did not deviate from Stuart Collins' report, but Edward was able to richly embellish such facts with intimate anecdotes, filling in the details of Catherine's history.

Rian listened to how Catherine's mother had died in childbirth, which in turn led to her father's breakdown. The excessive drinking and gambling had been his way of coping with tragedy. He also heard how devoted Catherine had been to her father, and he felt a strange mix of anger peppered with sadness as poor decision making accelerated the rapid decline of the family fortune. And finally, he learned how William Davenport had lost his own life. All of this being told by someone who'd known Catherine from the time she was a little girl. Who had played with her as a child. Who knew what made her laugh and what made her cry. Who probably stole a kiss from her when he himself was no more than a boy.

And with each new revelation, Rian felt the invisible cord that connected him to Catherine strengthen.

"I still feel terribly guilty about her father's death," Edward said morosely.

"You can't possibly take responsibility for the horse stumbling in a rabbit hole," Rian consoled.

"No, but it was my birthday, and I practically twisted my father's arm so he would invite them." He paused, sounding sad and lost in the memory. "It had been so long since I had seen Cat and, well, truth be told, I missed her."

"But you did get to see her that day?" Rian asked softly.

"Oh yes." He brightened considerably. "I'd been away for almost two years, but there was no mistaking Cat. She was so easy to be around. She made me feel as if we had only parted company the day before." His voice dropped. "I still remember how beautiful she looked."

The wistful tone caused the sharp claws of jealousy to pierce Rian's chest. Unable to help himself he asked the obvious question. "Were you in love with her?"

"Love? I don't know. Perhaps." Edward gave him a strange look. "I did care about Cat, and I still do. I thought we might make a good match."

"You never told her this?"

The bright red head moved in denial before Edward got up, retrieved the decanter, and refilled both their glasses. "No, but even if I had it would have changed nothing."

"Why ever not?" Rian hated himself for wanting to know. It should have been enough that this man-child before him had not possessed the courage to declare his feelings. If he had, Catherine surely would never have left here, and would have been spared a horrifying assault.

And she would never have come into my life.

"There were…objections," Edward said glumly as he sat down again.

"Your father?"

"Lord no. Papa adored Cat! Gave her his best horse to ride that day, and if you knew my father, you would have understood the significance of that particular gesture." He shook his head, saying, "I don't know how it is in your family, Mr. Connor, but in mine the fairer sex have always wielded the power in matters of matrimony. My mother has very strong opinions regarding such matters. She believes advantageous alliances are paramount in strengthening a family. I am quite convinced that in a previous life she must have been a very cunning royal advisor."

Understanding rushed over Rian. "And there was no advantage to be had by joining with your neighbor?"

The younger man eyed him speculatively. "It would have made me happy, and I think Cat also, but in some families that consideration bears little influence." Edward Barclay sighed. "In all fairness, I don't think my mother ever seriously considered Cat as a wife, but if she had, she would have dismissed her as being unsuitable."

"Due to the lack of fortune?"

He shook his head. "No, it was William's behavior that put an end to any chance of a betrothal. Mama would not have cared how poor he was if he had lost his fortune honestly. She simply could not forgive him his vices. The gambling, the whoring, his drunkenness."

"So Catherine had to pay the price for her father's weakness," Rian said bitterly.

"So it would seem, and I cannot tell you how sorry I am for that. I was not in a position to challenge my mother, and, well, it was just the way it was." He shrugged in defeat.

If you truly loved Catherine, you would have fought for her no matter what your mother said. If you had loved her then, if you loved her still.

"Do you know what happened after her father died?"

Edward shook his head. "That day was awful. As Cat was returning home with her father's body, we received word my paternal grandfather had himself passed away. We had to leave at once, and then, while we were gone, my Father took ill and also died." Edward looked decidedly gloomy and Rian couldn't really blame him. It was a hell of a way to remember your birthday. "By the time Mama and I returned," he continued, "The Hall was empty and Cat was gone."

"Don't you think it strange that no one knew where she was?" Rian asked. Edward Barclay might have many fine qualities, but his apparent inability to stand up to his mother, to allow her to rule his life, grated on Rian.

Picking up on the irritation in Rian's voice, Edward threw him an odd look. "I don't think I ever said that no one knew. Jacob Whitney knew. He was the Davenport's legal advisor," he added, anticipating the next question.

"And did you ask him where she had gone?"

"Of course I did." Now it was Edward's turn to sound irritable. "Especially as my circumstances had now changed."

"Changed?" Although Rian thought he understood the younger man's meaning, he wanted the clarification.

"Yes. With my father's passing, I inherited not just wealth, but his title also."

"And as the new Lord Barclay, you would be able to offer Catherine marriage," Rian finished for him.

"Exactly, and that was my intention, but as I said, she had already gone."

"The lawyer could not assist you?"

"He could not," Edward said firmly. "Mr. Whitney informed me that Cat had made him swear to secrecy regarding her situation. She wanted to be able to start life anew with no shadow of her past to follow her."

"Surely you didn't just leave it at that?"

Again the odd look. "No, Mr. Connor, I did not," Edward said slowly. "I wrote a letter explaining the recent tragedies that had occurred, and the subsequent change in my circumstances as a result. I prevailed upon Mr. Whitney to send the letter on my behalf, assuring him that he would not break any confidence by doing so." He gave a wry smile. "Your coming here, however, has answered a question that has haunted me since then."

"What question would that be?"

"Why I received no reply."

For a few moments there was silence between the two men, broken only by the soft huffing sound made by one of the dogs chasing rabbits in his sleep. Rian saw that the young man sitting opposite him had been hampered by his own peculiar code of honor. Believing he had done all he could in his pursuit of Catherine, it never occurred to him that his letter might not have reached its destination. The lawyer had assured him it had been sent, and that was all Edward needed to know.

I would never give up so easily, Rian thought.

"Perhaps if I spoke to the lawyer—what was his name?" Rian frowned as he searched his memory. "Whitney, was it?"

Edward nodded.

"Maybe if I spoke with him and explained the circumstances, he might be willing to tell me where Catherine was headed."

"It will be a rather one-sided conversation. The poor man recently suffered a stroke. It has left him quite unable to speak or move, I'm afraid."

Rian felt the ground being sucked from beneath him. "When did this happen?" he asked.

"Just recently as a matter of fact." Edward frowned and stared at the ceiling. "A week ago, if memory serves."

"Under what circumstances?"

"I understand he was in his offices when a fire broke out. Burned the building to the ground," Edward said gravely. "Nothing left at all. Jacob was lucky to escape with his life."

Burned to the ground along with any records or legal documents regarding Catherine and her family.

For a few moments nothing more was said. Edward stared into the fire and Rian began to process what he had been told. He looked at the young man sitting across from him. "I suppose it was providence that you had already purchased The Hall," he stated softly.

"What makes you think—" Edward shook his head. "Was it that obvious?"

"Lucky guess on my part," Rian told him.

"Well, all in all, I suppose it was."

"What compelled you to do such a thing?"

"Call it an act of rebellion to spite my mother." He made a sound that could have been a bitter laugh, making Rian think he had possibly underestimated the strength of Edward's backbone. "Perhaps if Cat had known I was the buyer, she might not have left."

"She never knew?"

Edward looked miserable. "I wanted to surprise her, so I acted through a third party. My agent instructed Jacob Whitney my wish to meet with the previous owner, on the pretext of discussing some changes I wanted to make to the house. Mr. Whitney told me afterwards that my good intentions did not have the desired effect. I merely hastened Cat's departure."

"Surely the man could have found a way to let her know without actually telling her?"

"I am certain he would have, Mr. Connor, if he himself had known I was the buyer."

The silence returned as each man contemplated the twists and turns of fate.

"And what are your feelings toward Catherine now?" Rian asked softly, finally breaking the silence between them. He had to know.

For a few moments Edward said nothing and Rian hoped that his own expression was sufficiently composed to hide his desire.

"I love Cat, Mr. Connor, and part of me always will, but I have to tell you that when I spoke of offering marriage before, it was with the intention of our betrothal taking place quickly."

"Before objections could be raised?" Rian asked quietly.

Edward nodded and looked somewhat embarrassed. "I'm a coward, Mr. Connor, I admit it, and my mother is a very formidable woman."

"So you are no longer in a position to offer Catherine marriage?"

"No. I am not." He refused to look at Rian, keeping his eyes fixed instead on the sleeping dog at his feet. "Had I known where she was..."

It would not have made any difference. You still would not have found the courage to defy your formidable mama.

"You are now spoken for?" Rian guessed. He found it difficult to be kind when a part of him wanted to reach out and box the young lord soundly about the ears. No matter his wealth, he would never be worthy of Catherine.

The bright red head bobbed a couple of times as Edward answered his question.

"And your Mother approves of the young lady?"

"Of course. Wilhelmina is her choice," Edward told him, glancing up quickly before returning his attention to the sleeping dog. "She comes from good stock."

"I'm sure she does," Rian agreed, unsure whether Edward was referring to his betrothed or the dog at his feet.

He stared at the boy sitting opposite him. He couldn't think of him as a man, no matter how prestigious his title. He was still a boy who was ruled by his mother, and Rian knew that if he hadn't found the courage to stand up to her by now, he never would. He wondered if Catherine realized what a tyrant her almost-mother-in-law was, and if she would welcome her narrow escape. Or would she have been prepared to fight the forbidding matriarch in order to secure her marriage to Edward Barclay? It was a question that would remain forever unanswered.

"Would you be willing to sell The Hall to me?" Rian suddenly asked. Edward whipped his head up and stared in astonishment. Rian was equally as dumbfounded.

"Why do you—" Edward broke off suddenly, and a defeated look appeared in his eyes as he acknowledged the presence of a better man. "Does she know?" he asked.

"Know what?" Rian asked with a frown wrinkling his brow.

"Why that you love her," Edward stated in surprise.

"Am I that obvious?"

"Lucky guess on my part."

"In answer, no. At least I don't think so."

"You've not told her then?"

"Not in so many words. The situation between us has become... complicated."

Edward frowned. "In what way?"

"A misunderstanding regarding a woman I was previously involved with." Rian was astounded to hear the words come out of his mouth, and wondered why he felt obliged to reveal such a detail to the young man before him.

"And is this woman still a complication?" Edward stated, genuinely curious.

"Not as far as I'm concerned." Rian tipped the glass and finished the last of his wine.

"But Cat doesn't know that, does she?" Rian shook his head. "Well, Mr. Connor, may I offer some advice?" The skeptical look on Rian's face brought forth a hasty clarification. "Oh, not about women in general—I would never presume—but about Cat?" Accepting Rian's shrug, Edward continued, "If the Catherine you know is still the same strong-willed girl that I grew up with, then you had best tell her your feelings as soon as possible." He paused before adding, "And then be prepared."

"Prepared for what?"

Edward's expression returned him once more to an affable host. "Cat never does anything halfheartedly, Mr. Connor. If she returns your affection, and your presence here is a good indication you believe it a possibility, then I would imagine you are about to enjoy an experience few men can boast of." Edward's smile, though warm and genuine, did not dispel the shadow that lingered in his eyes. The shadow that said *if only I had been braver, if only I had been stronger, if only I loved her the way you do.* "You're going to be a very lucky man, Mr. Connor." Edward said as he raised his glass and tipped it toward him. "I envy you."

Chapter 25

The hour was late when Rian returned to his lodgings. He'd accepted Edward's invitation to dinner but had declined, with regret, the additional offer to spend the night. Over another excellent meal they had discussed the transfer of ownership of The Hall. The conversation had disintegrated to good natured arguing as Rian thought Edward's asking price for the property too low.

"Trust me," he had told the easygoing young man, "I will make you earn the additional amount I am prepared to pay."

"How so?" Edward's face had been alight with curiosity.

"I would appreciate your acting as my agent."

"And what would my duties be?"

The eagerness in Edward's voice had made Rian hide a smile. No doubt anything to do with the Davenports was a chance to irritate his mother. "I would like you to reinstate as many of the original staff as want to return. I think Catherine would like that."

Edward nodded. "For such a short acquaintance it would seem you know Cat very well," he complimented.

Although he did not show it outwardly, Rian was pleased by his words. "Of course, I expect the house itself to be restored and returned to the way it was before."

Edward raised a brow. "That might prove costly."

Rian brushed aside the warning. "Funds will be provided, and I will pay a fair wage, but I would like the house to be ready as soon as possible." He paused before adding. "And if you could make sure the fountain is attended to, I would be grateful. I most particularly want it working again."

Edward nodded. "Very well. Regarding furnishings for the interior—"

"No," Rian cut him off. "Those will be Catherine's decisions to make. Just ensure that all the rooms are cleaned and one suite furnished with all the necessities for her comfort while she redecorates."

Edward's expression was one of cautious surprise. "Will you not also be in residence at The Hall?" He had assumed that Rian would be returning with Catherine, but something about the way he spoke told him that he should be prepared for the possibility of greeting his childhood playmate alone.

Rian propped his elbows on the table and rested his chin on folded hands. "Nothing is certain."

"In that case, would it not be prudent to prepare a suite of rooms for your own personal use?"

Rian chuckled softly. "Lord Barclay, if I have not secured a place in the lady's affections by the time she is ready to return, then I will not be residing at The Hall in any capacity."

The look in Edward's eyes reminded Rian that this was the younger man's childhood sweetheart he was talking about, but he didn't care. Edward had had his chance and had failed to seize it. Now he was betrothed to another, and his claim on Catherine was forever lost. Deciding it was best to steer the conversation in another direction, Rian turned to the more mundane matter of wages for the staff. Edward argued affably against the compensation being considered, and Rian allowed himself to be talked down to a sum more in keeping with what Edward currently paid his own household. He did not tell the young lord that he fully intended to revisit this subject again if he did indeed return to The Hall with Catherine.

Despite the lateness of the hour, the inn was still quite crowded as Rian made his way across the public room to the staircase that would take him to the upper floor and his bedchamber. The landlord smiled at him so broadly that Rian was momentarily taken aback. Up until this point he had only ever seen the man scowl.

"A pleasant evening with his lordship, sir?" The innkeeper's question stopped Rian, his foot hovering above the first staircase riser. He should not have been surprised. Every person in the inn, and probably the entire village, knew exactly where he had been all day. And with whom. He turned and looked down at the short, rotund man and could have sworn the noise level in the room dropped noticeably so no one would miss his answer.

"Yes, thank you. Lord Barclay is most hospitable."

"Aye, that he is," the landlord agreed, suggesting a familiarity that made Rian raise a questioning eyebrow. Did they also know he had just purchased The Hall? Of course they did. Cooks and grooms, Rian reminded himself silently. Hadn't Lord Barclay already warned him that his household staff knew more about what was going on than he did? He thought of the stoic expressions on the faces of the servants who'd waited on them during the evening meal as he and Edward had wrangled pleasantly over the transfer of ownership. No doubt the entire village had already committed to memory the name of Matthew Turner, the man who would be handling the transaction on Rian's behalf.

"I'd like to make an early start," Rian told the innkeeper, "so if I could settle my account first thing in the morning?"

"Of course, sir." The innkeeper sounded a little wistful, but as Rian reached the top step he heard the babble of voices rise with questions.

It had been a long day. A productive one, but that didn't make it any less tiring. Rian expected sleep to claim him instantly, but it did not. Tossing and turning, he found his thoughts returning again and again to examine the relationship between Edward Barclay and Catherine. His mind was filled with unasked questions because, despite Edward's admissions, Rian felt there was a great deal that had been left unsaid.

Whether Edward was betrothed or not, he wasn't actually married yet, and until that happened nothing could be taken for granted. A broken engagement, for whatever reason, would not bring the world to an end. Edward knew Catherine, and would always know her in ways Rian could never share. The young man admitted that he'd wanted to marry her at one time, and hearing the regret in his voice as he spoke, Rian suspected he still did. No matter what future his mother may have planned for him, if Edward could find the strength to break free of the maternal yoke, he could easily rekindle his prior affection for Catherine. And Catherine had already proved her mettle with Isabel, so Rian knew she could be formidable in her own right.

But that speculation now raised another problem. One that had Rian giving up trying to sleep at all. Throwing back the covers, he got out of bed and poured himself a brandy, downing it in one go as his mind refused to let him settle just yet. Would Edward still want Catherine once the full extent of what she had endured was known? No one could know for sure, but if the young lord's feelings were true, then it should make no difference. Not that Rian really cared about how Edward felt, but if Catherine were to feel rejected...

He shook his head. It was one scenario he refused to contemplate.

And what about his own feelings for Catherine? Didn't they deserve some consideration?

Ah, but though he is young and foolish, Edward Barclay has never caused her the heartache you have.

Up until now Rian had clung to the idea that Catherine would give him a second chance. And she would do so, not because she felt indebted to him, but because it was what she truly wanted. But even if she were to grant him her affection upon his return, how could he possibly accept it when she had no idea her childhood sweetheart still cared for her? And putting aside all his mama's aspirations for him, and his betrothal to another, Lord Barclay was still in a position to offer what he never could before.

Rian wondered if it had been wrong of him not to have been more truthful regarding the nature of his own relationship with Catherine. His words had suggested a depth of affection that might no longer exist, and he had dismissed Isabel's involvement as a minor difficulty hardly worth mentioning. Sighing loudly, Rian began pacing. He could not change what had been said, but what if Catherine had once loved Edward? Would she still? All at once Rian remembered the first kiss between them in the snow and then, more violently, the memory of her in the library crashed into his mind, and he could feel her once more in his arms and taste her on his lips.

No, if Catherine ever fancied herself in love with her handsome redheaded neighbor, it had been no more than a young girl's infatuation. Whether she could remember his face and name or not, no woman would have responded to a man the way she had to Rian if her heart truly belonged to another. If Edward had wanted her, wanted to prove himself worthy of her, then wouldn't he have done more to try to find her? If not for the efforts of Stuart Collins and the decision to send Rian on this quest, Edward would still have no idea where Catherine was, or what had become of her.

Rian returned to bed. Putting his hands behind his head, he lay back, staring up at the wooden beams that crossed the ceiling. He had furnished Edward with Catherine's whereabouts. It was up to his lordship to decide if there was enough feeling left to rekindle the passion. But Edward Barclay, though titled and wealthy, was still a young man, inexperienced where women were concerned.

Realizing he had been blaming some character flaw in Edward for his failure to act on his feelings for Catherine, Rian suddenly felt ashamed. The young man could not be held at fault for his youth and inexperience. And Rian knew nothing of the events that had shaped Lord Barclay's life since the day of his birthday celebration. It was too easy to reprimand Edward for being indecisive. Too easy, and completely undeserved.

Staring up at the crossbeams, Rian came to a decision. First thing in the morning he would send a letter to Edward, suggesting that he take the opportunity to visit Catherine so he could assure himself she was safe and being cared for. He would also let him know that he intended to delay his own return to Oakhaven, and spend a few extra weeks in the city. Of course Edward need not know the reasons behind this change in his travel plans, but Rian had the feeling that the younger man would welcome the chance to see Catherine alone. And it would allow both of them the opportunity to see if anything lingered between them beyond a youthful flirtation.

It was a risk, in more ways than one, but Rian felt he had no choice. If Catherine returned to him, granted him another chance at happiness, then he had to be sure that her feelings for any former suitor were resolved. And despite everything, Rian found he liked Edward Barclay very much. The young man possessed such a genial affability it was not hard to understand why Catherine, with all the sorrow in her young life, would be drawn to him.

He sighed, as the sharp pang of jealousy pricked him again. He would also need to inform Liam and Felicity not to be startled if a young redheaded man showed up at Oakhaven at some point in the near future.

* * * *

The wish for an early start the next morning was thwarted by the innkeeper knocking loudly on the door as Rian was packing his clothes.

"Beggin' your pardon, sir, but there's someone who wonders if he might have a private word with you."

Rian poked his head around the door but saw no one else standing in the hallway with the burly landlord. "Who?" he asked, noticing that the scowl was still pleasantly absent.

"It's just old Ned," the innkeeper said. Apparently further clarification was deemed unnecessary. Raising a brow, Rian wondered if it was possible to get used to such minimal conversations.

"And who might Old Ned be?" he asked, returning to his packing.

The innkeeper hovered in the doorway, nervously shifting from foot to foot. "He used to be the head gardener up at T'Hall."

"Well, if he's looking to be reinstated, then he needs to speak with Lord Barclay."

The landlord dropped his voice to a loud whisper. "No sir, he's not wanting to work."

"Then what does he want?"

"He won't say," the landlord told him. "I told him you was wanting to make an early start, but he can be a stubborn old cuss at times."

The corner of Rian's mouth twitched. "Well it's probably best not to keep him waiting then, isn't it?"

The innkeeper disappeared, then announced his return a few moments later by knocking loudly on the door. Rian was impressed. He hadn't credited the man with being so fleet of foot. At his command, the door was opened by the portly landlord, who now stood to one side as an elderly man slowly walked into the room.

Well, they definitely have the old part right, Rian thought.

The man's face was lined and weather beaten. His back was so stooped from a lifetime of manual labor that Rian couldn't begin to guess at his age. With great dignity Old Ned removed his cap, revealing a shock of snowy white hair that curled about the collar of his worn, but clean, shirt and nodded respectfully at Rian.

The innkeeper came forward and placed a pitcher of ale and two tankards on the table. "Mind your manners!" he hissed under his breath before leaving and closing the door behind him. Rian couldn't be sure which of them the remark about manners was meant for, until Old Ned spoke.

"Bah!" he exclaimed, looking at the closed door. "Telling me to mind me manners, like I've never spoke to quality before. Young pup!"

Rian stood by the hearth, his arms crossed in front of his chest with a grin on his face as he waited for Old Ned to remember why he was here. Finished with the innkeeper's impertinence, the man looked at Rian, fixing him with a stare that said he wasn't the doddering fool others might believe.

"You seem to have put him in quite a state," Rian said, gesturing to the closed door as the old man gave him a foxy grin.

"That's 'cause he knows I knows all his secrets," he cackled loudly, tapping the side of his nose with his forefinger. "He's worried I might be tellin' 'em to you."

Rian offered Old Ned a seat and then went about filling a tankard from the pitcher the landlord had left. "Are they secrets I ought to know?"

Watery eyes narrowed, almost lost in the wrinkles that surrounded them as the question was considered. Finally Old Ned shook his head. "No, but it don't hurt to let him think they might be."

He grinned again, revealing the two teeth he still possessed, and pulled the tankard toward him with both hands. His fingers were gnarled with age, but he had no difficulty in raising the beer mug to his mouth and taking a healthy swallow. There followed a copious amount of lip smacking before the mug was set back down and Old Ned wiped the foam off his upper lip with the back of his hand.

"Word about the village says you're going to be new master at T'Hall." There was a slight accusation in the old man's tone. "Is that true?"

"Yes, I suppose I am," Rian answered. *At least for the time being.*

Old Ned took another long draught of his ale, and repeated the lip smacking. "Word also says you knows Miss Catherine." His stare became surprisingly steely. "Is that also true?"

Rian knew he should have been annoyed at being so questioned, but he found himself intrigued by the old man. Edward Barclay's cook and groom had been quite busy in a relatively short span of time, it would seem. "Yes, that is also quite true," Rian told the old man respectfully, wondering where this conversation was going. He had already decided that if—*when*—he returned with Catherine, Old Ned was someone he needed to get to know better. The probable octogenarian grunted but Rian wasn't sure if it was in disapproval or not.

"I worked for her father, Master William that was. Took me on as a young lad, but it was all different back then. You never saw such gardens—the king hisself would've been proud to have them at his palace. I never did work anywhere else...."

He trailed off, lost in memories, and Rian realized there was no use in being impatient. The man would get to the reason for his visit in his own time. Accepting that the early departure was not going to happen, Rian poured himself a tankard of ale and joined Old Ned.

"Miss Catherine was always good to us, even when times was 'ard," Old Ned continued. "When there was no wages, she made sure no one had a hungry belly, and there was always wood for the fire." Rheumy eyes bright with emotion, Old Ned sniffed loudly and searched his pockets. Like a magician performing sleight of hand, he pulled a square of linen from a hidden pocket. He wiped his eyes and blew his nose, sounding like a rusty trumpet. Rian refilled Old Ned's tankard.

"Will you be seeing Miss Catherine afore long?" Old Ned asked.

"Hopefully," Rian replied, watching as the old man took another long draught of ale.

"Would you give her summat for me?" This time the foam was ignored, leaving Old Ned with a splendid mustache.

"Of course." Rian watched in fascination as from another hidden pocket arthritic fingers brought forth a delicate bundle which was placed reverently on the table. Wrapped in lace, it carried great significance. "What is it?" he asked the gardener.

"Heather."

"Heather?"

"Aye, she'll understand," Old Ned told him firmly. "It always was her favorite. Her mother's too."

"Then I'll make sure it gets to her, and tell her who it is from," Rian assured him.

"No need to do that. She'll know," the old man said softly.

With the current condition of Catherine's memory, Rian couldn't be sure of that, but he saw no point in crushing an old man's memories. After politely refusing another refill, the former head gardener stood and slowly made his way to the door. With his claw hand resting on the wrought iron handle, he turned and looked back at Rian.

"You'll do all right as master," Old Ned told him. "I'll no doubt be seeing you again."

Unexpectedly touched by the simple sincerity in the old man's voice, Rian thanked him for his words. "I'm not sure when I'll be in these parts again," he said truthfully.

Old Ned narrowed his eyes, his white brows becoming a line of frost across his weathered forehead. "I thought you said you knows Miss Catherine?"

"And I do."

"Then you'll be bringing her back home, or else she'll be bringing you!" he cackled. "Mark my words, one way or t'other, you'll be back afore long." And with that he pulled the door open, leaving Rian with the sound of his shuffling footsteps as he made his way down the hall.

The innkeeper's hasty appearance meant he had probably been hovering in an adjacent room. Rian smiled to himself. It was the way of things, but he was curious to know what secrets the man was worried Old Ned might spill.

"The carriage will be here within the hour, sir," the man said as he nervously wiped his meaty hands on the apron tied about his waist. Rian nodded and the man turned to go.

"Can you find me a courier?" Rian asked.

"A courier?" The innkeeper looked bewildered and Rian thought perhaps the man did not understand what he was asking.

"Yes, I wish to send a package and a letter south, and another to Lord Barclay," Rian explained.

"Well, my boy can take the letter to his lordship, and the coachman will be taking mail, sir."

He hadn't thought of that. By the time the landlord returned with his son, Rian was ready to leave. He had carefully enclosed the handkerchief with its precious contents within a sheet of heavy parchment, folded the corners together and sealed it with wax. He placed it in his pocket with his letter to Liam. Edward Barclay's letter he gave to the landlord's son, along with a gold coin for his trouble. The boy's eyes opened wide enough for Rian to know he had not held so much wealth in his hand before, and he wondered how much his father would allow him to keep.

Chapter 26

Foretelling the future was not a skill Mrs. Hatch possessed no matter how much Catherine might wish it. The few days that the housekeeper had predicted Rian would be gone had now stretched into almost two months. Liam had received a few letters, but had chosen not to share the contents with her. She could not fault him for the exclusion. Everyone was avoiding mentioning Rian around her. Everyone that is except Felicity, who refused to accept that he wasn't coming back soon, and that what had occurred between them was nothing more than a minor misunderstanding. Catherine could only admire her friend for her optimism.

February had come and gone, and blustery March had indeed roared in like a lion, and was now meekly making itself scarce, leaving behind signs of spring everywhere. The first snowdrops had long ago given way to chubby orange, purple, and white crocuses, while majestic golden daffodils heralded the coming of warmer days.

The ill-fated incident with the pink ball gown had indeed turned out to be the catalyst required to unlock a door in Catherine's mind. As a result her memories were returning at a startling rate. Each new day brought with it a reminiscence of her previous life, which she shared with Liam and Felicity, whom she now thought of as her family. She delighted Felicity one evening by joining her at the pianoforte in a duet, before proving herself to be quite an accomplished soloist as well. A hidden talent for mimicry, coupled with a wicked sense of humor, had Liam almost falling out of his chair as Catherine put her own spin on some of the conversations she had overheard the night of the party.

Other things, however, still eluded her, continuing to remain maddeningly just out of reach. Unable to tell either of them where she grew up, the name of the closest town or even what part of the country she called home was very frustrating. And the identity of the monster who'd assaulted her also remained hidden. Something that Catherine told herself might be better left unknown.

Alone, she spent a great deal of time reexamining the events of that morning in Rian's bedroom. She went over everything in fine detail and, after putting aside her shock at finding Isabel in Rian's bed, she listened carefully as Liam reluctantly repeated the conversation he had had with his brother.

"The decision is yours to make, Catherine," Felicity told her gently as they took advantage of the mild spring weather to gather daffodils.

"What decision?"

"Whether or not you can forgive Rian."

"What am I to forgive him for?" she asked sarcastically. "The naked harlot in his bed?" The look she gave Felicity said she was surprised her friend would even suggest such a thing. "I don't care if she does have a title," she added petulantly.

Putting the basket of flowers they had been filling on the ground, Felicity took Catherine's hand. "You have to forgive him for being a man. A man who can make very foolish and stupid mistakes."

Catherine felt her lower lip tremble. "I don't know if I can."

Felicity squeezed the slender hand she held. "I know it's hard, but try not to think about what happened that day. Just tell me what you feel here." She pressed her hand against her own chest, over her heart.

Catherine sighed, doing her best to control her trembling lip. "A part of me wants to hurt him as much as he hurt me, and then another part says I think I will die if he never kisses me again—"

"Kisses you?" Felicity grabbed Catherine by both her arms. "Rian has kissed you, and you never told me? Oh, shame on you, Miss Davenport!" The bright yellow flowers now forgotten, Catherine had no choice but to share what had taken place in the library. "And what if he never does kiss you like that again?" Felicity asked gently, picking up the basket of blooms with one hand and linking arms with Catherine with the other.

"That's something I don't want to think about," she whispered faintly.

"Then I think it's time you found out a few things about Isabel Howard."

"I thought you'd already told me all you know." Catherine cast her mind back to their prior conversation, before too much blackberry brandy had befuddled her senses.

"True, true. All _I_ know, but there's someone else who knows a great deal more about Lady Isabel Howard." Female curiosity reared its head.

Felicity was being mysterious. "And," she continued, "I think a change of scenery might be just the ticket to put the bloom back in your cheeks."

"I don't understand."

"I'm long overdue for a visit with Mama." Catherine gave her a puzzled look. "And you're coming with me."

They arrived back at the house to be told Liam was looking for Catherine. He had a package for her. "This was just delivered for you," he said, looking over the top of her head at his wife.

"Who is it from?"

"Rian," Liam said stoically, his face revealing nothing.

The last time Rian had given Catherine a gift, it had been an unpleasant experience for everyone involved, but it had also been responsible for putting her on the path to her continuing recovery. No matter how ugly the incident, it was universally agreed in hindsight that it had been a necessary one. But now Liam and Felicity held their breath as they waited for Catherine to break the wax seal and carefully open the parchment. The barest trace of fragrance lingered and it enveloped her at once, evoking emotions that were warm and wonderful, and made her feel safe, secure and loved.

"Darling, what is it?" Felicity asked, seeing Catherine's eyes glisten.

Carefully Catherine opened the folds of the lace handkerchief, taking out the small spray of purple heather that had been nestled within, its ends tied together with a piece of satin ribbon.

"It's my favorite," she murmured softly as she held the token out for them to see.

"It's simply lovely." Felicity admired the delicate spray. "Is there a note?" she asked, glancing at her husband.

"I received a letter from Rian, but he made no mention of this," Liam told her.

"It matters not," Catherine told him. "It is enough that he sent it." Her expression told them all they needed to know. "I shall take it with me when we leave." Catherine carefully rewrapped the spray in the lace handkerchief.

"You're leaving? Where are you going?" Liam asked.

"Oh, I thought I would take Catherine over to stay with Mama for a little while," Felicity said, patting her husband soothingly on the arm. "The change of scenery will do her good, and I think they would enjoy each other's company immensely." She did not mention the real reason behind their visit.

"Oh, of course. When were you planning to go?" It was not so bad. Pelham was less than an hour's ride by horse across country. A little longer by carriage.

"I thought after lunch," Felicity said, boldly kissing her husband on the mouth.

* * * *

Pelham Manor, though just as large as Oakhaven, was certainly a much grander house with its fine furnishings, tasteful decorations and well-manicured lawns.

"Don't you miss all this?" Catherine asked her friend a few days later as they walked through the beautifully laid out gardens.

The flower beds were much more formal in pattern and purpose with every bloom appointed its own designated space in which to grow. Catherine could appreciate the care taken in such a grand design, especially as each plant complemented its neighbor, but she secretly loved the wild feel to the gardens at Oakhaven. Suspecting the chaotic display owed more to accident than design, she'd admired the untidy disorder of the plants now beginning to burst forth. It wasn't hard to imagine the rambunctious riot of color that would assault them when summer was at its height. It was a gloriously appealing prospect. That didn't mean, however, she couldn't appreciate the almost military precision of the gardens at Pelham, and was now quietly noting how many different shades of green could be persuaded to grow together.

"Of course I miss being here," Felicity said in answer to her question. "This is where I grew up, where I was happy."

"Aren't you happy at Oakhaven?" Catherine's voice sounded worried.

"Yes, very much so, but it is a different kind of happiness. This"—she waved a hand—"represents the joy of my childhood."

"And Oakhaven is your adult life."

"Exactly, and there can be no comparison between the two. At Oakhaven I have Liam, and one day it too will look like this." Felicity spread her arms expansively.

"Truthfully?" Catherine didn't try to hide her disappointment.

"Oh, I don't mean the flower beds." Felicity lowered her voice as if afraid of offending the military row of hyacinths closest to them. "I love Mama a great deal, but I think this is all a little too perfect. It seems almost unnatural, don't you think?"

"Oakhaven has a different kind of beauty."

"Precisely! And that's why I'm not going to have any formally laid out gardens. Instead I shall simply allow the land to conjure up its own charm with each passing season."

"Oh Felicity, that's wonderful!" Catherine exclaimed, delighted her friend could recognize and accept the wild beauty of her new home.

"But the house itself is another matter altogether," Felicity declared with a determined air as she linked arms so they might continue walking.

The day before Felicity was to return to Oakhaven, mother and daughter sat in the salon taking tea together. Catherine, recognizing the need for them to share some private moments, had decided it was time she introduced herself to the stable's residents. Before leaving she gave Felicity permission to share with her mother as much detail regarding her ordeal as she thought necessary.

"Oh my word—how absolutely appalling!" Emily exclaimed on hearing only a brief synopsis.

"Quite, so you can imagine how pleased Liam and I were when it seemed that something had sparked between Rian and Catherine," Felicity told her mother.

Fully aware of Rian's recent affair with Isabel, Emily was mature enough to read between the lines. "What happened to extinguish it?"

Revealing her reason for bringing Catherine to Pelham, Felicity told her mother about the dreadful episode concerning Rian and Isabel.

"Well, that would explain the mournful look I see on her face when she thinks no one is looking," Emily remarked before sighing in exasperation. "Does she realize she's in love with him?"

Felicity shook her head. "I don't think so, Mama, but even if she does, Catherine will not admit to it. Not even to herself, nor I suspect, will she as long as she believes Isabel is still a threat."

"What a disaster. It's no wonder the poor girl is heartsick," Lady Pelham observed. "Men can be such asses!"

"Mama! I trust Papa is excluded from such an observation."

"Of course. Your father is a saint," her mother told her as she poured tea. "So, where is Rian now?"

"I honestly don't know. Liam said he had decided to travel up north to try to find out what he could about Catherine and her family."

Emily arched a finely plucked eyebrow. "And does Catherine know this?"

"We thought it best not to mention it," Felicity confided with a shake of her head.

"And she has no idea just how much the poor man is in love with her?" Emily handed her daughter a cup of tea, the translucency of the bone china revealing the darker liquid within.

"Mama—how can you possibly know that Rian is in love with her? His behavior has hardly constituted a declaration!"

"Hasn't it?" Emily sipped her own tea and gave her daughter a knowing look. "Only a man with a vested interest in the outcome needs a firsthand account of the events of Catherine's past. He could easily have dispatched a subordinate to obtain this knowledge, but he did not. Rian Connor went himself. I'd say that's a good indication of a man in love, wouldn't you? Are you certain Catherine is unaware of his feelings toward her?" she repeated.

"What she knows, and what she will admit to knowing, are two completely different things." Felicity thought back to Catherine's recollection of the incident in the library. "She has told me that Rian kissed her quite passionately, but she was also quite tipsy at the time, so her recollection of the facts might be suspect."

"Pish! I guarantee no woman would forget being kissed by Rian Connor."

Felicity stared at this woman who looked like her mother, but no longer acted like her. "Never mind that," she said, slightly flustered. "What we need to concentrate on is finding a way for Catherine to forgive Rian his appalling behavior with Isabel."

"Darling, don't do that. It's very unattractive," Emily reprimanded as Felicity began to worry her lower lip. "I shall tell Catherine what I know about Isabel when I think she's ready to hear it, and she will make whatever decision her heart tells her to. In the meantime, I think you should allow her to remain here with your father and me, while you return to your husband before he starts to feel neglected."

Chapter 27

Catherine had been a guest at Pelham Manor for over a month, and was thankful that it appeared she had not outstayed her welcome. Emily did not seem to mind her extended visit, finding her to be a delightful companion with a quick mind and sense of humor. For Catherine it was a chance to experience the mother figure she'd never had, and she could not help but wonder how different her own life might have been if the hand of fate had not been so cruel.

She also felt a strange sense of relief to be away from Oakhaven. Rian's presence lingered everywhere she went there, and expecting to bump into him every time she went around a corner had made her edgy. Being a guest at Pelham meant that Felicity was now able to step into her role as mistress of Oakhaven, and spend time alone with her husband without fretting over Catherine. But her friend still managed to return to her former home regularly, and, as she always stayed overnight, there was ample opportunity to visit with both her parents and Catherine.

It was during one of Felicity's visits to Pelham that Liam received a visitor. Having been forewarned by his brother, he was not terribly surprised when a young man came to call, one with shocking red hair.

"Lord Barclay, welcome to Oakhaven." Liam greeted him with some curiosity, mainly because Rian's letter had expressed doubts the young man would actually make the trip.

"Please, call me Edward," the visitor said after giving the customary bow in greeting. "And you, I trust, are Liam Connor?"

"Indeed I am."

"Then as you show no surprise, I can only assume you are forewarned of my purpose in visiting you?"

"My brother did mention it, yes."

"Is he here?" Edward asked, looking about as if he expected the older Connor to materialize out of thin air.

Liam shook his head. "I'm afraid business is keeping him in town."

"Pity. I very much enjoyed his company." He paused before asking, "And Cat? Where is she?"

"Who?" Liam looked slightly bewildered.

"Ah, your brother didn't tell you everything, I see," Edward said with a grin. "It's a childhood nickname. One I doubt I will ever outgrow. I meant to say Catherine."

"I am sorry to have to tell you that Catherine is at present enjoying the hospitality of my wife's family on the neighboring estate."

Seeing Edward's crestfallen look, Liam chuckled and waved a hand. "Lord Barclay—"

"Edward."

"Forgive me, Edward. Allow me to offer you some refreshment, and a bed. We can ride over to Pelham in the morning, and you may see Catherine then."

Liam thought it quite charming to see how his lordship's face brightened at the prospect. It made him look quite boyish. The arrival of their unexpected guest brought Mrs. Hatch to them, and she informed Liam that Lord Barclay's room was already prepared, and supper was waiting for him in the dining room.

"Does Cat know I am here?" Edward asked Liam as he sat down at the long, polished dining table.

"How could she? You have only just arrived," Liam answered with a smile. Youthful enthusiasm was hard to dislike.

"I thought perhaps your brother might have told her he had met me."

"Rian has not yet returned home since visiting with you. He has not seen Catherine."

The expression on Edward's face made Liam wonder if his brother knew just what he was doing.

* * * *

Emily glanced up from the piece of embroidery she was working on and looked thoughtfully at Catherine, who sat reading, totally absorbed by the pages of the book she held in her hand. As she watched, Catherine absentmindedly pulled at a lock of hair and began twisting it around her finger. Emily smiled. So that explained why one curl was always out of place. It had been quite a change of pace to have Catherine stay with them. Her presence affected the entire household, and the staff had become quite enchanted by her, especially when Catherine spent as much time in the kitchen as she did in any of Pelham's grand drawing rooms. Emily was pleased to see that although Catherine shared many similarities with her daughter, there were enough differences to promise their friendship would remain fresh and interesting.

As more of Catherine's memory returned, it became apparent to Emily that, like her own daughter, Catherine's education had been varied and wide ranging. She showed a love of art and literature, coupled with a sincere appreciation for music. She possessed a working knowledge of French and Italian that was good enough to allow conversation in either language. There was, however, a severe dislike of mathematics, although, much to Charles Pelham's delight, Catherine seemed to enjoy the sciences. He confided that his daughter had never shown an interest in this part of her education, but now he found a partner who pored over scientific manuals and was willing to play devil's advocate in order to present an opposing point of view on most subjects.

Emily would sit quietly listening to them discuss concepts that, like her daughter, she had no grasp of. Not because of a lack of intelligence, but more a lack of interest. The rise and fall of their voices as they argued good naturedly became a pleasant background song to her ears. As far as the Pelhams were concerned, Catherine was welcome to stay as long as she wished.

But Catherine had brought with her a dark side too. Nightmares. Not every night, but enough that her disturbed sleep was marked by the shadows under her eyes. It seemed the door that had been opened by the incident with the pink ball gown was gaping ever wider, allowing dark recollections to come through and manifest themselves in her dreams.

Woken by her personal maid, Emily had run to Catherine's room the first night, finding the young woman thrashing in her bed. She seemed to be in a place between wake and sleep, muttering incoherently, and soaked with perspiration. At first Emily had been afraid to reach out to her, but then maternal instinct had overcome any reservations. Holding Catherine tightly in her arms, she had stroked her matted hair and whispered soothingly until the young woman sagged against her.

Catherine's only reference to the incident was a soft thank you at breakfast the next morning. Emily inclined her head slightly, and smiled in acknowledgment, believing it to be an isolated incident that would not be repeated. But when it happened again the two women were forced to speak candidly about the matter. Not wanting to cause Catherine further distress, Emily was fully prepared to let her return to Oakhaven, thinking that the change in surroundings might be the reason for the recurring dream, but Catherine pleaded to remain.

With Emily she was developing a relationship that, although quite different from her affection for Felicity, was already important to her, and she was reluctant to give it up so soon. Both women came to the conclusion that the nightmare was definitely linked to her assault, and Catherine voiced the opinion that perhaps the cocoon Oakhaven had wrapped about her had been keeping it at bay. Knowing she would never be whole until she had confronted this part of her life, Catherine was determined to do so.

"Do you remember any details about the dream?" Emily asked her gently one morning. Felicity had stayed over the previous night, but was still abed. As always, Catherine had initiated the discussion.

"Just vague images, nothing specific," Catherine told her with a shake of her head. "It's more a sense of things. Sounds I think I can hear, a feeling of terror, and a smell…"

"A smell?" Emily asked, surprised at this odd detail.

"Yes, something foul and rank, diseased, decaying."

"Is Rian involved in the dream in any way?" Emily asked quietly. "Not that I'm suggesting he's diseased or decaying."

"Rian would never hurt me…not in that way."

"Darling, I do not doubt you, but if you cannot remember the details of the dream, how can you be so certain?" Emily had no wish to cast doubts on Rian's character; rather she wanted Catherine to face her conviction, and actually say aloud her reasons for defending him.

"Because whenever I dream of him it is in another place, and his behavior is very…different."

The high blush of color staining Catherine's cheeks told Emily all she needed to know about the difference between the dreams. "Do you dream of him like that often?" she asked softly, taking Catherine's hand in her own.

"Yes, and it's always after…so I know it isn't him in the nightmare."

"You always dream about Rian after the nightmare is over?" Emily thought this a significant admission.

"When I can go back to sleep," she admitted in a small voice.

Feeling her hand tremble, Emily put her arm around Catherine's shoulder and held her compassionately. Whatever horror Catherine was still experiencing, Emily was determined to help her through it in any way she could.

"And are these dreams about Rian…romantic in nature?" She lowered her voice and felt Catherine stiffen before she nodded in response. Through the curtain of blond hair Emily could see the flush on her cheeks deepen.

"Although I'm not sure 'romantic' is quite the right word," Catherine admitted with naïve honesty.

"Ah, I understand." Emily could feel her own cheeks warming.

"You don't think it means—" Catherine lifted her head. A dark, smoky hue colored her eyes and Emily wondered if they always looked so when she was passionate about something, or if it was only when Rian Connor was the subject.

"No, I do not believe that Rian is a part of your nightmare," she reassured Catherine, "but I do believe he is part of the answer."

She brushed a stray lock of hair from Catherine's forehead. "Tell me, do you love him?"

"I don't know," she confessed, surprised by the question. "Sometimes I think I do, but then there's always…*that woman.*"

"Ah yes…Isabel."

The way Emily spoke her name made Catherine turn her head and look at her with a different kind of awareness. "Felicity said you knew her… knew things about her."

"Only too well." Emily sighed and looked thoughtful. She patted Catherine's hand before continuing. "John Howard, Isabel's late husband, was a good friend to both Charles and me. In fact, his first wife, Amelia, was a great friend of mine. We all felt her loss keenly when she died, none more so than John. He had been a devoted husband, and I always felt it a shame that they never had children. But after her death something changed inside him, and he was never quite the same man again."

"I know how that can be," Catherine said softly as the memory of her father's despair suddenly filled her.

"John took Amelia's death very hard. He stopped associating with anyone who had known her while she was alive. He refused all invitations sent to him and became something of a recluse." Emily squeezed Catherine's hand. "Grief takes hold in many different ways. The next thing we heard, he had become obsessed with a young girl, and before anyone could dissuade him, he had married her and she was now the new Lady Howard. Isabel was very young and very beautiful. It was easy to see why John had become so besotted with her, but within five years he was dead and she was left a very wealthy widow."

"I'm so sorry," Catherine said, hearing the sorrow in Emily's voice.

"Yes, well, perhaps it is better for John, and in all fairness I cannot say that Isabel did not bring him some measure of joy in the time he had with her, but"—her voice hardened—"allow me to illuminate the character of Isabel Howard."

Half an hour later Emily finished talking and Catherine rang for tea. It had been thirsty work. Handing her a cup of the hot liquid, Catherine spoke. "But what of Isabel's family?"

"Yes indeed, what of them? Isabel *claims* to be the daughter of a disgraced and impoverished aristocrat who died when she was an infant. Her mother also has now passed, conveniently succumbing to some illness just before Isabel wed John. Whether or not he met the woman, no one knows. Whatever verification exists to substantiate her birth, her husband was the only one who ever saw it."

"You don't believe her, do you?"

Emily sipped her tea and shook her head. "In my experience many young women who wish to improve their social standing *claim* a great many things. They are all revealed as frauds eventually."

"And you think this will be the case with Isabel?" Catherine was fascinated both by the intrigue as well as Isabel's audacity if Emily's suspicions were true.

"Undoubtedly." The older woman's voice was firm. "I think it just a little too convenient to have no living relative to vouch for you."

"But surely if her husband saw the verification?"

"You have had just a small taste of Isabel's determination to get her hands on something she desperately wants. How much more forceful and clever do you imagine she would be in securing her future in the first place? Whatever documentation she provided to convince John of her heritage, or what poor woman she paraded around as her mother, I will go to my grave with the certainty that both were false. However, suspicion and proof are two very different matters."

Catherine looked thoughtful as she nibbled on a tea cake.

"So are you telling me that finding Isabel in Rian's bed was somehow Isabel's design?"

"Can you honestly believe it was anything else?" Emily put down her tea cup. "Isabel has never made a secret of her feelings for Rian, feelings I might add that he has never publicly reciprocated. Now I ask you, which of them do you trust?" She held up her hand and her voice softened. "No, you don't have to answer me, Catherine. You know in your heart what the answer is, but now you have to make a decision."

Catherine gave a wry smile. "Your daughter gave me much the same advice recently."

Picking up her cup, Emily smiled over the rim. "Clever girl, I wonder who she learned that from?"

At that moment Felicity joined them. She had been feeling a little peaky that morning and had been lying down in her bedroom.

"Feeling better?" Catherine asked solicitously.

"A little," her friend replied. "I hope I'm not coming down with something."

Emily pursed her lips but said nothing, a small smile tugging at the corner of her mouth. It was still too early to speculate; a few more weeks and then it would be certain. "Catherine, be a dear and ring for more tea, would you?"

Catherine had her hand on the bellpull when the door to the salon was opened by a footman announcing Liam's arrival. Emily frowned, wondering why the man had thought it necessary to announce her son-in-law. Usually Liam simply found them wherever they might be. If the sudden shriek that filled the air had not made Emily clutch her bosom, then the sight of Catherine launching herself at the young man who followed Liam into the room surely did.

"Edward!" Catherine squealed in delight.

Chapter 28

"What do you think is going to happen?" Felicity asked as she looked over her mother's shoulder at Catherine and Edward walking down the terrace steps, arm in arm.

Once introductions were made, and the young man's identity was revealed, conversation had become oddly strained. Felicity and Emily knew nothing about the young man seated across the room from them, and Liam knew barely any more. However, the fiery redhead couldn't take his eyes from Catherine, and she, in turn, alternated between giddy delight and embarrassment over her lack of decorum. It was Emily who suggested Catherine show Edward the gardens, giving them a chance to speak to each other in private.

"Should they not have a chaperone?" Felicity asked, worriedly.

"Why? He's a childhood friend, my dear, and I think if Catherine felt unsafe with him, she would have let us know." Finding no reason to disagree, Felicity repeated her earlier question.

"Who can say?" her mother answered with a shake of her head.

Once Catherine and Edward had disappeared from view, Emily took her daughter's hand and moved them away from the window. "So tell us what you know about this young lord," she instructed her son-in-law.

Liam had remained seated, observing with keen interest the reaction Edward's arrival had produced. Of course, his interest was directed not so much at Lord Barclay, but rather at how Catherine responded to him.

"All I know is that Edward and Catherine have known each other since they were children, growing up on neighboring estates just like we did." He nodded at his wife. "Well, from Catherine's obvious delight, we know that to be true," Felicity said, "but I'm curious how Lord Barclay knew Catherine was here."

"Rian told him."

"Rian told him?" Felicity gasped, taken aback.

"Mmm, yes. I gather after his meeting with Lord Barclay he thought it would be improper of him *not* to tell his lordship exactly where Catherine was, and how to find her." He gave his wife an apologetic look. "He is a link to Catherine's past, and quite a strong one from all accounts."

"And you didn't think to share this with me?" Felicity huffed.

"I apologize, my darling, but I didn't want to bother you with something that I wasn't sure would actually happen. The tone of Rian's letter seemed to indicate a certain hesitancy on the young man's part. I think my brother will be most surprised to learn Edward Barclay accepted his offer to visit."

Somewhat mollified, Felicity asked, "Did Rian happen to say how close this childhood friendship was?"

"Whatever are you thinking?" Emily asked, voicing the concern before her son-in-law could.

"I'm just wondering if an understanding exists between them." Felicity turned her attention back to Liam. "Well? Did Rian mention anything to that effect?"

"There was never a formal declaration."

"Nothing formal?" Felicity pounced on the distinction like a cat chasing a bug. "But there is an existing affection between them?"

"I think," Liam said with a twinkle of amusement, "Catherine has demonstrated that most effectively. Rian believes Lord Barclay still cares for her, but was never in a position to make her an offer until recently."

"Do you suppose that is what has brought him to our doorstep?" Emily asked with some concern.

"It is, I believe, a safe assumption," Liam concurred.

Felicity went to stand before the window again. She wanted to be able to judge Catherine's state of mind the moment she saw her. "I still don't understand why Rian would tell a potential rival where to find her," she said.

"Don't you?" Her mother seemed surprised at her daughter's lack of insight. It was normally so keen. "He is offering Catherine a choice, and will abide by whatever decision she makes."

"So, she has forgiven the incident with Isabel?" Liam asked.

Emily picked up her embroidery and held the needle between thumb and forefinger. "Yes, I believe she has, even if she doesn't quite know it herself yet."

"I'd wager Rian would not have been so generous with his invitation if he was aware of that!" Felicity said.

Coming to stand behind her, Liam rubbed his wife's arms reassuringly. "It would be a wager you would lose, my darling," he chided gently.

"You think knowing Catherine has forgiven him would make no difference to Rian?"

Emily spoke before Liam could answer. Resting her needle she looked at her daughter. "I think even if Rian already knew he was forgiven, he still would have sent young Lord Barclay to Catherine."

"But he risks losing everything."

"And no doubt my brother believes what he could gain is worth that risk."

* * * *

Arm in arm, Catherine and Edward walked through Emily's formal garden, neither saying a word. Never before had they been at a loss for conversation when in each other's company, but events had now made them strangers. After a few stilted tries, Catherine halted her steps and looked up at Edward, emotion making her eyes shine too brightly. "It's alright, Cat," he hushed reassuringly, using the pad of his thumb to wipe the moisture from her cheek. "You don't have to say anything. It's a beautiful day. Let's simply walk, and enjoy the gardens."

She squeezed his arm, grateful for his understanding, but then something told her Edward had always understood her. They continued walking, meandering past the meticulous flower beds and through the uniformly shaped hedgerows, until they reached a secluded place far from prying eyes. A massive beech tree, no doubt a sapling when the House of Stuart was restored to the throne, invited them to sit beneath its leafy canopy. Taking off his coat, Edward spread it on the ground, and, after settling his back against the broad, sturdy trunk, he took Catherine in his arms. He held her to him as she wept quietly.

Catherine couldn't help but be reminded of another pair of arms that had held her while she cried. Edward's were just as strong, just as safe, but there was something missing, and when the last of her tears had washed out of her, she looked up with a guilty smile. He smiled back, his bright blue eyes twinkling, and taking her hand in his, he raised it to his lips and gently kissed her fingertips.

"I have missed you," he said softly.

"And I you," Catherine told him.

Although most of her memory had restored itself, gaps still remained. However, Catherine felt her recollection concerning Edward was complete. It was wonderful to be able to speak of things from her past without the need for explanation. Edward knew all the places she described, the memories she recalled. He was an anchor to the past, giving her the freedom to be herself.

She didn't think that she consciously adopted a façade with either the Connors or the Pelhams, but, if she was honest with herself, she couldn't be sure. Were the mannerisms she used her normal behavior, or a reflection of theirs? How could she possibly tell the difference when she couldn't remember what normal felt like? At least with Edward Catherine was confident he would soon tell her if she was behaving in a manner that was not her own. Or that of the person he knew her to be.

Pushing herself back from him, Catherine looked up into his face with a quizzical expression. "Edward, how did you know where to find me?" She would have been amused to know Felicity was asking the very same question.

"Rian Connor told me," he answered as he studied her reaction. Rian had told him that Catherine was unaware of his visit north, and her puzzled expression confirmed this.

"Rian?" she queried faintly. "You know Rian?"

Edward nodded. "Yes. He came to visit me."

"He visited you?" She spoke slowly, as if sounding out the words would give her some insight into what she was missing.

"I'm sure he didn't come with the intention of visiting me, Cat. We met by chance while he was exploring the grounds at The Hall."

"But why would he be at The Hall?"

"He told me he was looking for information."

"About what?"

"About you, of course."

Edward smiled, seeing a familiar furrow appear between her brows. It was the same one that always showed up whenever she was wrestling with a problem. He knew she was trying to decide if he was being deliberately infuriating, or just delighted to have something to tease her about. There was a familiarity to his banter that told her more often than not she found him frustrating, but she decided it didn't matter. She was too happy to be annoyed with him.

"So what did you tell him…about me?" Heat flooded her face and she turned her head, but not before Edward noticed the blush on her cheeks.

"All that he wanted to know." His voice became serious with no hint of mockery or goading. He caught her chin with his fingers and gently turned her face back toward him. "He's a fine man, Cat, and I like him."

"Yes, he is a fine man, and I like him too." The words slipped out before she could stop them, but Edward said nothing. Content to simply hold her in his arms, he encouraged her to resume her place against his chest. "Edward, what happened to you after Papa died?" Hearing the steady rhythm of his heart, Catherine could have sworn it skipped a beat. "The servants said you had left, but you know you could have told me why yourself. I would have understood."

She flinched at the sound of him cursing out loud. Pulling back her head, she saw a rare glimpse of anger filling his normally good natured blue eyes. It lingered for only a moment before being replaced with a weary understanding.

"I did write to you, Cat. I made certain I sent a note to tell you we had just received news of my grandfather's death, and that I would send further word as soon as I was able." His mouth twisted in a bitter smile. "I take it you never received any of the other letters I wrote, did you?" Catherine shook her head, even though she was overjoyed to hear he had not abandoned her. "Damn my meddling, interfering mother! I should have known better than to trust her where you are concerned." The anger in his voice was also tinged with sorrow.

"What does your mother have to do with it?" Catherine asked, sitting up and twisting around to look at him.

"She assured me she had arranged to have my letters, *all* my letters, sent to you." He looked thoroughly miserable. "Ah, Cat, I have punished myself a thousand times over for that night. If I could go back and change things I would. You do know that, don't you?"

The anguish in his voice erased all the doubts she hadn't realized she'd been holding ever since that tragic night. Tears threatened to spill again as Edward told her his version of what had taken place the night of his birthday ball. Apologizing to their guests, many of whom were already staying overnight, Edward had delayed his own departure long enough to pen the note to Catherine, which she never received. He and his father had left within the hour on horseback. His mother was to follow once everyone had departed, but as they galloped south, they ran into a violent storm which soaked them both before they were able to find shelter. Arriving at their destination the next morning, Edward's father dismissed his mild headache and chills as being of no consequence. By week's end there were two burials being performed instead of only one.

Consumed by his own grief, Edward reached out to the only person he felt would understand. He did not rebuke Catherine for not responding to him, for she had her own grief to deal with. Her father, too, had died unexpectedly. His mother's reluctance to leave her husband's grave, coupled with Edward's responsibilities as the new Earl, kept them away far longer than he had intended. He did not mention that an overheard, secondhand conversation while meeting with his bankers had facilitated his purchase of The Hall. But by the time he returned, leaving his mother and grandmother consoling each other, Catherine was gone. Bewildered and hurt by her disappearance, Edward felt as if he had another loss to mourn.

"I'm so sorry," Catherine said, feeling his heartache as keenly as she had felt her own. "I liked your father very much."

He kissed her cheek. "Hush, it wasn't your fault."

The air, heavy with the warmth of the day, covered them like a blanket as they lost themselves in its tranquility. Holding hands, and lying on the sweet-smelling grass side by side, Edward whispered, "Cat, what happened to you? Where did you go?"

Now it was her turn to hesitate, wondering how to answer him. "I don't know. That part of my memory still eludes me." She turned her head and gave him a wry smile. "I was hoping that you might be able to tell me, but if I had already left before you returned, then you would not know either."

"The Hall had to be sold—"

"I'm well aware of that," she interrupted, "but that alone would not have been sufficient reason for me to leave the place where I grew up. The fact I am here says I obviously made my way south, but why would I venture to a place where I know no one? Can you answer me that?"

Edward sat up, his expression one of confusion as he waved a hand in the air. "So you are saying you do not know either the Connors or the Pelhams?"

Looking slightly embarrassed, Catherine also sat, replying with a nod of her head.

"Then how is it you are with them now?"

"What did Rian tell you?"

"He said you were living with his brother and sister-in-law. That you had suffered a misfortune resulting in some memory loss. He gave no other details."

"It's true. Rian found me wandering and alone on the docks of London, and was kind enough to give me shelter." She gave him a searching look. "He did not tell you any of this?"

Edward shook his head, and then the grin she remembered so well suddenly lit up his face, breaking the somber mood. "Well, thank God you were still able to recognize me!"

Laughing, Catherine ran her fingers through his hair. "As if I could ever forget this."

The mood between them lightened, even as their discussion reverted once again to a somber tone.

"What happened to you, Cat, before you were found by Mr. Connor?"

"I don't know, but I am certain that my reason for going to London is linked to whoever it was that hurt me. I am positive the two are connected."

"Hurt you? What do you mean hurt you?" His nostrils flared as he took hold of her hands.

Edward's reaction told Catherine that Rian had actually shared only the minimum of information, and she was grateful for his tact. The truth would be better coming from her. She would be able to gauge just how much to tell her childhood friend. It was hard to know how to begin, but then she reminded herself this was Edward. He had known her all her life.

Seeing her hesitate, Edward spoke. "Cat, if it's too distressful, you don't have to tell me—"

She put her fingers against his mouth to silence him. He pressed his lips against the smooth skin and she smiled.

"It's all right, Edward. My concern is for you hearing it."

He responded by reaching for her and Catherine allowed herself to be pulled back against him for no other reason than it felt good to be in his arms. As she began, she felt as if she was relating a tragedy that had happened to someone else. A distant acquaintance known to both of them. In many ways it was a repetition of that awful day with Rian, when she lay in his arms and told him, but there was a difference between then and now. A difference she felt at once.

If, for some reason, Edward decided what had happened to her had now tainted her in some way, then so be it. She would be hurt and disappointed, but she would move on with her life and not hold him at fault. Had Rian shown a similar feeling, she would have been devastated. And that was enough of a difference to be meaningful.

Chapter 29

Catherine continued with her story until it was done. The girl she described, the one who had suffered, no longer existed. She *had* been changed, but Edward said nothing. He did not need to. And in his silence Catherine found her answer.

It was late afternoon when the main house came once more into view. The sun was making its descent toward the horizon as they walked arm in arm. Each was reassured that their feelings for each other, though undeniably altered by the consequences of their separation, had remained for the most part intact. The childhood friendship had matured and strengthened and would survive. They had almost reached the same terrace where Liam's life had been forever changed, when Edward suddenly stopped and, placing his hands on her shoulders, turned Catherine to face him.

"Cat, we have known each other most of our lives, and I'm sure you know how much I care for you...." He trailed off as his face reddened to match his hair.

Taking his hand in hers, Catherine led him up the wide marble steps to a small alcove where a decorative wrought iron bench was situated. She sat, beckoning him to join her. Edward might have been older in years, but in all the ways that mattered, she was the mature one, and always had been.

"You are also very dear to me, Edward, and always will be."

"As you know, I now have wealth and a title..." He faltered and Catherine squeezed his hand, encouraging him as he struggled to find the right words. "I always thought we would make a good match, and though I am already promised, I will gladly break—"

"No, Edward! Say no more, please."

Stunned by his confession, along with his willingness to be censured for severing his engagement, Catherine was reeling. Edward's mother had apparently not allowed the inconvenience of mourning to prevent her from securing a suitable wife for her son, but she would not—could not—allow him to forsake the young woman for her. Deep down, no matter how much he professed his love, she knew a part of him would always resent her for it.

"Even if you were free," Catherine told him, "we both know it would not be possible. Your mother would never permit it, and I would not force you to choose between us."

He closed his eyes and sighed, acknowledging the truth in her statement. "Nevertheless. I would have been a good husband to you, Cat. You would have wanted for nothing."

She stared at him, feeling a lump in her throat. Yes, he would have been a good husband, and had circumstances been more favorable, they would have enjoyed a nice, comfortable union. But that was before a dormant part of Catherine had been awoken. As much as she cared for Edward, she now knew something between them was missing. Passion. She never dreamed of Edward the way she dreamed of Rian. Yes, he would have been a good husband, but he would also have been the wrong husband.

"That you are still willing to marry me, even now, is honor enough," she said with a smile. "Any woman would consider herself blessed to be your wife."

"And if I were free and if my mother adored you?"

"It would make no difference, Edward. What I feel for you, what I have always felt, is the affection of a sister for a brother. Not that of a wife for a husband. I love you Edward, but I am not *in love* with you. Any more than you are in love with me. You are my dearest friend, and I hope never to lose that friendship."

Roughly he pulled her into his arms and hugged her tightly. "I think I always suspected as much," he mumbled, his lips at her temple, "but I needed to be sure. Please don't think less of me for doing so."

Appalled that he would ever imagine her capable of such a thing, Catherine protested, "Of course I don't think less of you!" The worry that lined her brow was for him alone, and he kissed her forehead, wanting to smooth away her concern.

"Do you like her?" she asked as he released her from his embrace.

"As much as I am able," Edward replied. "I hardly know her. We have met only twice."

"Promise me you will be kind to her. After all, she has had even less say in this forthcoming marriage than you." She gave his chin a gentle shake.

"Let her get to know you, and see what a truly remarkable man she has married. Spend time with her, Edward. Talk to her. Discover what makes her happy, as well as what makes her sad."

"I'll do my best." They smiled at each other and slipped effortlessly back into the easy comfort of their friendship. "And you must promise me you will do the same."

Her laugh was more of a startled squawk. "I doubt I shall ever become a wife."

This time it was his hand on her chin, and he raised her head until she had no choice but to see the disbelief on his face. "What about Rian Connor?"

"What about him?" Catherine could feel the flush rising as it warmed her neck.

"That's who you're in love with, isn't it?"

"In...love?" She hesitated and bit down nervously on her lower lip. "No, I think you are very much mistaken. I'm grateful to him of course, for all he has done for me, but I'm not in love with anyone."

"You're lying, Cat. I can always tell."

Spluttering with indignity, she pulled free of his grasp and got to her feet. "I think your memory is at fault, Edward. I'm not the same girl you remember."

"Yes, you are," he contradicted. "In all the ways that matter. Tell me, if you care nothing for the man, why do you get so agitated whenever his name is mentioned?"

"I do not!" Her denial was vehement, and she stepped away and turned her back on him.

With a hand on her shoulder, Edward turned her back around. "Cat, your face is flushed, you refuse to look at me, and"—his glance raked over her bosom—"you'll faint if you don't catch your breath. You can deny it all you want, but you're in love with Rian Connor. It's written all over your face." Catherine's finger found the errant lock of hair that had slipped free and began corkscrewing it. "You haven't told him, have you?" Edward asked.

She shook her head as her finger worked double time. Worried that she might actually pull her hair out, Edward stayed her frantic motion with his hand. He was tempted to ease whatever insecurities plagued her, but he was not at liberty to do so. Rian might not have confirmed his feelings for Catherine with words, but neither had he denied Edward's guess. And it would be presumptuous of him to reveal such a confidence. All he could do was push Catherine in the right direction, and hope she would discover the truth for herself.

"Tell him, Cat. You might be surprised by his response."

She arched a brow and gave him a skeptical look. "The situation is not as simple as you think. There is a difficulty you know nothing of."

"Then tell me. Perhaps I can help." He arched a brow of his own and, as she seemed no longer concerned with her hair, he let her go.

Now she began pacing, her heels tapping a smart staccato across the tiles. Edward watched, saying nothing. He knew from experience she would speak soon enough. Coming to an abrupt stop, Catherine turned and faced him. Her hands were balled into small fists that she held stiffly at her sides. "There's another woman," she declared, thrusting her chin out as if daring him to dispute her words.

Unable to disclose that this was a fact he was already aware of, Edward simply said, "And?"

"And? That's all you have to say? *And?*" Torn between bafflement and anger at his attitude, Catherine threw her hands up in despair, declaring, "I knew you wouldn't understand!"

"Come, Cat, this is me, your best friend in the whole world. Tell me what you mean. You never had any difficulty in the past getting me to see your point of view. What is this woman to you?"

"Nothing." Her voice trembled slightly as the vision of Isabel, wearing only Rian's bedsheet, suddenly filled her head.

"Then why is she a difficulty?"

"Because she was with Rian before, and she *knows* him." Catherine's voice caught, and she turned her head, feeling a trickle of moisture slide down the side of her nose.

Edward gently pulled her in close so her head was now buried in his shoulder. He understood exactly what she had meant.

"Cat, Cat, hush now," he whispered, his mouth against her hair. "He's a grown man, a man of the world. Of course he has known other women." He began to rock her gently in his arms, moving soothingly from side to side. Catherine gave herself over to the comfort of his swaying, following where he led as her sobs slowly subsided.

"What are you afraid of, Cat?"

She tensed. "That he w-w-won't want me."

All her insecurities tumbled out, and she tried to move away, but Edward would not let her go. He had never known Cat to be afraid before, but then he had never known her to be in love before.

"You think he won't desire you because of his experience with this other woman?" Catherine nodded, refusing to look up at him. "She may have meant something to him once, but I doubt she means anything to him now."

Her head snapped up and despite the wetness of her eyes, he saw a flash of temper in them, which to his way of thinking was a good thing. An angry Cat was preferable to the helpless, despondent one he had been holding.

"How could you possibly know that?" she growled out between clenched teeth.

Now it was his turn to sound exasperated. "Cat, what do you suppose would make a man such as Rian Connor travel north in the first place? He talked not only with me, but anyone in the village who would give him the time of day, trying to find out all he could about you."

His words caught her off guard. It was something she hadn't fully given herself time to consider when Edward first told her he had met Rian. Instead she had allowed herself to become consumed by thoughts of Isabel's prowess in the bedroom, letting it cloud her thinking.

"Odd behavior for a man occupied with thoughts of another woman, don't you think?" Edward moved his hands to her shoulders and shook her gently, waiting for her to grasp the significance of his words.

"No." She pulled away from him. "You've not seen her; if you had you would think differently. Any man would."

The vulgarity he uttered made her cover her mouth with her hand in shock. He closed the distance between them, and stared down at her with a look of barely concealed frustration on his face.

"Do you love him?"

Dropping her hand from her mouth, Catherine looked back at the stranger that had replaced the even-tempered, good-natured man she thought she knew. "I-I-I," she stammered.

"It's an easy question, Cat, yes or no."

"I'm not—I don't..."

"Come on, Catherine! Tell me the truth."

"Stop it! You're bullying me!"

"Do you love Rian Connor?"

"Yes! Yes, I love him! I've loved him from the very first moment I saw him. He's all I think about from the moment I wake until I fall asleep again. And even then I don't escape him, for in my dreams he's—"

The realization that she was about to unveil details too intimate to share made Catherine recover her mouth with the same hand she'd used only moments ago. Edward might be a dear childhood friend, but he was also a man. Her face was burning, though whether from fury or embarrassment, she could not say.

"Is he worthy of your love, Cat?" Edward asked in a tone that was now both sympathetic and envious. Afraid her tongue might be possessed with the ability to act independently, Catherine simply nodded.

"Good. I think so too," Edward told her.

She clutched his arm. "What should I do?" Her voice was hesitant and hopeful all at the same time.

"Trust in yourself, Cat. You cannot continue without knowing if he loves you back, and there is only one way to find out."

Her mouth had suddenly gone dry and she swallowed, the movement a painful rasp. The truth of Edward's words continued to ring in her head. There was only one way to find out. She thought back to the first time she had kissed Rian after their tumble down a snowy embankment. And later, when he found her in the library. She recalled the warmth of his mouth against her skin, the feel of his fingers brushing across her bodice, the hardness as he pressed himself against her. He had wanted her then, but that was before he took Isabel to his bed.

Would he want her still?

...there is only one way to find out.

Suddenly everything became clear. She would confront him, tell him how she felt, and then pray it would be enough. Pray that *she* would be enough. Reaching for Edward's hand, Catherine twined her fingers with his.

"I'm not sure I know how to tell him," she confessed.

Edward's laugh was kind as he raised her hand to his mouth and brushed his lips across her knuckles. "You'll find a way, Cat," he assured her. "You always do."

Embracing Edward's unshakeable faith in her, Catherine took comfort in the certainty of his smile. In her mind she saw Rian gazing down at her. Dark hair falling across his forehead, eyes aglow with something more than desire. It was a look that held the promise of something stronger, a feeling that was deeper than physical passion. It was the look of a man in love.

**Don't miss the dramatic conclusion of the
CORSETS AND CARRIAGES saga.
Salvation is available for pre-order now!**

"I will not be a wife in name only."

Rian Connor's proposal of marriage should have been the happiest moment of Catherine Davenport's life. He is her savior, her tutor in the ways of flirtation, the man she wants for her lover. But two impediments bar the way: the vicious assault that may have ruined her ability to enjoy any man's touch; and the vindictive woman who will stop at nothing to regain Rian's affection.

"There can be no turning back once you have given yourself to me."

One exquisite night of completely mutual pleasure proves to Catherine that with Rian, the physical side of their union will bring only joy. But even her new husband cannot protect her from the diabolical scheming of his former mistress. Delivered into the hands of the madman who once delighted in tormenting her, Catherine is swept back to the place where it all began. And this time, the price could be her future with the man she is finally free to love . . .

Meet the Author

Carla Susan Smith owes her love of literature to her mother, who, after catching her preteen daughter reading by flashlight beneath the bedcovers, calmly replaced the romance book she had "borrowed" with one that was much more age appropriate! Born and raised in England, she now calls South Carolina home, where she lives with her wonderfully supportive husband, awesome son, and a canine critique group (if tails aren't wagging then the story isn't working!). When not writing, she can usually be found in the kitchen trying out any recipe that calls for rhubarb, working on her latest tapestry project, or playing catch up with her reading list. Visit her at www.carlasmithauthor.com

Printed in the United States
by Baker & Taylor Publisher Services